TORN

ALSO BY K.A. ROBINSON

Twisted
Book 2 in the Torn Series

TORN
BOOK 1 IN THE TORN SERIES

A Novel

K.A. ROBINSON

ATRIA PAPERBACK

NEW YORK   LONDON   TORONTO   SYDNEY   NEW DELHI

ATRIA PAPERBACK

A Division of Simon & Schuster, Inc.
1230 Avenue of the Americas
New York, NY 10020

First Atria Paperback edition September 2013

ATRIA PAPERBACK and colophon are trademarks of Simon & Schuster, Inc.

For information about special discounts for bulk purchases, please contact Simon & Schuster Special Sales at 1-866-506-1949 or business@simonandschuster.com.

The Simon & Schuster Speakers Bureau can bring authors to your live event. For more information or to book an event, contact the Simon & Schuster Speakers Bureau at 1-866-248-3049 or visit our website at www.simonspeakers.com.

Designed by Dana Sloan

Manufactured in the United States of America

10 9 8 7 6 5 4 3 2 1

Library of Congress Cataloging-in-Publication Data

Robinson, K.A., date.
 Torn : a novel / by K.A. Robinson. — First Atria Paperback edition.
    pages cm. — (Book 1 in the Torn Series)
  1. Women college students—Fiction. 2. Triangles (Interpersonal relations)—Fiction. 3. West Virginia University—Fiction. I. Title.
PS3618.O3285T67 2013
813'.6—dc23

                                            2013020224

ISBN 978-1-4767-5213-6
ISBN 978-1-4767-5215-0 (ebook)

This book is dedicated first and foremost to my husband for putting up with countless nights of me being glued to my laptop; to my parents, without whom I wouldn't be who I am today; to my son for bringing so much joy to my life; and to my Ninjas and my Cougars. You ladies know who you are. Love you all.

TORN

FIRST SIGHT

My friends often tell me that I would be late for my own funeral. As I heard someone knocking on my dorm room door, I rolled over and glanced at the clock. My eyes widened at the time, and I scrambled out of bed thinking they're probably right. I ran to the door and threw it open, only to see my best friend Logan staring at me with amusement on his face.

"Good morning, Chloe. I see you're going to make us late, as usual."

Logan was one of the most attractive guys I had ever seen. With his sandy blond hair, blue eyes, and ripped body, he's every woman's wet dream. The fact that he was one of the sweetest people I knew just gave him extra points. I had no doubt that he would have several women chasing after him once they noticed him around campus.

"Oh my God, I can't even be on time for our first day!" I shouted as I made my way around my room hunting for something to wear. I quickly found an old pair of jeans and a black Stone Sour T-shirt that I had thrown down beside my bed. I ripped my pajamas off and threw them on my bed before jumping into my jeans and shirt.

"Well, at least you had on underwear and a bra before you did that," Logan mumbled, staring at me with a devilish look in his eyes.

"Very funny, Logan. It's not like you've never seen me in a bikini. Underwear and a bra are pretty much the same thing."

I rushed over to my dresser and grabbed my brush, running it through my hair before pulling it into a low ponytail to keep it out of my face. It was a good thing I wasn't the type of girl who messed with makeup much, or we really would have been late. With my blond hair, blue eyes, and blemish-free fair skin, I was often referred to as a porcelain doll by my friends. Not that I was pretty, just average enough to blend in with every other female out there—at least that was my opinion anyway.

The only thing that could possibly make me stand out on a campus full of thousands of blond girls was what my other best friend Amber liked to refer to as my blond rocker-chick look. While most girls around here wore the cute pink look or the camo look, I preferred to take a darker approach to life: almost every shirt I owned had some kind of rock band on the front, and I had both of my ears gauged out slightly. My hands were usually covered in rings, and I felt naked if I didn't have at least five rubber bracelets on each wrist. I liked my look, but Amber had always insisted I scared more men away with it than she could count.

I grabbed my bag off the desk and headed out the door, locking it behind me.

"Seriously, Logan, I am so sorry. I was sure that I would be up on time today. I guess I didn't hear my alarm clock again."

He looked over at me and grinned. "I wouldn't expect anything less of you. The fact we managed to end up in the same dorm is probably a blessing. Without me as your unofficial alarm clock you really never would make it to class."

I linked our arms together as we stepped out of our dorm and headed across campus to our first class. "What would I ever do without you as my hero?"

"Hmmm, I'm going to guess you'd be late every day."

I elbowed him in the ribs. "Thanks, Logan, you're the best."

We made it into the building and found our classroom with only a moment to spare. Glancing around the room we found two empty seats in the last row and quickly sat down, hoping the professor at the front of the room wouldn't notice our almost late arrival. As I sat my bag on the floor, I glanced at the guy sitting next to me and my heart nearly stopped.

I had never seen a man as gorgeous as he was in my entire life. Whereas Logan was all light and sweet, he was the physical embodiment of the stereotypical bad boy. His hair was so dark it could be considered black, and it hung down into his eyes and around his face in a shaggy yet attractive mess. I couldn't see the color of his eyes, but they looked as dark as his hair.

I noticed that he had piercings in his eyebrow and his lip, as well as a few tattoos poking out of his shirtsleeves on both of his arms. As I stared at the tattoos, I wondered if he had any others hidden under his shirt. Not that I was the type to fall for the body-modification, bad-boy type—despite my own appearance—but this guy could have worn his hair dyed pink and in pigtails and pulled it off looking hot.

As if he somehow sensed my eyes locked on him, he glanced up at me. I quickly looked away, blushing furiously that I had been caught staring at him. I chanced another glance and saw he was still watching me, which made my blush deepen. He must have noticed it from the smile appearing on his face as I quickly turned away from him again.

The rest of class, I refused even to look in his direction. I listened to the professor go over everything, taking notes when I thought I needed to. Before I knew it, class was over and I was putting my books into the bag sitting at my feet. As I threw my bag over my shoulder, I noticed my hot neighbor already walking out the door. I stood and headed out of the building with Logan by my side.

As we made our way down the stairs I saw him standing only a few feet away from us smoking a cigarette. I noticed him smirking at me out of the corner of my eye. I kept my focus on the conversation I was having with Logan as we made our way past him, refusing to give him the satisfaction of catching me staring at him again.

"Hey, do you know that guy?" Logan asked when we were out of earshot.

Lost in my thoughts, I looked at him confused, "Who?"

"That guy standing back there, he keeps staring at you."

I glanced over my shoulder to see him referring to the hot guy still standing there smoking, still staring at me with that damn smirk on his face.

"Oh, I have no idea who he is," I said as I turned away from him before he could notice that I was blushing from being caught yet again.

Logan and I finished the walk across campus with an easy silence. It had always been this way with us, I always felt comfortable and safe with him as long as we had been friends. He transferred to my school our freshman year of high school and was assigned the seat next to me in Mrs. Jenkins's English class.

We had instantly bonded over guessing whether her hair was real or a wig and the rest was history.

We had spent every moment of high school attached at the hip, which had caused problems with some of his old girlfriends. They were convinced that we were secretly together or that he had a crush on me. We had always laughed the rumors off, but I had felt guilty more than once about ruining some of his past relationships.

Our next class, Spanish, went much like the previous one, except the hot guy was nowhere to be seen. I actually felt kind of relieved, seeing as every moment I was within a mile of him my cheeks were permanently red. I had no idea what my problem was when it came to him. I did not get flustered around men, yet with one look he could almost bring me to my knees. I needed to get a grip.

Once the professor dismissed us, we headed across campus to grab some lunch. Logan and I had nearly identical schedules on Monday, Wednesday, and Friday, but our Tuesday and Thursday schedules were totally backward from each other. My only saving grace was the fact that his first class on those mornings was at the same time as mine, so I knew he would make sure I was up and out the door on time.

I glanced up at him as we grabbed our food and headed toward an empty table to eat. He really was gorgeous, even as his best friend I had noticed this. Truthfully, when I had first met him, I had a slight crush on him, but after getting to know him so well, my feelings had changed from a crush to friendship. Without him around, I really would be lost.

When the time came to apply for colleges, I had flipped out for weeks until I knew that we would be going to the same college. I had kept up a perfect 4.0 GPA all through high school so I had several options available, but Logan was determined to attend West Virginia University and I wanted to be with him. When we both received our acceptance letters in the mail on the same day, I had rushed to his house and tackled him with excitement. I knew college would change us both, but I hoped that we would always remain best friends. I don't think I could handle it any other way.

"What? Do I have food on my face?" he asked as he wiped at the imaginary food on his chin.

"No, why?"

"Well, because you have been staring at me for the last five minutes."

I grinned up at him. "Sorry, I was just thinking about how I would be lost without you here with me. You know that right?"

He pulled me into a tight hug. "Don't ever worry about that, Chloe, you will always have me. We will be old and gray and still together."

I hugged him back. "I'm glad. Hopefully my future husband and your future wife won't mind us being permanently attached to each other."

His face grew tight at my words and I looked at him in confusion. "What'd I say?"

His face quickly relaxed and he smiled at me. "Nothing, I was just thinking that you will never find a guy good enough to be your husband. Speaking of guys not good enough, what was up with that guy who was sitting next to you this morning? He was staring at you like he wanted to eat you alive."

I rolled my eyes. "I have no idea what you're talking about. He wasn't staring at me. He just happened to look up when we did. There was no way a guy like that would ever be interested in me."

He frowned at my words. "Chloe, you're crazy. Any guy with eyeballs can see how beautiful you are."

I started to give a sarcastic reply, but he cut me off.

"That is, until you open your mouth. Then they run in terror."

I punched him in the arm. "I have a wonderful personality, thank you!"

He laughed at my disgruntled expression. "I'm just kidding. In all seriousness though, you really are great, Chloe. I hope you're right about him not being interested in you though, I don't like him."

I laughed. "And you would know you don't like him *how*? You've never even talked to the guy."

"I don't have to. I know his type, the whole bad boy vibe he puts off. He's probably a total womanizer and you're better off if you stay away from him."

"Seriously? Why are we even talking about this? The guy isn't into me and that's that."

If only I'd been so lucky.

. . .

Logan and I parted ways after lunch. He had another class and then planned on spending the rest of the afternoon downtown applying for jobs, and I had promised to meet up with my other best friend Amber after her last class. Amber and I had been friends since middle school, bonding over our mutual taste in heavy metal instantly. Whereas Logan and I were close, Amber was like my twin, on the inside at least.

Her features couldn't have been more different from mine if she tried. Her skin was a naturally tanned color and her hair was a dark brown. She had these amazing green eyes that could make anyone do her bidding, and a perfect size-six figure. My blond hair and blue eyes were nice, but I often felt boring and self-conscious when I stood next to her. The only thing I had going for me when she was around was my D-cup breasts, which might bring me attention from time to time, but they tended to get in my way more than anything.

Even with her amazing looks, she was one of those people who had a heart of gold; not only was she gorgeous on the outside, but on the inside as well. She had always been there when I needed her, and I loved her for that. There were few people who could put up with me like she did on a full-time basis.

I sat on the bench outside her building for a few minutes before she emerged, shielding her eyes with her hand from the sun glaring down at us. She noticed me and waved, walking over to where I sat.

"Hey, girl! How'd your classes go?"

I smiled, and we started walking toward our dorm. "They were good, a bunch of boring stuff over and over mainly."

She nodded as she walked alongside me. "Yeah mine were the same. I'm so glad we decided to only take a few classes this semester until we get adjusted."

She and I had both decided to go easy on the classes our first semester and squeezed by with the bare minimum to be considered full-time students, unlike Logan, who had enough classes for two people.

"Anyway, have you seen some of these guys walking around here? I think I'm in love!"

I laughed at her boy craziness, but a certain tattooed guy popped into my head. "Yeah, I noticed a couple."

She stopped dead in her tracks and spun to face me. "What?

You noticed someone? I thought for sure you were a nun in hiding!"

I elbowed her in the ribs. "I am not a nun. There just hasn't been anyone to catch my interest. We can't all be as boy crazy as you are."

"Whatever. So, who is this guy?"

I fidgeted a little and glanced at my shoes, which was a total mistake. Amber knew the shoe staring was my thing when I was trying to keep something from her.

"Don't you dare look at your shoes, woman! Spill!"

I sighed and looked up at her. Her eyes were practically glowing with excitement, waiting for me to spill my guts to her. "I don't know his name or anything. He is just a guy who was sitting in the seat next to me this morning."

She raised her eyebrows at me. "And what does this mystery guy look like?"

I glanced around, making sure that no one was around us before answering her, "He's cute I guess. His hair is so dark it's almost black, and he has these beautiful, piercing eyes. Oh, and these really hot piercings in his lip and eyebrow. And he had some tattoos poking out of the bottom of the sleeve of his shirt, but I couldn't tell what they were."

Cute was the understatement of the year, but I wasn't about to start gushing at his hotness in front of her—she really would combust from the excitement—so I kept it to the bare minimum.

As I spoke I saw her mouth dropping in slow motion. "You don't like just any guy, you like a bad boy. Holy shit, I'm pretty sure hell just froze over, my little Chloe crushing on the bad boy!"

She pretended to faint and I elbowed her again. "Shut up.

I don't like him, I just find him kind of attractive. What is this, middle school?"

She busted out laughing at me, "Touchy aren't we? Sorry, I'll stop bothering you about the tattooed, pierced, and kind of attractive bad boy."

We started making our way across campus again and were nearly to the dorm before she spoke again. "So I know it's a Monday and all, but some girl in my English class invited me to a party across campus at one of the sorority houses. Will you please come with me? I need my wing woman!"

"I really shouldn't. I still have a couple of boxes to unpack, but I'm sure your roommate would be glad to go with you."

She looked at me with those big green eyes and her lower lip sticking out in a pout and I started feeling guilty. "Please, Chloe? I saw Chad today and I really need a night out. We won't even have to stay late, I promise!"

The Chad she was referring to was the ex-boyfriend she had been with since the summer before our senior year. He had seemed like a really good guy, and I had truly liked him. That is, until she surprised him by stopping at his house one day un-announced and catching him in bed with Carrie Jenkins, head cheerleader and the biggest slut in town.

The weeks following had been brutal. Amber had never seen it coming, and neither had I for that matter. After count-less nights of staying in her room all night with tubs of ice cream and enough tissues to keep Carrie's bra stuffed for a year, I was finally able to coax her out of her house just before we moved into our dorms. I knew Chad was here on campus as well, but I had hoped that she wouldn't have to see him, at least for a while.

I sighed and pulled her into a hug. "All right, I'll go, but only because I have that super cute dress I've been dying to wear."

She squealed and started jumping up and down. "Yay! And I love that dress, I told you so when I bought it for you! Plus, I have the cutest shoes to go with it!"

She grabbed my arm and pulled me into the dorm and up to her room. As soon as we were inside, she started rummaging through boxes in her closet and pulled out a pair of killer red heels.

I smiled as she handed them to me. "Thanks. I'm going to head to my room and try to get the rest of my stuff unpacked before tonight. I'll meet you back here around eight o'clock?"

"Okay, that works for me."

I gave her one last hug before leaving and making my way up to the floor above where my dorm room was located. Even though Amber and I hadn't ended up being roommates, fate must have been smiling on us. Logan, Amber, and I had all ended up in one of the few coed dorms on campus. We were stacked on top of each other with Amber on the first floor, me on the second, and Logan on the third. It was good to know if I needed either one of them they were just a set of stairs away.

I unlocked my door and stepped into the havoc I had left in my wake this morning. Groaning, I started gathering my dirty clothes and throwing them into the hamper by my closet. After I had managed to find my floor, I moved on to the boxes stacked against the wall. Did I really want to unpack all this stuff? That was a dumb question, of course I didn't, but I couldn't very well live out of boxes for the next year. I grabbed the top one and started unpacking the clothes inside. I had already put most of my clothes away this weekend, but there were still a couple of boxes like this one with the sweatpants and baggy shirts I used as pajamas sometimes.

I managed to get a couple boxes put away before my phone

started playing "Blood" by In This Moment, and I grinned as I grabbed it off the bed.

"Hey, Logan, find any jobs?"

He groaned in frustration. "I've already applied to half the town, so I'm sure I'll find something. There are still a few places I want to check out though."

"That's cool. I'm trying to get the rest of this crap unpacked. I was going to suggest you come over and help me, but I guess that idea is out."

He laughed at me. "Yeah, I think I'd rather be applying for jobs than helping you put your underwear away. Actually, on second thought . . ."

"Well, when you put it like that, I can't really blame you. If you're free before we leave you should come with Amber and me to a party at one of the sorority houses."

"I think I'll pass on this one, but just be careful. Don't leave your drink alone, and if you need me to come get you just call me, okay? You know I worry about you."

I rolled my eyes at his words. "Yes, Dad. I promise to be good."

"I'm serious, Chloe. I don't know what I'd do if something happened to you."

"I know that, and I promise I will be careful. I should probably go and try to get the rest of these boxes sorted. I'll call you when I get home, promise."

"All right, just remember to call me later, or I'll be beating on your dorm room door in the middle of the night in only my boxers."

I laughed at him. "Well, as much of a thrill as that would give the girls on this floor, we wouldn't want that. Talk to you later."

I hung up and threw my phone back on the bed. I loved how protective Logan was of me, even if he made me feel smothered at times. He had always been this way, and it made me feel safe to know he was always there for me.

I managed to get all my boxes unpacked with a little over an hour to spare, so I decided to take a shower. Grabbing my bathroom bag, I made my way to the showers, which were almost completely empty with the exception of a few girls standing by the sinks. Not wanting to push my luck, I took the fastest shower on record before heading back to my room.

I left my hair in a towel to dry as I dug through my now excessively cramped closet to find my dress. I found it pushed against the back wall and quickly started trying to pull it out before any of my other clothes could drag me into the mess and hold me prisoner for eternity.

When I managed to untangle it from the disaster that was my closet, I held it up in front of me and smiled. I had to agree with Amber, the dress really was gorgeous. The bottom was skintight and ended several inches above my knees. The top of it was a halter top with a built-in bra, which was lucky for me since the back was too low cut for me to wear one. It wasn't my usual style, but I loved it.

I quickly squirmed into it before pulling my hair out of the towel and running the brush through it as I blow-dried it. My hair was almost to my waist and took forever to dry, so I rarely spent the time required to blow-dry and straighten it, but tonight was my first college party and I wanted to look my best. After I got my hair under control, I started applying my makeup. My roommate, Rachel, walked in just as I was finishing and flopped facedown on her bed groaning.

"Rough day, Rachel?"

She groaned again and nodded. "Remind me again why I signed up for all these classes?"

I laughed as she rolled over to face me.

"Hot damn, woman, you look amazing. And FYI, if that dress comes up missing and finds itself in my closet, it wasn't me. I swear it."

"Thanks for the warning. I know how these things grow legs and walk straight into someone else's closet, but mine usually end up in Amber's somehow."

"So where are you headed looking like that?"

"There's some party at a sorority house Amber is dragging me to. You're welcome to come if you want."

She considered my offer for a minute before shaking her head. "No thanks, I've had a rough day. I'm just going to curl up on my bed and read. I don't think I could take on a party tonight if I tried."

I had seen Rachel's schedule the day we moved in and I knew she wasn't kidding. Her days started first thing in the morning and except for lunch, ran solid up until early evening. The girl was crazy in my opinion, but her parents had pushed her to take everything she could.

Rachel was what you would call a sexy nerd. She was one of the smartest people I had ever met, but with her long red hair, perfect face, and amazing figure she was a total babe by anyone's standards. When I had first met her, I was terrified she was going to be one of those self-absorbed girls, but with her down-to-earth personality, I had liked her within the first ten minutes.

"All right, but next time you're going with me even if I have to drag you." I glanced at the clock before slipping into my shoes and heading for the door. "I don't think I'll be out late, but if I am I promise to be super quiet when I come in."

She grinned up at me. "Don't worry, I'll probably still be between the pages with a certain Mr. Maddox. Lord knows I can't put him down once I start."

I laughed at her current book obsession as I walked out the door. "Can't blame you there. Later."

I made my way back down the stairs carefully so I wouldn't break my neck in Amber's amazing but super-high-heeled shoes. As I reached her room, I knocked once before heading in.

"Hey! What the hell? Oh, it's just you. Don't do that to me!" Amber yelled as a welcome.

She was standing in just her bra and a super chic miniskirt, staring at her closet like the perfect shirt was about to jump out at her.

"I have nothing to wear!"

I raised my eyebrow as I pointed at her closet. "You have about a million shirts in there, surely you can pick out something."

She finally pulled out a cute yellow tank top and threw it over her head. "I guess this will do. Come on, we better hurry or we'll be late."

"Can you even be late for one of these things?"

She rolled her eyes as she breezed by me and headed out the door. "I don't know, but if you can, Lord knows you would be."

I tried to smack her, but my heel caught on the carpeting in the hallway and I nearly fell down.

She started laughing like an idiot at my usual clumsiness. "That never gets old. Seriously though, gravity has never been kind to you."

I stuck my tongue out at her back as we made our way out the door and across campus to our first college party.

CHAPTER TWO

FALLING FOR YOU

I walked up the steps of the huge sorority house, Amber following close behind. There were students everywhere, all looking completely wasted even though it was only an hour into the party. I pushed through the door and was blasted with music loud enough to make my ears bleed. I had no idea who it was, but they were doing a cover of Chevelle's "The Red," and they were amazing.

Amber came up beside me and motioned toward the table holding more alcohol than I cared to think about. I grinned and nodded—tonight was about having a blast, hangover be damned. I grabbed her by the hand and marched over to the table, grabbing a cup and filling it to the top.

There were several guys standing next to us at the table, and they smiled approvingly as they took in my dress. I gave them my best flirty smile, and as the band switched to "Pour Some Sugar on Me," two of the guys approached us.

"Hey, I'm Ben. This is Alex. Care to dance?"

I grinned and nodded, noticing Alex was practically undressing Amber with his eyes.

Ben led me to the center of the dance floor and we started dancing close, more grinding than any actual dance moves. As we moved, he put his hands on my hips to pull me closer, if that were possible. We had only been dancing for a few minutes when I glanced up across the sea of people and locked eyes with the singer of the band. My breath froze in my chest. It was him. Mr. Tall, Dark, Tattooed, and Pierced from my morning class. And he was staring straight at me. I dropped my gaze, suddenly shy.

I finished dancing with Ben as the song ended and made my way back to the drink table, as far from the singer as possible. Much to my dismay, Ben followed.

He stared down at me, more at my low neckline than at my face.

"Want to get out of here?" He grinned naughtily at me, leaving no doubt as to where he wanted to go.

"No thanks, I think I'm just going to hang out here."

He looked disappointed, but shrugged and walked away. I glanced around for Amber, seeing her and Alex locked around each other on one of the couches pushed against the far wall. I grinned: about time she started actually trying to move on. Not that I was the type to hook up with random guys at parties, but she deserved some fun after all the heartache she'd had with Chad over the summer.

I hung around the party awhile longer, refilling my cup a few times and dancing with a couple different guys, but I refused to go home with any of them. Not my style, unlike several of the girls I'd seen sneaking upstairs to the bedrooms above throughout the night.

I listened to the band, which I was blown away by, but I refused to glance back up at the singer, afraid he'd be looking at me again. I mentally hit myself. There was no reason to be all nervous around this guy, he had never even talked to me. I wasn't going to let some random guy make me crazy. I glanced up to the stage, but the band was packing up; they had finished their set while I was thinking about him.

I decided to call it a night, even though the party was still in full swing. My head was slightly fuzzy and I knew if I stayed any longer I'd end up drunk off my ass passed out on a couch, or worse. If I called Logan like that, he would surely lock me in my room for the rest of the year. I pushed through the crowd to the door, texting Amber so she would know I'd left.

As soon as I made it out the door I sighed in relief. I hadn't realized how hot it was inside and feeling the cool evening air on my skin helped to clear my head a little. I started walking in the direction of my dorm when the spike on my heel caught in a crack on the sidewalk. I flew forward and landed face-first with my ass sticking straight up in the air.

"Damn these shoes!"

I muttered curses as I tried to stand when a hand grabbed me firmly by the arm and stood me up. I tried to balance myself, but the heel had broken off of the shoe and I wobbled, falling against whoever had picked me up. Strong male arms wrapped around me and pulled me into his chest, keeping me from falling all over again. I glanced up to thank my savior, but the words lodged in my throat when I saw it was the lead singer holding me. I stared at him, unable to think, or move for that matter.

He cocked his head to one side, looking down at me. "You okay?"

His voice pulled me back to reality and I realized I had just been standing there staring into his eyes for longer than I cared to think about.

I cleared my throat and nodded. "Yes, thank you. My stupid shoe caught in the sidewalk."

"Yeah, I saw."

I stepped away from him, careful not to lose my balance again, and glanced over his shoulder to where the other members of the band were loading up the equipment into the back of a van. The color in my face drained as I realized he was directly behind me when I fell. I knew that anyone behind me had seen pretty much everything thanks to the short length of my dress, and to make things even better I had worn a thong tonight so he really had gotten a show. My face heated and the corners of his mouth turned up as if he knew what I was thinking.

"No big deal."

I knew he was trying to make me feel better, but at this point I was done. A person can only take so much embarrassment before they die of shame.

"Well thank you for helping me. I appreciate it."

"Not a problem."

As he spoke, I watched his eyes travel the length of my body and I knew I needed to leave before I did something stupid.

"Well, thanks again. I'd stay and chat, but I need to get home." I turned quickly and removed both my shoes, dreading the now endless barefoot walk back to my dorm.

He grabbed my shoulder and turned me back toward him. "Where are you headed? My car is right over there. I can drop you off instead of making you walk without shoes."

Doubt about getting a ride from a complete stranger clouded my thoughts as I looked up at him. If Logan knew he would absolutely kill me. I chewed my lower lip, debating before nodding my head. "Oh, well okay, if you don't mind. It's only three blocks over to my dorm. I can walk though, it's not that far."

The thought of being in a car with this stranger made my stomach quake. As handsome as he was sitting next to me in class, being up close and personal to him was a whole other matter. I had never seen someone with such dark brown eyes, and the way his dark hair hung in his eyes, it took everything I had not to reach out and push it back. When he had pulled me against his chest I had felt pure, hard muscle and the shirt he wore was fitted enough that I could see those muscles beneath it. I almost blushed as I started picturing what he looked like without a shirt on.

"It's not a problem. Wait here and I'll pull my car over."

I nodded as he turned and started walking to the lot across the street to get his car. I watched him walk away without guilt as I stared at one of the nicest backsides I had ever seen. He glanced back once, and I quickly averted my eyes, hoping he hadn't noticed me checking him out. How many times can one person embarrass themselves in one night?

A minute later he pulled up next to me and I almost rolled my eyes. A guy that looked this good should not have a car this sexy. I knew next to nothing about cars, but I knew this one was old, even though it looked brand new. The exterior was a glossy black with chrome wheels, and as I opened the door and hopped in, I saw the inside was all new and black as well.

"Nice car," I commented as I closed the door behind me.

"Thanks, it's a 1969 Mustang. I rebuilt pretty much all of it. She's my baby."

He patted the dash affectionately, and I laughed at him. "Oh no, don't tell me you're one of those guys who loves their car more than any woman."

He laughed. "No, I wouldn't say that, but she is pretty close to my heart."

He peeled out of his spot and headed toward my dorm. It

was quiet for a minute as I racked my brain for something intelligent to say. I figured that I'd only get this opportunity once and that I'd be home in five minutes tops, even with traffic, so I didn't want to waste it.

"I'm Chloe, by the way."

"Drake Allen. Nice to meet you, Chloe."

I grinned. "Well, now that we got the whole awkward introduction thing over with, I feel better."

He busted out laughing. "Yeah, glad we got the awkward part of the evening over."

My face instantly turned blood red, thinking of the view he had seen tonight, and I looked out the window hoping he wouldn't notice. Apparently he did, because he laughed again.

"Sorry, I didn't mean to embarrass you. Think of it this way: with the introduction we had, I won't forget you anytime soon."

My face felt even hotter, if that was possible, and I groaned, hiding my face in my hands. "Oh my God. I think I'd like to die right now, thank you."

He kept chuckling as the light turned green and he turned onto my street. We pulled into the parking lot across from the dorm, and he put the car in park, waiting for me to get out. I didn't want to leave yet, so I said the first thing that popped into my head.

"Your band is pretty amazing, you guys rocked at the party tonight."

His eyes lit up and I could tell I'd hit on a subject he was happy to talk about.

"Thanks. We play every Friday night down at the bar across town called Gold's Pub. You should stop down some night and check us out. The bar is awesome and just between the two of us, they don't card."

Was he asking me to meet him again? No, he was probably just trying to get more fans. There was no way a guy this hot could be interested in me.

I glanced at him again, taking in just how attractive he was. His lip ring caught my attention as it glimmered from the reflection of the street light outside. I wondered what it would feel like to kiss him with that in. Pulling myself away from any thoughts of his lips, I quickly smiled at him and opened the door. "Good to know, I'll stop down sometime. I'd better head inside. Thank you for everything."

He smiled back at me. "Yeah, no problem. Good night."

I quickly grabbed my shoes and got out of the car, watching for any pebbles or glass that I might step on as I closed the door. I started to walk away when he rolled the window down.

"Hey, Chloe?"

I turned back to the car and leaned down to the window. "Yeah?"

He had the oddest look on his face, but stayed silent. Finally after what felt like an eternity, he smiled at me. "Watch out for cracks from now on, okay?"

. . .

How I made it up my room without breaking my neck, I'll never know. I even managed to sneak in without waking Rachel up, who was out cold with her book across her chest. All I could think about was Drake, with his flirtatious nature and charming smile. That smile could make me forget my first name, so it was understandable that one minute I was walking away from his car and the next I was sitting on my bed in a daze.

I admitted to myself that I was attracted to him from the

moment I saw him, but now that I had actually talked to him, it was ten times stronger. He seemed like a nice guy if my first interaction with him was any indication of his personality. He could have embarrassed me endlessly from what he had seen, but he played it off like nothing to help put me at ease, and I truly appreciated that from him.

I fell back into my pillow and groaned. Men had no spot in my college plans; they had never had a spot anywhere, truthfully. Although I wasn't planning on becoming a nun anytime soon, Amber had been right about me not ever being into any guy. Sure, there had been dates. I wasn't even a virgin—I had lost that to my cousin Danny's best friend Jordan when I tagged along with my mother to road trip and visit my aunt one summer—but no one had ever caught my eye since.

Thoughts of my mother brought a sigh to my lips. To say my mother was flighty would be an understatement. She had become pregnant with me at seventeen. She had been a hardcore partier, and I was a result of a drug-and-alcohol-fueled night with some man she didn't even remember. She had managed to contain her drug use while she was pregnant with me, but she had continued to smoke and drink, which had resulted in me being born almost a month early.

Soon after I was born, she had gone back to using drugs and partying, leaving me with whoever would watch me. More often than not, it was someone who was a complete stranger to me, since my grandparents had disowned her when she informed them of her pregnancy and her only sister lived hours away.

When I was around seven or eight years old, she started bringing me to the parties with her and would leave me alone for hours. As I got older, she would let me stay home by myself, leaving me home for days at a time, sometimes weeks. By that time, I had become good friends with Amber, and often stayed with her when my mother took off.

By the time I was a freshman in high school, her trips had become multiple-month events, and Amber's parents, Dave and Emma, had transformed their guest room into my own bedroom. They had bought me school clothes every year, Emma took me prom-dress shopping, they had even ordered my graduation cap and gown. While they became parents to me, my mother's visits became less and less frequent, until I saw her only a couple of times a year.

I was thankful when she was gone. My mother had always held a grudge against me over my birth, and when she drank at home with just the two of us, she often became violent toward me. I spent most of my childhood trying to cover the bruises she left all over my body. The physical wounds had healed long ago, but they left me bruised and battered inside. That, and the venom she often spewed at me, left me feeling that I could never truly trust anyone and that I really was as worthless as she said. Logan and Amber had broken down my barriers slowly, and I thanked every deity out there for putting them in my life.

One summer, I had decided to tag along with her for whatever reason. We lived in West Virginia, but she took me from state to state, as far away as Colorado, mostly by bus or cramped into the back of one of her friend's cars. We ended up at my Aunt Jennifer's home in Ocean City, Maryland, and I quickly formed a close friendship with my cousin Danny.

He and I had only met a couple of times, but my mother and I stayed with them for over a month, so I started tagging along with him and his best friend Jordan. I became close friends with Jordan as well, and one night we were with a group of kids on the beach partying. Danny had left with some random girl, so Jordan and I decided to take a walk down the beach together.

We found ourselves hidden by some rocks, only a few feet from the ocean, having drunk sex. Being the sweet guy he was, though, he made it romantic and gentle, and I loved him for it. Even though I rarely spoke to either of them, Jordan would always hold a special place in my heart.

Thoughts of my mother and my past sobered my excitement over Drake. It had been over a year since I had seen her, and sometimes I missed her. I knew she loved me in her own crazy way, but she hadn't even been able to pull herself away from her life for one night to attend my graduation. I sighed again and rolled over on my bed just as my phone started playing Logan's ringtone. I had forgotten to call him.

I grabbed my phone and answered it before the noise woke up Rachel. "Hey, Logan, I'm home."

"Thanks for calling me."

"I just walked in a couple minutes ago. Amber met some guy and stayed though, so go call and yell at her."

He stayed silent for a moment and I thought he really was going to call her, but his next words surprised me.

"You mean you walked back by yourself this late at night?"

His voice was lined with anger and I bit my lip. Telling him Drake had brought me back would probably make him angrier than the thought of me walking home by myself. I decided to be honest, in case I slipped up later.

"Actually, I got a ride with someone." I waited silently on the blowup that my words would surely bring.

"And who was this someone?"

"You remember that guy who was sitting beside me this morning in class?"

He groaned into the phone. "You got a ride from some guy you don't even know? Why didn't you just call me, Chloe?"

I felt slightly guilty at the concern in his voice. I had debated on calling him, but the need to be alone with Drake had won out.

"It's not like that. I was walking home, but my heel broke on my shoe and he was there, so he offered me a ride. It was fine, Logan, honest. He just drove me back here and dropped me off. He didn't try anything with me."

I heard him muttering curses under his breath. "Well, it could have ended a lot worse. Next time you need a ride, you call me, understand?"

Sensing the anger fading to worry in his voice, I smiled. "Of course I will."

"You better, Chloe. I don't know what I'd do if someone hurt you. You're important to me—you know that, right?"

My heart swelled at his words. "Yes, I know. And you're important to me too. You're like the brother I never had."

Expecting some kind of remark about me being an annoying little sister, I was surprised by the silence on the other end of the line.

"Logan, are you still there?"

"Yeah, I'm here, but I've got to go. I'll talk to you tomorrow, okay?"

"Um, yeah I'll see you tomorrow. Night."

I plugged my phone in to charge, wondering what on earth went on inside Logan's head sometimes.

CHAPTER THREE

I'VE GOT YOUR NUMBER

I somehow managed to wake up on time the following morning. It might have had something to do with the fact that I was hoping to see Drake somewhere on campus during the day. With that in mind, I took extra care getting dressed and even applied a small amount of makeup. I grabbed my bag and stepped outside my door just as Logan came out of the stairwell.

He took one look at me and grabbed his chest. "Oh my God, it's a miracle! She's on time! I think I'm having a heart attack from the shock of it all!"

I made my way past him and into the stairwell.

"Don't get used to it, you're still my alarm clock. Today was just a fluke."

He laughed as we stepped out of the stairwell and threw his arm over my shoulders. "Oh, Chloe, don't worry. I know this won't happen again anytime soon. Besides, if it did, my heart couldn't take it."

I tried to elbow him, but he moved out of reach. "Shut up, asshole, and walk me to class."

He laughed again and wrapped his arm back around me. "Bossy little thing this morning, aren't we?"

I ignored his comment as we made our way to my building. His class was a few buildings down from mine, so he had decided to take it upon himself to make sure I made it to class. When we stopped outside of my class to say good-bye, he surprised me by kissing me on the cheek.

"What was that for?" I asked as he pulled away.

He glanced over my shoulder into the class and then back to me. "Just didn't want any guys getting any ideas about you while we're apart."

I smiled at his overprotectiveness. "Gee, thanks. Now if you'll excuse me, Mr. Overprotective, I need to head inside. I'll meet up with you later this evening, okay?"

He smiled down at me and nodded. "My last class lets out at six o'clock, so I'll drop by your room after that and we can grab something to eat."

I waved as I made my way into the classroom. Scanning around for a seat, I noticed Drake sitting in the back corner grinning at me. My heart stopped as he pointed to the chair next to him. With my heart hammering in my ears, I made my way over to him and took the seat.

"Morning."

He gave me that wicked grin of his as he spoke. "Good morning, Chloe. I see you managed to make it from your dorm to here without any cracks getting in the way."

My face instantly turned red and he busted out laughing. "You're never going to let me live that down are you?"

His gaze traveled down my body and back up to my eyes before answering. "Nope, but with you wearing jeans, it wouldn't be nearly as fun to watch today as it was last night."

I smacked his arm and felt electricity shoot from my fingers up my arm at the brief contact. "Shut up or I'll move to a different spot. I don't have to take your torment for the next two hours."

"Oh, she threatens. I'm scared now."

I stuck my tongue out at him as I turned back toward the front of the class, pulling my book out of my bag. "You should be."

He was silent for a moment, so I glanced up at him and my breath caught at the look in his eyes. They looked as if he wanted to devour me on the spot and I gulped.

"What?"

He leaned toward me slightly as he spoke. "Stick that tongue out at me again and see what happens."

My mouth dropped open at his words, and I quickly looked away as the professor entered the front of the room. Once class started I tried to ignore him, but it was impossible. I kept glancing at him, and every time he would be staring at me with those lust-filled eyes. I wiggled uncomfortably in my seat at his scrutiny, and he grinned. The professor called a break halfway through, and I stood, stretching my arms above my head to get the kinks out of my back. My shirt pulled up, revealing my belly-button ring, and I caught him staring at it.

"What are you looking at?"

He pulled his eyes up to my face and grinned. "Got anything else pierced?"

I gave him the sexiest smile I could muster as I replied, "Wouldn't you like to know?"

He grinned at me as he stood. "I'm going outside to smoke, want to come with me?"

"Sure, why not? Maybe I'll get some secondhand smoke, that'll really make my day."

We made our way outside to a group of other students smoking. Drake lit up and glanced at me as I stood awkwardly next to him.

"What's wrong with you?"

"Nothing, just trying not to breathe."

He started laughing loudly, and some of the other students glanced our way at his outburst. "You just say whatever comes to mind, don't you?"

I gave him a sheepish grin. "Logan tells me I have no filter. It drives him nuts most of the time, I think."

"I like it, it's refreshing. Most people never really say what they think. They worry about what everyone else will think, but you just put it right out there."

"Thanks, I think."

"So is Logan the one who was with you in class yesterday?"

"Yeah, that's Logan. He's my unofficial alarm clock and self-appointed bodyguard."

"Ah, I see. Overprotective boyfriend as well?"

I laughed, surprised at his way-off-base observation. "Um, no, definitely not boyfriend. He is my best friend though."

He frowned at my words. "You sure about that?"

"What do you mean?"

"Just that I saw how he looked at you yesterday. It definitely wasn't as a friend."

"I have no idea what you're talking about. Logan is just Logan, he doesn't look at me any way except as a friend."

He shrugged his shoulders. "Whatever you want to believe, but trust me, I'm a guy, I know that look. It's the *I want in her panties* look."

I rolled my eyes at him. "Whatever. We aren't like that."

He stomped out his cigarette and we made our way back

into the classroom without speaking. His words worried me. There was no way Logan thought of me like that: we were best friends and nothing more. But what if he was right? I tried to think of Logan in a different way and failed miserably. Sure, he was extremely attractive, but he was like a brother to me. If he did care about me like that, it would ruin everything.

I thought about all the times I had changed clothes in front of him, and he had never acted like it bothered him. Sure, he would make some kind of smart-ass remark, but nothing he said ever indicated it got him worked up. I sat down in my seat and sighed. I hadn't expected this when I sat down next to Drake. I glanced over at him and he was grinning at me again.

"Now what are you thinking?"

"Nothing really, just that you're insane with the whole Logan thing."

He leaned toward me again and whispered into my ear, his breath against my skin making me shiver. "You want to know how I know I'm right? Because when I look at you, I do it the exact same way."

At his words, I felt tingling between my legs and my mouth dropped open in shock. This boy was a total flirt. I started giggling and rolled my eyes as he leaned back and grinned at me.

"You know, when I say stuff like that, I don't expect the girl to laugh at me."

"Drake, you are such a flirt and you know it, but I hate to break it to you, it doesn't work on me," I lied with a straight face. I had known this guy all of two days, and he got to me like no one else had. He started laughing again, and I felt the tingles between my legs reappear.

"You know what, Chloe? I think you and I are going to end up being great friends."

I couldn't suppress my grin at his words. "I don't know, guess we'll have to wait and see."

I somehow managed to survive the rest of the class with Drake giving me that smoldering stare of his. As soon as we were dismissed, I darted out of my seat to escape him, but he quickly caught up to me, trying to make small talk as we made our way across campus to the cafeteria. As we walked in, I spotted Amber sitting off to the side, waving at me like a mad woman to catch my attention.

I laughed and waved back to her before turning to Drake. "Well, Amber seems to be flagging me down, so I guess I'll see you later."

He glanced at Amber behind me and grinned. "What, you aren't going to invite me to eat with you? I'm crushed."

My stomach seized at the thought of having Amber and Drake at a table together. I had yet to tell her about last night, but I knew she'd go crazy over him. I looked him over from the corner of my eye and really couldn't blame her, he was sex on legs. I glanced back at his face, and he was standing there with a smirk on his face, waiting for my answer.

I sighed dramatically before motioning him to follow me. "I guess I can put up with you if I have to."

We made our way to Amber, and I saw her eyes widen and her mouth drop at the sight of him.

"Amber, Drake. Drake, Amber." I threw my backpack into a seat and turned to Amber. "Now that introductions are over, I'm going to grab something to eat."

I walked away without glancing back at either of them to get my food. Seeing as Drake was going to be eating with us, my appetite had all but disappeared, so I grabbed just a soda and a bag of chips. After showing my ID and paying, I glanced over at our table, and my stomach dropped at the sight of some bleach-blond bimbo standing next to Drake and rubbing his arm.

My temper instantly flared, and it took every ounce of self-control I had not to walk over to her and rip her arm off. I made my way slowly back to the table, taking deep breaths and reminding myself I was not the crazy jealous girl I was acting like. I slid into my seat next to Amber, giving her the brightest fake smile I could muster, completely ignoring Drake and the bimbo. Amber raised her eyebrows, but said nothing about our company as I asked her about her morning class. It was a pitiful attempt really; next I would be asking her about the weather.

Drake seemed oblivious to my attempts to ignore him and his company as he plowed right into the middle of our conversation while Blondie settled herself onto his lap. "So Amber, were you at the party with Chloe last night?"

I raised my eyebrows at the girl, but she simply smirked at me, assuming I was jealous. She was right of course, but I wasn't about to let her know that. Amber cleared her throat, and I glanced in her direction to catch her trying to hide her smile. I was so busted, and I knew she'd be pumping me for information as soon as we were alone.

She turned her gaze to Drake. "Yeah, I was. Why do you ask?"

"I just wondered if you heard us playing. Chloe here seems to think we were the most amazing band she has ever heard."

I snorted. "Please, I said you were good, but I've heard better." I turned back to Amber. "Please don't encourage him, I don't think I can handle it if his ego gets any bigger."

Drake smirked before putting on a hurt face. "Is that what you really think, Chloe? I'm deeply hurt, I thought we had something special."

Amber and I giggled as Blondie leaned in closer to him and ran her hand down his chest. "I'm sure I can think of something to make you feel better."

Drake pushed her hand away and glanced over at me. "Not now, Chrissy. Why don't you run along, I'll find you later."

She pouted as she stood up.

"Fine, Drake, be that way, but you know where to find me," she said as she leaned down and kissed him deeply on the lips, staying attached far longer than necessary in my opinion.

I felt my stomach tighten, and I had to look away from them before I did something stupid. She finally pulled away, smirking at Amber and me before stalking away, swinging her hips extra hard. Unable to contain myself, I glared daggers at her until she was out of sight. I glanced around the table to Drake and Amber once she was out of sight, and both of them were staring at me.

"What?"

Amber coughed as she tried to cover a laugh. "Nothing sunshine, not a thing. Anyway, Drake, I had no idea that was you playing last night. You guys sound insane, I loved it."

I nibbled on my chips as they talked about the band, stealing glances at Drake when he wasn't paying attention.

"So how did you guys meet anyway?" Amber asked, turning her attention to me.

I wasn't planning to tell her about the incident after the party while Drake was around, so I shrugged. "I had to sit by him in my morning class yesterday, and the one today. I was desperate for human interaction so I ended up stuck with him."

Drake grinned at me. "She's lying. I saved her ass last night, literally. So she was groveling at my feet this morning."

Amber glanced between us. "What happened last night?"

I was going to kill Drake for telling her.

"Well, I was walking home from the party last night and the heel of my shoe got caught and broke. Due to my natural grace, I fell down and Drake helped me up and gave me a ride home."

"Wait a minute! You broke my shoe? Just when were you planning on telling me about that?"

I couldn't help but laugh at her missing the part about Drake giving me a ride home and skipping right to her damaged shoes.

"Sorry Amber, I'll buy you a new pair."

"You better! Until then, I'll just borrow those awesome black pumps you have. Actually, I was planning on dragging you to that club down on Fifth Street tonight. I'll wear them then."

"I can't go tonight. I'm hanging out with Logan after he gets out of class."

"Oh, come on! You can hang out with Logan anytime. Come with me tonight, we can get our dance on! Pretty please?" Amber stuck her bottom lip out at me and gave me her best puppy-dog eyes.

"I don't know, Amber, I already promised him. I guess I could check and see if he wanted to come too. Let me text him and see."

I reached for my bag and started digging through the contents, trying to find my phone. After a few minutes and a few muttered curse words from being stabbed by random objects, I pulled my hand out defeated.

"I must have forgotten my phone in my room. I've got some time before my next class. I'll run and get it."

Amber clapped her hands and threw her arms around me. "Thank you! I know he'll say yes, he can't deny you anything."

Drake coughed, and we both looked up to see him watching us with an amused look on his face. "He can't deny her anything? He sounds more like a whipped boyfriend than a best friend."

Amber looked at him like he had grown a second head. "Logan and Chloe? Have you lost your ever-loving mind? They might as well be brother and sister. The day they get together I'll give you my favorite pair of Chucks."

"Whatever you say, you know them better than anyone. So am I invited to this club tonight or are you two going to completely ignore me like you have been for the past five minutes? Mention shoes and you're both gone."

"Rule number one: never get between a woman and her shoes, and yes you can come keep Chloe company tonight. I'm sure she doesn't mind."

My cheeks flamed at her words. "Listen, I've got to go get my phone, but you're welcome to come with us if you want."

I stood and started to grab my bag from the chair, but he got to it first and threw it over his shoulder.

"I don't have class until later, I'll walk with you."

I nodded as I quickly turned away from him, trying to hide my grin. He was seriously carrying my bag for me, and he was going to walk to my room with me. Where we would be alone. With my bed. My stomach twisted from the nerves, but I quickly pushed it aside as we left the cafeteria and made our way toward my dorm. He was just being friendly, and from the way that blonde, Crissy, had hung all over him, he had much better options than me. Why would he ever go for Plain Jane me when he had *those* kind of options?

We walked beside each other in silence for a few minutes before Drake spoke. "So do you like to go to clubs and parties or does Amber force you?"

"She usually has to force me to go, but once I'm there I have fun. I mean, I like to party and dance, I just don't like being in crowds, especially with a bunch of super drunk people."

He nodded his head in agreement. "I can understand that. This might sound stupid since I'm in a band and all, but I hate crowds too. But without crowds there would be no reason to perform. Plus, with crowds come groupies, and you've got to love the groupies."

He shot me a sly smile and I nodded. "Exactly, I mean how could you be a man whore with no groupies?"

"Hey now, I'm not that bad. It's not my fault they show up in next to nothing and flock to me. I mean, look at me, can you blame them?"

I rolled my eyes. "You really are full of yourself, aren't you?"

"Always. You know, the groupies are great and all, but they aren't the ones that really catch my attention."

I glanced up at him and noticed the serious expression on his face. "Oh really, and what kind of girl really catches your attention?"

We had made it to my building by this time, and he was standing in the doorway, blocking my entrance. The serious look was still on his face as he stared at me.

"The ones who don't try, who don't fall all over themselves with me, and who aren't impressed because I'm in a band. But they also have to have a sense of humor, and give me attitude right back when I give it to them." He cleared his throat. "Of course they have to be smoking hot as well, or the rest is just a waste."

I laughed as I pushed him aside to open the door and make my way up the stairs to my floor. "Wow, you were really starting to sound deep there, glad you redeemed yourself at the last minute."

I pulled my key out as we reached my door and unlocked it. Stepping inside the door, I took my bag from him and threw it and my key on the chair next to the door as I started searching the desk for my phone.

Drake walked in behind me and went straight to my bed, flopping down on it like he owned the place.

I glanced back and raised an eyebrow at him. "Don't just stand there, please make yourself at home."

He grinned at me as he kicked his shoes off and put his arms behind his head. "Thanks, I think I will."

I turned back to the desk and continued my search. Unfortunately my phone was nowhere to be seen, so I moved to my bedside table and started moving papers and other junk out of the way before opening the drawer. My phone wasn't there either and I groaned.

"I have no idea where I put the damn thing."

He pulled his phone out of his pocket. "What's your number? I'll call it for you. I have to ask someone do this for me all the time. I lose my phone more than I use it."

I recited the number to him and stood still, straining my ears to listen for it as he dialed. After a few seconds I heard "Bury Me with My Guns On," my unknown ringtone, coming from the bed, but it was muffled. I dropped down to my hands and knees, searching under my bed, but it didn't sound like it was under there.

I stood back up as the ringing stopped. "Dial it again, it's here next to the bed, but I can't find it."

He redialed and the muffled ringing started again. I crouched down next to the bed and realized the sound was coming from underneath him.

"Hey dumbass move, I think you're on it."

He looked over at me and grinned. "Make me."

I grunted as I started trying to shove him off the bed. As soon as I touched him I felt tingles running up my arm, but I ignored them. He refused to move, so I shoved on his hips harder as he laughed at my pitiful attempts.

"Is that all you've got? What a wimp."

At his words I started pushing him even harder, but my hands slipped from his hip and I tumbled down onto him. My breath was sucked out of me as I landed on top of him and I felt those tingles everywhere my body pressed against his. I tried to shove away from him, but he grabbed my arms and pulled me up so I was fully on top of him, chest to chest, stomach to stomach, hips to hips. He was hard everywhere I touched, and I felt my cheeks turning red as I looked at him.

His eyes had darkened until they were black with hunger as he stared at me, and a smirk appeared on his lips. "You know baby, if you wanted to get on top of me all you had to do was ask."

He released my arms, but I was frozen, staring into those beautiful eyes. I glanced down at this mouth—if I moved an inch I would be kissing him. I shook my head to clear my crazy thoughts and pushed myself off of him before I did something incredibly stupid.

"Whatever, jackass, you made me fall so don't try to blame me."

He gave me an easy smile, but I could still see the hunger in his eyes. "You're right, I just wanted an excuse to get you on top of me. It worked though, didn't it?"

I ignored his comment and started trying to shove him again. "Will you please move so I can get my phone?"

He rolled to his side so I could check the bed, and sure

enough my phone was sitting right below the pillow. I snatched it up and unlocked it. I had a couple texts from Logan asking how my morning was going, and one from Amber.

Amber: **Don't think I didn't hear that boy say he gave you a ride home. I want details when we're alone. Xoxo**

Me: **He's here now, I'll fill you in later.**

I sent Logan a text asking him to go to the club tonight, and he replied almost instantly.

Logan: **Yeah, that's fine with me. I'll come to your room after I finish class. Wear something hot!**

Me: **You're hilarious. . . . I'll see you then.**

I glanced up at Drake and saw him watching me. "He said it's fine."

Drake nodded as he rolled onto his back again. "All right, guess we're going clubbing tonight. You have a fake ID?"

I shook my head. "No, but I wasn't planning on drinking anyway."

There was no way I was getting drunk with Drake around me. Plus Logan would drive me crazy trying to watch out for me if I did. I did not need another embarrassing moment like the night before. I stood there awkwardly as Drake watched me from the bed.

"Well, I guess I'll see you later tonight then. I've got your number so I can text you when we leave. You can meet us there." I hinted for him to leave, but he stayed where he was.

"Are you trying to get rid of me?"

"No, not at all. I just figured you had better things to do than hang out on my bed."

He grinned at me. "Nowhere else I'd rather be."

"So how long have you been in your band?" I asked to change the subject as I moved across the room to sit on Rachel's bed.

"I've been with them since I was sixteen. I've lived here in Morgantown with my uncle since I was ten. My mom and dad died in a car wreck so he took me in."

I didn't know what to say to that so I just nodded.

"It's okay, you don't have to freak out or anything, it was a long time ago and I'm over it."

"Yeah, well I really don't know what to say to that besides I'm sorry."

"Nothing to be sorry for unless you were the drunk driver that hit them. Anyway, are you from around here?"

"No, I grew up in Charleston. My mom and I have a complicated relationship, so by the time I was fourteen I had pretty much moved in with Amber and her parents, they took me in like I was their own. Everyone talks about what a great school WVU is, and since Amber and Logan both applied here I did too. So here I am. Yay, Mountaineers."

I waved my imaginary pom-poms, and he laughed. "Nice."

We sat in silence for a few minutes until I looked at the clock.

"Wow, I'd better get going, my class is a fifteen-minute walk from here." I stood and grabbed my bag as Drake sat up and slipped his shoes on.

He walked past me and out the door before turning and grinning. "At least some good came out of you losing your phone."

I looked at him confused. "What?"

He held his own phone up as he turned to walk away. "I've got your number now."

CHAPTER FOUR

DRUNK MEN TALK TOO MUCH

I was slipping on my favorite pair of skinny jeans when I heard a knock at the door. Assuming it was Logan or Amber, I yelled for them to come in as I buttoned my pants and grabbed a fire-engine-red halter top out of the closet, a gift from Amber. I turned to greet them and screamed. Drake was standing in my door with a drop-your-panties grin stretching across his face.

"What the fuck are you doing here?" I yelled as I clutched my top to my chest.

His eyes dropped to my covered chest before coming back up to my face. "I figured I'd just meet you here since Amber and Logan are. I have to say, if this is how you greet me every time, I might just drop by more often."

"Oh, shut up and turn around so I can put my shirt on!"

He kept the smile on his face as he turned around. I quickly threw the shirt on and adjusted it, making sure everything was covered.

"All right, you can turn back around."

He turned and sat down in the chair next to him as I dug

through my massive pile of shoes until I found the ones I was looking for.

"Next time you knock, let me know it's you."

"Would you still greet me like that?"

"No way, hence the reason for telling me it's you."

He shook his head. "Not a chance then."

I sighed as another knock came on my door. Feeling a little bit cautious after what had just happened, I walked over and opened it. Amber and Logan were standing there, and Amber pushed through. "All right, woman, where are those heels I want to . . ." she stopped midsentence as she caught sight of Drake. "Well hello, hot stuff. What are you doing here?"

Logan walked in behind her and glared at the sight of Drake sitting so relaxed in my room. "That's what I'd like to know."

"Hey, Amber, and Logan, right? I was just sitting here while Chloe gave me a striptease."

My eyes darted to Logan and saw his face turn a light shade of pink at Drake's words. "Shut up. He's kidding, he just showed up a minute ago so we could all go to the club together."

Logan was still glaring at Drake, but his face had lost the pink hue. I quickly grabbed the heels Amber wanted and threw them at her, trying to hurry before Logan ripped into Drake.

"Here, Amber, let's go!" I grabbed my key and some cash and stuffed them in the pocket of my jeans before walking to the door. Everyone stepped outside, Amber hopping on one foot as she put her shoes on.

"Slow down, woman! Where the hell is the fire?"

I ignored her as I locked up and we made our way outside. Drake's car was sitting by the curb, and he motioned us to it.

"I figured we could all ride together."

I walked past him and slid into the backseat, Logan sitting down next to me as Amber and Drake sat down in the front. Drake started the car and we were off. The ride to the club was uncomfortably silent, and I was glad when we arrived.

As soon as Drake parked, I jumped out as Logan came around behind me and put his arm around my shoulder. Drake glanced at us and shook his head as he led the way to the club entrance. Luck was actually with us for once: there wasn't a line, and we were quickly let in. The other three had fake IDs, so I was the only one who had to have their hand stamped *Under 21*.

I sighed heavily as the bouncer let us pass by, and Logan looked down at me grinning.

"What?"

"Nothing, I wasn't planning on getting drunk, but a drink would have been nice since I'm not driving."

"Maybe if you're good, I'll slip you a shot or two."

I grinned up at him as he took my hand and started weaving through the crowd on the dance floor to one of the few unoccupied booths in the back.

"Have I told you you're the best lately? Because just so you know, you are."

He smacked me on the butt as I slid into the booth beside him. "You have, but it's always nice to know I'm appreciated."

Drake sat down across from me, and Amber slid in next to him as Logan stood and motioned toward the bar. "I'll buy the first round. I know what you want, Amber, and Chloe, you'll just have to share mine." He glanced at Drake. "What do you want?"

"Just get a Jack and Coke."

Logan nodded as he turned and disappeared into the crowd of swaying bodies.

I turned to Amber as one of my favorite Lady Gaga songs started playing. "Come on, hooker, let's dance!"

I stood and grabbed Amber's hand, leading her into the center of the chaos. I released her once we reached the floor and started swaying to the beat of the music. My hips moved as I raised my hand above my body, my head falling back as I let the music take over. Amber grabbed me and pulled me to her as she put her leg between mine. We moved in perfect synchrony, as only two people who had danced together for years could. We stayed like that for a few minutes before separating, each moving to the rhythm.

I felt someone come up behind and pull me close. I turned to see an attractive guy smiling down at me as he moved with me. Suddenly he was jerked away from me roughly, his eyes going wide with shock.

Logan stood behind him, looking extremely pissed off. "Back the fuck off, asshole, she's with me!"

The guy glanced at me before throwing his hands up in surrender as he walked away from us. "Sorry, bro, my bad."

I sighed as Logan grabbed me by the arm and pulled me off the dance floor and back to the table. Drake was sitting by himself watching us closely as we approached.

I threw myself in the booth and turned to glare at Logan. "Care to explain what that was all about?"

"That guy was all over you! I was just trying to help!"

"He was not all over me, we were just dancing, Logan! He was barely touching me! I don't know what the problem is, but you need to get over it!"

"I don't have a problem, but I'm not about to watch some guy hang all over you! He was watching you and Amber before that, and as soon as you broke apart he went after you. But by all means, if that's the type of guy you want then go for it! When they use you and throw you away, don't come crying to me!"

He stomped away before I could yell at him again. I watched him disappear into the crowd with my mouth hanging open. He had always been protective of me, but since coming to college it had already gotten out of hand after only a few days. I was going to have to sit down with him and have a serious conversation. He was not my brother or my protector, he was my best friend, and I needed to set boundaries.

I glanced around the table and noticed Drake staring at me. "What?"

"Now do you believe me?"

"What are you talking about?"

"What I said earlier, Logan has some major feelings for you. You'd have to be blind to not see it after that little show."

I glared at him. "Don't even start with me tonight, Drake, I'm not in the mood."

He sighed and shrugged his shoulders. "Whatever, go ahead and live in that little oblivious Chloe bubble, but don't say I didn't tell you so."

I grabbed an unopened can of soda off the table and popped it open, trying my hardest to ignore Drake. I was seriously pissed off at him for suggesting that crap again, but what he said was bothering me. I hoped he was wrong, but that little voice inside my head said maybe he wasn't so far off base. Maybe what I had taken for brotherly protectiveness was something more, and if it was I was totally and completely screwed.

I looked up as a little redhead in a dress short enough to be a shirt approached the table and smiled at Drake. I groaned internally as she bent down to rest her elbows on the table, giving Drake a clear shot of her overly exposed cleavage. His eyes dropped to her chest before returning her smile.

"Can I help you with something?"

She batted her eyes in what I think was supposed to be a sexy way as she leaned in closer to him and whispered in his ear. "I'm Molly, I came over to drag you onto the dance floor with me. You want to dance?"

Drake nodded as he stood. "I'm going to go dance with Molly. You all right here by yourself?"

"Yeah, I'll be fine. Besides, one of us deserves to have fun."

He gave me a sympathetic smile before turning and wrapping his arm around her. I watched as they too disappeared into the crowd and mentally gagged. Drake had no problem in the women department, that much was clear. That fact was a good enough reason for me to ignore my stupid crush.

I sat by myself, watching everyone else enjoy my good time. A few guys glanced my way, but apparently I was giving out bad vibes since no one approached me. Just as I finished my drink, Logan appeared out of nowhere with two shot glasses in his hands and sat down beside me.

He pulled me into his arms and kissed my forehead. "I'm sorry, Chloe, it just bothers me to see guys hanging all over you like that."

I looked up at him and saw remorse in his eyes. Suddenly feeling guilty for yelling at him, I snuggled up into his arms and laid my head on his chest.

"I'm sorry too, I shouldn't have yelled at you. I know you were only looking out for me. You know how independent I am, and it just bothers me when you go all badass caveman on me."

I felt his chest shake with laughter under my head. "Caveman, huh? I'll take that as a compliment. Listen, I felt bad for ruining your night, so I brought us both a shot. Consider it a peace offering."

He grabbed a shot glass off the table and handed it to me before picking up his own. Clinking our glasses together, we threw the shots back. My face twisted up at the bitter taste, and he laughed at my expression.

"Am I forgiven?"

I nodded as he grabbed Amber's drink off the table, downing it all in one drink. "Sure, as long as you let me dance without ripping someone's head off."

He smirked as he stood and pulled me up with him. "Since I'll be the only one dancing with you, I can agree to that."

I laughed as he led me onto the dance floor. He stopped in an open space and turned around, pulling me into him. I turned so that my back was against his chest and started grinding against him to the beat of the music. As we danced together, I felt the leftover anger drain away, and I relaxed further back into him. We danced together for a few songs before I looked up and noticed a petite blonde sitting at the bar watching him.

I turned to face him and motioned to her. "That girl is staring at you like she wants to eat you alive. Go talk to her, buy her a drink or something."

He shook his head. "I'm fine here with you."

I pulled away from him. "Seriously, I'm worn out. I'm going to go sit back down, and you," I shoved him in her direction, "are going to go buy her a drink. Have a few yourself, I'll be your protector for once."

He studied my expression. "That wouldn't bother you?"

I gave him a questioning look. "What, you buying some girl a drink? No, definitely not. Now go before she disappears."

His expression turned angry at my words, and I looked at him completely confused.

"Why are you looking at me like I pissed in your Cheerios?"

He shook his head and turned away. "No reason. I'm going to go talk to her. Maybe if I play my cards right I'll even get laid. That'd make you happy, wouldn't it?"

My eyes widened in shock at his words. Logan had never spoken to me about women like that.

"Um, sure. Whatever makes you happy."

He gave me one last glare before walking over to her, leaving me alone and completely confused. I started walking back to the table, trying to figure out what had just happened. I had no idea what I said to make him so mad.

Just as I reached the edge of the dance floor, I felt hands wrap around my waist, and I was pulled back into a warm, hard body. I instantly knew it was Drake as my body started tingling at the contact.

"Where do you think you're going?"

I turned to look at him, and my breath caught at how close his face was to mine. I pulled away slightly, trying to remember how to breathe. "I'm tired, I was going to go sit down at our table for a while."

He shook his head as he pulled me against him. "No way, you've already danced with Amber and Logan. I think it's my turn. I mean, after all, I was the one who gave you a ride tonight."

His eyes twinkled in amusement as the double meaning sank in.

"I don't know, that ride was awful quiet and awkward. It was kind of quick too."

I smiled sweetly at him as he laughed. "Come on, dance with me."

I nodded as he settled his hands low on my waist. I started moving in time with the music, brushing against him. He turned me so I was facing away from him and I started grinding my ass against his pelvis. My body hummed at the close contact as I slowly slid down his body and back up, lifting my arms above my head and wrapping them around his neck as he slid his hands from my waist down to my thighs and back up again.

We continued to dance tight against each other, and I felt him growing hard behind me. Feeling him like that shot lightening straight between my legs and I moaned, laying my head back onto his chest as I pushed myself back tighter against his now bulging cock. He lowered his head so that his lips brushed my neck, then my ear. "Do you feel what you're doing to me, dancing like that?"

I moaned again as his hands slid between us to cup my bottom.

"You're one of the sexiest women I have ever seen and you have no idea just how beautiful you are, do you? You have no clue the effect you have on men, on me."

All thoughts of ignoring my feelings for Drake suddenly disappeared at his words. I turned to face him and wrapped my arms around his neck, my breathing shallow. I stood on my toes so that I was eye level with him, leaning in to kiss him. I stopped when our lips were less than an inch apart.

"Do you want to kiss me?" His breath tickled my lip as he spoke.

Before I could respond, Logan appeared out of nowhere and shoved Drake away from me. I had been leaning into him and I stumbled as he fell backward. Logan reached out and grabbed my arm, pulling me into his chest.

"Chlooooe! Are you okay? I've got ya, baby girl," Logan slurred into my ear.

I could smell alcohol on his breath as I untangled myself from his arms and stepped away from him. "What are you doing, Logan? Are you drunk?"

He stumbled forward and reached for my arm again, but I pulled away.

"No way, Chloe, I'm not drunk! I'm fine, I saw that asshole," he pointed at Drake, who had come up to stand behind me looking extremely pissed off, "trying to maul you so I came to help."

His eyes were glazed over, and he swayed as he spoke. There was no doubt about it, he was drunk. He had obviously thrown several shots back to get this wasted in the short period of time since I had left him.

"Drake was not mauling me, we were just dancing. And you are definitely drunk, my friend. Come on, let's get you home." I glanced over my shoulder at Drake. "Can you find Amber while I get him to the car?"

His eyes went to Logan. "Why don't I get him outside and you find Amber?"

I shook my head. "I don't think that's such a great idea, he's not exactly your biggest fan. Seeing as he's completely trashed, I think you'd both be safer if I went with him."

Drake hesitated for a minute before nodding and handing me his keys. "All right, I'll find Amber and be out in a few."

I turned back to Logan and wrapped my arm around his waist. "Come on big guy, let's get you to the car."

We made our way slowly through the crowd, bumping into several people as we went, and out the door into the cool night air. I kept my arm wrapped around Logan as he stumbled and swayed his way along beside me. We finally reached the car, and I unlocked it. I opened the passenger door and gently shoved him inside after I moved Amber's seat out of the way. He fell into the seat, groaning as I closed the door and made my way around the car and opened the driver's door, pushing up Drake's seat and sliding in beside Logan.

As soon as I sat down, he lay down in the cramped space, resting his head on my lap. I sat running my fingers through his hair as he mumbled something and started snoring softly. Logan never drank this much, and it worried me.

When he woke up the next day, I was going to have a talk with him about this crap. I had spent too many nights trying to take care of my drunken mother—when she would let me—to have to take care of Logan like this. I closed my eyes and let my head fall back and rest on the headrest as I listened to his snores.

I was starting to doze off when one of the doors opened and my eyes flew open at the sound. Drake and Amber got in the car, and Drake turned to face me, holding out his hand for the keys. I gently pushed Logan's head out of the way as I grabbed them out of my pocket and tossed them to him. He caught them and turned to start the car without a word. He peeled out of the parking lot, tires squealing as he flew down the road back to our dorm.

Amber looked back at us with concern. "Is he okay? Drake said he was pretty wasted."

I nodded. "Yeah, he just needs to sleep it off."

Drake glanced at me in the rearview mirror. "Is he always that much of an asshole?"

"Shut up, he just had too much to drink."

Drake turned his attention back to the road, and I sighed.

This night had been a disaster, except dancing with Drake, that had definitely been the highlight of the evening. We rode the rest of the way in silence. Drake pulled up in front of our dorm and stepped out. He pushed his seat forward and grabbed Logan to pull him out of my lap.

"Hey, asshat, wake up. We've got to get your sorry ass upstairs."

Logan groaned as he opened his eyes and let Drake pull him out of the car. I quickly exited and ran around the car to help Drake walk him inside. We made our way slowly to the building, one of us on each side to help support him as Amber rushed ahead and opened the door to let us in. We told Amber good night at the entrance and turned to the stairwell.

Getting him up the stairs was a nightmare, but somehow we managed. As we reached his door, I put my hand in his pants pocket and pulled his keys out.

"Next time you reach in my pocket, move your hand to the left a little," Logan grumbled as he leaned against the wall with Drake supporting him, his eyelids fluttering open slightly.

I smacked him in the chest before unlocking the door and stepping back to let him and Drake pass through. Drake walked him to his bed and shoved him down onto it.

Logan groaned and rolled to his side as his eyes landed on me. "Come help me, Chloe."

I walked over to the bed and started pulling his shoes off. Drake stood off to the side, watching me with a strange expression.

"Thanks for your help, Drake, but I've got it from here."

He smirked. "Yeah, I'm sure you do."

He waved as he left, closing the door behind him, and I went back to the task of getting Logan semiundressed. I pulled his socks off and moved to stand beside him and started tugging on his shirt.

"A little help would be nice, you know."

Logan slowly sat up as I pulled his shirt over his head.

"All right, lie back down and stay on your side in case you throw up." I grabbed a garbage can and sat it beside his bed. "And aim for this, I'm so not cleaning up your puke."

He laughed as he rolled to his side. "Yes, ma'am. Come lie down with me for a little while."

"No thanks, I'm beat and my own bed is calling my name."

"Fine," he grumbled as I bent down to kiss him on the cheek.

Just as I reached him, he grabbed my waist to pull me down on top of him and turned his head so that my lips pressed to his. Before I could react, his arms pinned me on top of him and he was kissing me hard on the lips. I tried to pull away as his tongue slipped into my mouth, but he was holding me too tight. He finally released me and I jumped off the bed.

"What the hell, Logan?"

He just grinned up at me and closed his eyes. "I've been wanting to do that all night. I love you, Chloe."

Before I could respond, he was already asleep. I groaned as I stomped out the door and made my way to my room. I unlocked my door and threw my keys on the desk before falling onto my bed. My eyes went to Rachel's side of the room before returning to staring up at the ceiling above my head. She was already passed out for the night, and I listened to her soft snores as I pictured Logan drunk upstairs. What the hell had just happened in there? Logan had no right to kiss me, not even drunk, and I intended to add that to the growing list of topics we needed to discuss.

My mind drifted away from my drunken best friend and back to the dance floor with Drake. I had been so close to kissing him, and if Logan hadn't shown up when he did, I knew without a doubt I would have. I kept telling myself to stay away from him, but then completely ignored my own advice. I had my future planned out in my head: focus on school, graduate with a psychology degree, move far away to keep my mother from finding me, and get a great job.

There was no room for Drake or any guy in my plans, and I liked it that way, yet he kept shoving in without even realizing it. I decided then and there, since I couldn't ignore the fact that I already had feelings for Drake, that I would just let the cards fall where they may and pray I left with my heart still intact in the end.

My thoughts were interrupted as my phone beeped with a new text message. I grabbed it off the nightstand and saw it was from Amber.

Amber: **You make it back to your room okay?**

Me: **Yeah, I'm in bed now.**

Amber: **Okay good, I wanted to make sure Logan didn't knock you down the stairs or something. That boy was out of it. I've never seen him like that.**

Me: **Yeah I know. I don't know what's up with him. We're going to have a long talk tomorrow.**

Amber: **Don't blame you. Anyway . . . I saw you and Drake** dancing tonight, it looked like you were having sex on the dance floor. ;-)

Me: Shut up ho, we were just dancing. Seriously, what is up with everyone being against my dancing?

Amber: Sure, whatever helps you sleep at night. You know you want to lick that boy from head to toe.

Me: Good night Amber . . . -_-

I quickly turned off my phone before she could respond. I stood and threw it on the nightstand before grabbing my bathroom bag and went to take a much-needed shower with thoughts of licking certain parts of Drake running through my head. A cold shower it was then.

CHAPTER FIVE

CONFESSIONS

The next morning, I woke up extra early so I could talk to Logan before class started. I dressed quickly and grabbed my bag off the table, locking the door silently behind me as I tried not to wake Rachel. I made my way up the stairs to Logan's room and knocked softly, afraid that he was still asleep, or maybe even still drunk. A few seconds later the door swung open, and Logan stood there looking like he had been run over by a truck.

"Rough night, tiger?" I asked as I pushed past him and sat down on his bed.

He held his head and groaned. "Do you have to talk so loud?"

I giggled and whispered an apology.

"So what are you doing up this early? I don't think you've ever been awake this early in your life."

My eyes were suddenly mesmerized by my shoes as I debated on what to say first.

"Quit staring at your shoes. It's a dead giveaway that you're trying to avoid me. What's up?"

I took a deep breath as he sat down beside me and waited for me to start talking. "I wanted to talk to you about a couple things actually. Just let me say what I have to say then you can fight with me, okay?"

He nodded and gave me a confused look. "Okay . . . Go for it."

"All right, listen. I know you are just trying to watch out for me, and I love knowing that you care enough to do it, but you have got to back off with the whole overprotective brother thing."

He opened his mouth to speak, but I put my hand over it.

"Let me finish. You and Amber know everything that happened with my mom, so you know I am more than capable of taking care of myself. You have got to let me live my life, Logan. I'm going to do something stupid from time to time, I'm going to get hurt. Hell, I might even get stupid drunk and have a crazy orgy, but they're my mistakes to make and I need to make them. You can't shelter me from everything, and honestly, you're smothering me to death." I lowered my hand from his mouth and waited for him to speak.

He sighed and his shoulders slumped. "I didn't realize I was smothering you, Chloe. Honest. I promise to try to back off, but sometimes I can't help it. Protecting you is second nature to me."

"All I can ask of you is to try."

He pulled me into his arms and hugged me. "Is that all you wanted to talk about?"

I pulled away from him gently as I spoke. "No, I wanted to ask you to try to be nicer to Drake. He seems like he likes to hang out with us, which means he is going to be around. It would make me feel a lot better if I didn't have to worry about you ripping his head off every time I turn around. Can you try to get along with him for me? He's a really nice guy, you might even be friends if you tried being nice to him."

Logan frowned. "I don't like the way he looks at you when you're not looking. He wants you, and anyone with eyes can see it."

I shook my head, even though I was starting to think he did after dancing with him last night. "We're just friends. Please try to get along with him, for me."

He sighed and ran a hand across his face. "All right, I'll try. But I'm not promising anything."

I smiled at him. "Thank you, that's all I'm asking. Now, what was up with the drinking last night? I have never seen you that drunk before."

"I've just had some stuff going on in my head. I started talking to Chastity and ended up drinking more than I planned. I'm sorry if I acted like an idiot, I don't remember much after I was at the bar with her."

"The girl I showed you, that's Chastity?"

He nodded. "Yeah, she seemed nice from what I can remember."

I laughed. "I'm glad. So you don't remember anything after you were at the bar?"

"Not really. I remember you getting me to the car, Drake hauling my ass in here—none too gently might I add—and you taking my shoes off. That's it."

My stomach dropped as I realized he didn't remember kissing me. I had no idea if I should tell him or not.

"What's wrong, Chloe? You have an awful look on your face."

"Um, you don't remember anything after that?"

Logan shook his head. "No, nothing. Why? Did I do something stupid? I did, didn't I? I can tell by the look you're giving me." He took my hand in his. "Tell me what I did. Please."

I looked at our hands as I whispered, "You pulled me down on top of you and kissed me."

He dropped my hand and jumped off the bed. "I did what?"

"You kissed me."

He ran his hands through his hair as he paced in front of me. "I didn't try anything else, did I?"

I shook my head no as he dropped down to his knees in front of me and rested his head on mine. "I'm so sorry if I made you feel uncomfortable, Chloe. I wasn't myself. Please tell me you aren't mad."

"Of course I'm not mad. I just, I don't understand why you did it."

We sat in silence for a moment as I waited for him to speak. When he didn't, I lifted my head to look at him. "Logan? Why did you kiss me?"

He raised his eyes to stare into mine and I had to force myself to breathe. Drake had been right, and it had taken me until this moment to realize it. When I looked into Logan's eyes, I saw love. Not brotherly love, but something else entirely, something that was accompanied by lust. My breath caught in my throat as he leaned down and lightly brushed his lips against mine before pulling back.

"I've told you for years that I loved you, you just misunderstood what kind of love I felt."

I sat frozen on the bed, unable to process what he was telling me.

"Look at me, Chloe."

I raised my gaze to meet his.

"This doesn't change anything between us, understood?

If you don't feel the same, I understand. Just think about it, okay?"

I nodded as he kissed me on the forehead.

"I'm going to skip our morning class. I'll catch up with you at lunch, okay?"

"Yeah, I'd better go or I'm going to be late." I stood up and grabbed my bag off the bed beside me. "I'll see you later, Logan."

My mind was still reeling from the conversation with Logan as I took my seat in class. How had I missed it all these years? And even though he told me that it didn't change anything, to me it changed everything. I had never considered Logan as anything more than a friend. Sure, I knew he was attractive, but I had never really thought about it. To me, he was just my Logan, my best friend. Now I wasn't even sure how I was supposed to act around him, or if any feelings I had for him could be turned into something more.

"What has you in such deep thought over there? Trying to solve world hunger?"

I jumped at the sound of Drake's voice. "You scared the crap out of me! Where did you come from?"

He raised his eyebrows. "From what I learned in anatomy, I came from my mother. But if you're referring to just now, through the door."

I couldn't help but laugh at his reply, "You think you're hilarious, don't you?"

"Yeah, and I've been told that several times. So back to my original question, what were you concentrating on so hard when I came in?"

I bit my lip as I debated on telling him what had happened between Logan and me. Deciding I'd rather avoid a long *I told you so,* I shrugged my shoulders.

"Nothing really, just worried about Logan," which really was the truth, even if he didn't know exactly why I was worried.

"I see. Is Pretty Boy still hung over?"

"Yeah, I checked on him before I came to class. He's going to skip his morning class and sleep it off. He looked like crap."

Drake laughed. "Seeing as he could barely stand up last night, I'm betting crap would be an understatement."

"Leave him alone, he had a rough night."

"All right, I'll leave him be since he isn't here to defend himself. Did you have fun last night?"

My stomach tightened as I thought about us dancing together, and I stared at my desk as I answered. "Yeah, I did."

He leaned over so that he was only a few inches away from me and I glanced up to see his eyes smoldering.

"I did too. Too bad we were interrupted before things started to get interesting. We'll have to do it again sometime soon."

I was saved from replying when a couple girls walked over to us. "Hey, you're in that band, Breaking the Hunger, with Adam and Eric, aren't you? Drake right?"

Drake turned away from me to give them his trademark sexy smile. "That'd be me. What can I help you lovely ladies with?"

The brunette who had spoken before stepped closer to him and slid a piece of paper into his hand. "Why don't you call me sometime, maybe I can help you."

She smiled sweetly as she turned back to her friends and walked away to sit on the other side of the room.

I glanced at the note in his hand. "What was that all about?"

He looked up at me and grinned before opening up the folded note to read it.

"That," he motioned to where the girl was sitting, glaring at me from across the room, "was Xanda, and apparently if I call her at this number she will give me a good time."

I rolled my eyes as I turned away from him, trying to hide the hurt I was feeling. He wasn't mine, and I shouldn't be bothered by other girls giving him their numbers. "Nice, you get around a lot, don't you?"

He grinned at me as he tucked the note into his pocket. "I told you before, gotta love the groupies."

The rest of my morning flew by, and soon I was making my way to the cafeteria to meet up with Logan and grab some lunch. He was standing outside looking pale with a pair of sunglasses on to hide his eyes.

"Feeling better?"

"Not really, but I figured I should probably make it to at least a couple classes today."

He held the door open for me as I walked past him and into the cafeteria. We grabbed some food and sat down at an empty table next to the doors. I devoured my food like I hadn't eaten in weeks as Logan watched me with a look of disgust.

"There is no way I'm going to be able to handle food. Here, take mine," he said as he slid his sandwich over to me.

"You need to eat, it'll make you feel better."

"No thanks, I'll take my chances."

We sat in an uneasy silence with him staring at me. I couldn't think of a single thing to say that didn't involve our conversation from this morning. The chair next to me was pulled back and Drake dropped into it.

"Dude, you look like shit."

I hid a smile as Logan pinched his lips together.

Drake turned to me. "What are you guys doing later? I

thought we might go hang out at the bar I play at." He glanced up at Logan as an evil smile spread across his face. "Grab a beer or two, and something to eat."

Logan turned a light shade of green and stood up. "I've got to go. I'll text you later, Chloe."

He was out the door before I could reply and I turned to glare at Drake. "That wasn't very nice."

"What'd I say?"

"Don't try to play innocent, you know exactly what you did."

"Whatever. So what do you say? Want to go to the bar tonight? You can bring Amber too."

I shook my head. "No thanks, I've been out the last two nights, I need to fit some actual studying somewhere in my college life."

He shrugged his shoulders as he stood up. "Suit yourself, but if you change your mind, you have my number."

I watched as he walked out the door with the brunette from class, I think he said her name was Xanda, following him. I had no doubt he'd find someone to entertain him while I was studying.

CHAPTER SIX

MY HERO

The rest of the week passed quickly, and before I knew it, I was sitting in my room Friday night going over some of my assignments due on Monday. I had stuck to my word, working on assignments and studying Wednesday and Thursday nights, and it appeared I was going to be doing the same tonight. *What a way to spend my Friday night,* I thought to myself as I sighed for the thousandth time and threw the book shut.

Amber had a date tonight with Alex, the guy she had met at the sorority party, and Rachel was nowhere to be found, so I was on my own for the night. I stood up, deciding I could at least make a trip to Starbucks and get some caffeine in me for an all-night study session. I grabbed my car keys and headed for the door, leaving a note for Rachel in case she came home and wondered where I went. I was walking down the stairs, dreaming of a pumpkin spice latte, when I ran into Logan.

"Hey, where you headed to?" he asked cheerfully.

"I'm going to make a run to Starbucks. I need caffeine if I am going to get any work done tonight."

He rolled his eyes at me. "You and your caffeine addiction—

as much coffee as you drink you would think you could manage to drag yourself out of bed in the mornings on time."

"There is nothing wrong with my caffeine addiction, but since you're being so rude, you can guarantee I won't be bringing you a cup back."

"Somehow I think I'll survive."

I chuckled to myself as I waved good-bye and made my way out the door to my car. Things had been less strained over the last few days with Logan, and I was thankful to be getting back to normal with him. Both of us had been busy, but we still managed to at least text each other a few times throughout the day.

I started my car and headed across town to get my coffee fix. Lucky for me it was only a little way across town, and before I knew it, I was pulling into their drive-through and ordering my latte. The boy opened the window to take my money, and I almost passed out from the coffee smell coming from inside. I would live here if only I could afford it! He handed me my coffee and I noticed a *Help Wanted* sign hanging in the window.

"Hey, can I have an application too please?"

He smiled and grabbed an application from under the counter. "Here you go. Get it back as soon as you can, we're desperate!"

I took the application and thanked him. I decided to pull over and fill out all the information in the parking lot. It was pure luck that I had a major Starbucks addiction, and since I had worked at the one back in my hometown my senior year, I already knew how to make most of their drinks.

I got out of my car and headed toward the doors. As soon as I opened them, I was assaulted with the coffee smell again. Yeah, I could definitely stand working here. I marched over to the counter and handed my application to the woman standing behind the register. I noticed her name tag read *Janet* as she looked over it, noting I had already worked at a Starbucks.

"Can you start on Monday evening at five o'clock sharp? We need someone for the evening shift, and based off your schedule preferences it should be perfect."

I almost jumped up and down. I had been contemplating getting a job, and this one had all but fallen right into my lap.

"Sure, I'll be here!"

She told me what I was expected to wear, and I thanked her as I walked back out the door, all but skipping to my car. I guess my coffee addiction had finally paid off. I couldn't wait to tell Logan.

I jumped back in my car and made my way toward the exit. Just as I started to pull out I noticed a bar across the road—Gold's Pub, where Drake said his band played every Friday night. I glanced at my dashboard. It was almost nine o'clock, so surely his band would be playing soon. I made a split-second decision before pulling across the road and into the bar parking lot. The lot was packed and I had to hunt for a spot, finding one in the very back, next to a shiny black 1983 Mustang. I guess that answered my question about him already being here.

I grabbed my coffee and headed inside. Once the guy by the door—who looked like he was an escaped convict on the run—let me through without carding me, I managed to find an empty table in the back. Just as I sat down, I saw Drake and his fellow band members take the stage. My breath caught when I noticed him; he seemed to look sexier every time I saw him.

Glad to be hidden by the shadows in the back, I openly stared at him as they started into their first song. It was fast but heavy and had me entranced at once. At the party they had covered other bands, but this wasn't a song I knew, and being heavy into rock music, I assumed it was one of their own. His voice was as amazing as I remembered it, and he knew it. He gave a cocky look out across the bar and to the women already standing by the stage. When he got to the chorus he belted the lyrics out, almost screaming.

> *Just follow me,*
> *I'll take you there,*
> *Stand by me,*
> *Have no fear,*
> *When we're together the world stands still,*
> *Just follow me,*
> *Stand by me,*
> *I'll make it worth your while,*
> *Have no fear,*
> *Just follow me,*
> *I'll take you there*

The lyrics were catchy and I instantly started swaying in my seat to the music. Drake could definitely control an audience—he had the women eating out of the palm of his hand with the smoky, sexy looks he was giving them. When the song ended, they all started screaming out his name. He grinned at them, signaling the guitar player to start the next song. Soon the drummer—a girl, amazingly enough—started in, followed by the guy on bass.

This was a slower song, and as Drake started singing the lyrics, his face took on a thoughtful, almost helpless look. He closed his eyes as he sang, almost whispering on some of the lyrics. It was the most beautiful, heartfelt song I had ever heard. The second time he sang the chorus, I already knew the words by heart.

Hold me close,
I need to feel you there,
When the rest of the world's gone,
All I need is you in my arms,
So hold me close,
Keep me safe,
I need to feel you there

I loved the song, and I loved watching Drake perform it. He was absolutely amazing, and I wanted to tell him so. As he finished the song and started back into another fast, heavy song, I decided I would catch him after the show and let him know. The band played a few more songs before finishing up. They grabbed their instruments and jumped off stage as I pushed through the crowd to approach them.

He didn't notice me at first, since there were more women than I could count gathered around him and the other guys. I saw the girl who played drums grin and roll her eyes as the bass player grabbed a girl and headed out the door, holding his guitar in one hand and her on the other. Drake had an arm around some blond girl in a skirt shorter than my dress the night of the party when he glanced up and saw me. He untangled himself from her, whispering something in her ear as he continued to stare at me.

She pouted as she glanced up at me, but nodded and headed over to a table with her friends, throwing glares my way as she went.

He walked over to me with a huge grin on his face. "Hey! You made it!"

I smiled shyly up at him. "Yeah, I was in the area and thought I'd stop by. You were amazing, even better than you were at the party, if that's possible."

He gave me one of those earth-shattering grins that made my knees weak.

"Thanks. I'm going to hang out here and have a couple beers. Care to join me?"

"Uh, yeah sure, I can stay for a few." My stomach was in knots as he took my hand and led me across the room to the table the girl drummer was sitting at.

Drake motioned to me. "Jade, this is Chloe. Jade is the drummer in our band."

I smiled and nodded in her direction. "Yeah, I noticed you playing! You're really amazing!"

Jade gave me a quick once-over, smiling as if she approved.

"Why, thank you! I've been playing since I was ten. The drums have always been my thing."

She had the cutest southern accent when she talked, and I instantly liked her. She was a pretty girl, with warm brown eyes and dyed black hair that had red streaks running through it. It fell halfway down her back in gentle waves. I had noticed earlier that she was tiny, probably three or four inches under my five foot five, but she gave off an air of confidence that told me she was not someone to push around.

Drake stood up and headed to the bar. "I'll get us a couple of beers, be right back."

I watched him walk to the bar, and noticed several other women staring at him as well. He reached the bar and the bar-tender, a woman of course, skipped over the people already standing there and went straight to Drake. She grabbed him three beers and handed them over the bar, leaning forward enough that he had a full shot down her low-cut shirt. I rolled my eyes and turned back to Jade before I lost my Starbucks.

Jade seemed to notice my discomfort, and gave me a sympathetic smile but didn't say anything. I knew from the short time we had spent together that Drake tended to have lots of women around him all the time. That is, lots of willing women around. We sat in silence as Drake made his way back to the table. I couldn't help but notice how well he looked in his fitted black T-shirt and distressed jeans that hung low on his hips. There was no denying the boy had a body, and I found myself thinking yet again about how he would look with his shirt off.

I shrugged the thought off, knowing that probably every girl here was wondering the same thing, or in some cases, not having to wonder at all. I'd seen him start to leave with the blonde after all, and as sexy as he was, he had to be getting some on a regular basis.

He finally made it to the table and set our beers down in front of us. "Here ya go, guys. So I can see you two were in deep conversation over here, don't let me being here stop you."

Jade and I both laughed, knowing neither of us had said a word to each other while he was gone. It wasn't her fault really, I was always so shy around new people and I never knew what to say.

Jade started talking to him about some show they were doing in a couple weeks, and they were deep in conversation before too long, completely ignoring me. As I sat there watching them talk so freely, I suddenly felt out of place. I looked around the room trying to distract myself and noticed a *Restroom* sign across the room. I stood, excusing myself, and hurried across the bar and into the bathroom.

I stood at the sink, looking at my reflection in the mirror above it. With no makeup and in my old University sweatshirt and torn jeans, I looked completely out of place here. All the other women in the bar had dressed to impress, and I had no clue how Drake had even noticed me with a room full of them.

I sighed, wondering why Drake had asked me to sit with him, and then completely ignored me. If this was some kind of game to him, I had no intention of playing. I knew I had developed an attraction to him as soon as I saw him, and it had grown stronger over the week as I talked with him, but I wasn't about to put myself out there to get hurt if all I was to him was just a game.

I left the bathroom and started walking back to the table. As I walked by the bar some guy caught my arm.

I stopped and looked at him questioningly. "Yes? Can I help you with something?"

He smiled at me. "I was just wondering if I could buy you a drink?"

I started to decline, but decided why not. "Uh, sure, but only one. I've got to drive home in a few."

I sat down at the bar and ordered a rum and Coke.

The guy looked at me surprised. "Wow, most girls go for the girly drinks."

I shrugged my shoulders. "I'm not most girls."

He grinned at me as the bartender set my drink in front of me.

"Obviously not. I'm Nick, by the way."

"Chloe, nice to meet you, Nick."

I took a sip of my drink and winced a little as it burned its way down my throat. I didn't know why I had suddenly gotten so upset over Drake ignoring me, and something strong would take the edge off. Nick and I sat and talked for a while, mainly about my school, my new job, and just random things. He had informed me he had recently graduated from college and was working at a local advertising agency as their accountant. I was impressed that he had already landed such a great job so soon after graduating.

As we talked he ordered me another drink, then another. The first two I was okay with, but the third one made me nervous. I did have to drive after all, and I told him so.

"I forgot about that. I'm really sorry. But you've already had two, and I'm sure they will catch up to you soon, so you might as well enjoy this one too. I'll pay for a cab for you, that way you're safe."

He seemed genuine so I nodded. "All right, that sounds reasonable, but I'm not drinking anymore after this one."

The other two, and my beer before, were already starting to make me feel dizzy, and even though Nick seemed like a nice guy, I was not about to get stupid drunk with him. We kept talking and I started to feel like I was floating. I was laughing at everything he said, even if it wasn't that funny. Somehow his hand had ended up resting on my leg and I hadn't felt the urge to move it.

I turned and glanced around the bar, and caught Drake staring at us with a pissed-off look on his face. I waved at him, but he didn't return the favor, he just kept staring at us.

I turned back around, suddenly uncomfortable, and looked at Nick. "I think I'd like for you to call me that cab now. It's getting kind of late."

He seemed disappointed, but nodded and pulled out his cell phone, calling the cab company. He hung up a minute later and stood.

"They'll be here in a few. I'll wait outside with you."

I nodded. "Okay, sounds good. Let's go."

I stood and started walking toward the door when I remembered I'd left my purse at Drake's table.

"Wait, I need to grab my purse from my friend's table. I'll be right back."

I made my way across the room and walked up to Drake's table, stumbling as I went. I realized I really was drunk.

"Hey, I'm heading home. Thanks for inviting me to stay."

Jade smiled and said good night, but Drake was glaring at me.

"You are not driving home, Chloe—you can barely stand up!"

I flinched at the anger in his words. "I'm not driving. Nick called me a cab. It's probably outside waiting by now, so I'll see you later."

I grabbed my purse and attempted to march across the room before he could say another word. I managed to reach Nick without falling, but just barely. I stumbled into him as we started out the door, and he had to grab me and hold me around the waist to steady me as we went. He kept his arm around my waist as we walked across the parking lot.

"Thanks for tonight, I had fun." I had barely finished the sentence when I stumbled again. "Maybe too much fun."

Nick laughed at me as he led me to a car on the side of the lot. "We can stand over here by my car until the cab gets here."

He wrapped his arms around me and pulled me close, tilting my head up so he could see my face. Before I knew what was happening he leaned down and kissed me roughly. I tried to push him away, but he was stronger than me and I couldn't get him to let go.

"Stop!" I yelled into his mouth, but he only laughed and pushed me up against his car.

His hands started traveling down my body, and he reached behind me, grabbing my ass. I started to cry as I tried to shove him again.

"Please stop. Please," I begged him, but he ignored my pleas.

This could not be happening to me, not again. I could not be standing in a bar parking lot being molested by some nice man I had just met.

"Just shut up. You know you want this."

He grabbed my hips and pulled me away just enough that he could get his hands to the front of my pants. He held me against the car with his body and put one hand over my mouth as he started undoing the buttons. I was sobbing uncontrollably and still trying to push him off, but the alcohol had made me fuzzy. I knew what was going to happen, and I wanted to die before he touched me. I made one last attempt to break free, when suddenly he was pulled off of me. I slid down the side of his car to the ground as I watched someone holding him to the ground, punching him in the face over and over.

"You stupid fucking asshole! I'll fucking kill you if you ever come near her again."

My heart rate increased as I realized Drake was my savior. Nick was attempting to fight back, but I could tell he was no match for Drake. Drake straddled him, keeping him pinned to the ground as he sent blow after blow down onto Nick's face. After what seemed like hours, he gave Nick one last punch, knocking him out, and stood up. He turned to me and approached me slowly, as if he was afraid I was going to run.

"Chloe, it's me, Drake. Are you all right, sweetheart?"

I nodded as he finally reached me and sat down next to me, pulling me into his arms as I realized I was still sobbing uncontrollably.

He just sat there and held me as I soaked his shirt with my tears until my sobs started to subside. Even after I stopped crying, I leaned into him, unwilling to move away from the safety his arms provided.

"Chloe, we need to call the cops before he comes to, which I'm assuming will be soon."

I looked over to Nick on the ground and a chill went up my spine. The police would be called, I'd have to press charges, tell my whole story to a bunch of cops, stand in a courtroom, and be berated by some attorney. I didn't have it in me to go through all of that, to have other people see how vulnerable I'd made myself. I just couldn't do it.

I looked up at him and shook my head. "No, I can't do it. I just want to go home. We were both drinking and I'm sure he wouldn't have done it otherwise."

Drake looked like I'd smacked him across the face. "Are you kidding me right now? That piece of shit tried to rape you. Drinking or not, it doesn't matter—what he did was wrong."

I couldn't stand to look at his face and see the disappointment. I lowered my gaze as I shook my head again. "No, I'm not doing it. I just want to go home. I'm calling a taxi and leaving before he wakes up."

I grabbed my cell phone out of my pocket and started searching for the nearest taxi service.

"You're really serious, aren't you?"

I glanced up at him and saw the anger radiating from his eyes. "Yes, I am."

I started dialing the number when he grabbed my phone from my hand.

"Well, you're not going home by yourself. I live right around the corner; you can stay with me tonight."

Before Nick I would have been practically jumping up and down to have this opportunity, but now I refused to go with him. I felt so much shame because he knew what had almost happened to me. Underneath that, I felt fear. Even though he had saved me, he was a male as well, and I didn't even really know him all that well.

"No, thank you. I would rather just go home. I'm not feeling as drunk, but my head's starting to throb and I just want to go to bed."

He stepped forward, grabbed my arm, and all but started dragging me across the lot.

"Well, I'm not taking no for an answer. You shouldn't be alone after what happened tonight. You can go to my house and sleep in my bed."

I jerked my arm from his grasp. "I'm *not* sleeping with you."

He sighed and turned back toward me. "I know you're not sleeping with me. You can have my bed, I'll take the couch."

CHAPTER SEVEN

WELCOME HOME

Drake finally convinced me to go with him after much kicking and screaming on my part. As we pulled up to a house just a block away, I realized he wasn't kidding about living right around the corner.

"Why do you even drive? You could walk faster."

He grinned, the first one I'd seen since Nick. "I could, but then I wouldn't be able to show my car off to the ladies."

I rolled my eyes as I stepped out of the car and toward the house. It looked small from the outside, and as far as I could tell in the dim lighting on the street, it was either light blue or gray. He unlocked the door and held it open for me as I stepped inside. He flipped the light on as he closed the door behind us, revealing a small entryway that sat between a kitchen and a living room. A hallway led into darkness across from me, where I could only assume the bathroom and bedroom were. He hung his jacket next to the door and headed into the kitchen.

"Do you want something to drink?" he asked over his shoulder.

"Um, no I'm fine," I replied as I inspected his kitchen. It wasn't huge, but it wasn't tiny either, and while the appliances weren't brand new, they were nice.

"Do you own this place?"

He shook his head. "Nah, I rent off my Uncle Jack. He's currently deployed overseas so I'm living here by myself until he gets back, probably another year or so."

"Ah, I see. Well, it's a really nice house."

He smiled as he leaned against the counter. "Thanks."

His expression turned thoughtful. "Are you really okay?"

I looked at the checkered floor tiles as I nodded. "Yes, I'm fine; I just want to forget about it."

And I did. I also wanted to forget about Nick lying in the parking lot still unconscious as we pulled away. *I hope he gets mugged,* I thought venomously.

"Please don't tell anyone what happened. Please."

Drake shook his head. "I won't, but you really should call the cops before it's too late. He deserves to be behind bars. I'd like to kill him for what he tried to do to you."

The anger in his voice softened my heart. This man seemed to really care, even though he barely knew me.

"No, just drop it."

He huffed as he pushed himself away from the counter and headed toward the doorway.

"Fine, let me show you where the bedroom is. I'm sure you're tired. You can shower too if you want."

A shower sounded wonderful to me. I wanted to scrub every minute of the night off of my skin.

"Yeah, I could definitely use a shower, but I don't have any clothes to change into."

He seemed uncomfortable for a minute, bouncing from

foot to foot as he spoke. "You can wear my clothes and I, uh, have some girl underwear and bras someone left here."

My eyes widened, and I couldn't help but to ask why he had women's underwear in his house.

"Well, a couple of them left extra clothes, but never came after them. Don't worry though, most of them still have their tags."

My cheeks reddened at his words. I had assumed he got around, but this was proof in black-and-white lace.

"Okay, that's fine. Just show me the bathroom and where they're at."

He led me down the hallway and flipped on a light inside the bedroom. The room was not what I'd expected from him, but then I remembered he was renting. The walls were a light cream color, bare of anything sentimental, almost as if he didn't really live here at all.

I giggled as I noticed the color of the carpet. "Really? Pink? You never struck me as that type of guy."

He rolled his eyes as he dug through a drawer and pulled out a pair of boy shorts and underwear. "Shut up. I'm renting, remember?"

I grinned. "Of course."

He threw the underwear at me and started digging again. There were an awful lot of silky-looking panties in there.

"What size bra do you wear?"

My mouth dropped open at the question. "That's none of your business, thank you very much."

He gave me a sly look. "I'm trying to find something for you. I guess you'll have to make me guess."

He stared at my chest, unashamed for a full minute longer than was necessary in my opinion. My cheeks warmed and I crossed my arms.

He grinned and turned back to the drawer. "Let's see, I'm going to guess D?"

Could my face have got any warmer? It seemed like all I did was blush when he was around.

He finally pulled a bra from the drawer, something far sexier than anything I wore, and threw it at me. I glanced at the tag and smiled to myself. Thirty-six D, he'd nailed it first try. He pulled a pair of jogging pants and a T-shirt from another drawer and handed them to me as well.

"Bathroom is directly across the hall. Yell if you need anything."

I turned and headed across the hall to the bathroom. Just as I started to shut the door, his hand caught it. He had a playful look in his eyes.

"Looks like I guessed right on the bra," he said as he laughed and closed the door in my face.

. . .

I showered quickly and slipped on the borrowed clothes. I smelled Drake's shirt as I slid it over my head. He always smelled so good, a mixture of his body wash and his natural male scent. This was getting ridiculous, even his scent turned me on. I stepped out of the bathroom and yelled good night down the hall toward him before making my way into his bedroom. I curled up in his covers, which also had that amazing Drake smell, and closed my eyes.

I tossed and turned, but I couldn't seem to get comfortable. It wasn't the bed really, my thoughts were in total chaos after what had happened to me. If Drake hadn't come out of that bar, who knows what would have happened to me, besides the obvious. *Rape.* It was such a dirty word, and it brought tears to my eyes. *No! You are not going to cry again.* I sniffled as I shifted under the covers yet again.

Sometime later in the night, I woke up screaming as the images of my nightmare followed me into consciousness. I sat straight up in bed as I tried to control the sobs racking through my body. I had relived it all again, only this time I had been running from him. Suddenly, I felt arms around me and I screamed again, thinking Nick really was here.

"Shhh, it's just me. You're safe, Chloe. I won't ever let him touch you, I promise," Drake mumbled into my ear as he rocked me in his arms.

At the sound of his voice, I relaxed. I owed so much to him—he had kept me safe before, and here he was again, protecting me.

"Thank you, I mean it. If you hadn't been there . . . If you hadn't been here now . . ." I trailed off, unable to continue.

He hugged me tighter and kissed the top of my head. "Don't worry about it, Chloe. I'm here for you. Lie back down, I'll stay with you until you fall asleep."

My distrust from earlier was gone, and instead of being afraid to have him in the bed with me, it made me feel better, safe. I snuggled down into the covers beside him and laid my head on his chest, wrapping my arm around him.

"Will you stay with me tonight? I don't even want to think about waking up alone again."

He hugged me tight. "Of course I will. Just close your eyes and get some sleep, sweetheart. I'll be right here when you wake up."

I smiled at him and closed my eyes, snuggling into him as tightly as possible. Within a few minutes, I had a new fear. Being this close to him, smelling him, being wrapped around him, had me going insane. The thoughts running through my head weren't helping either. I had never been so comfortable and uncomfortable at the same time in my life. I slid my hand down his chest to his stomach, trying to get comfortable, and I felt him stiffen.

I pulled my hand back suddenly. "I'm sorry, I didn't mean to make you uncomfortable, Drake. All you had to do was tell me, I'll roll over."

He grabbed my arm as I started to roll away from him. "No, it's not that, Chloe. It's just, I have this beautiful girl in my bed wearing my clothes, snuggled up against me, and I can't touch you, no matter how much I want to. I would never do that to you after what happened."

My heart did a nervous flop. He wanted me? I couldn't see how he would even notice me when he had all of those women following him around. He had to be joking with me; there was no other explanation for his words. I scooted up and looked at him grinning.

"Yeah right, I bet you say that to all the girls lying in your bed."

Instead of laughing at me, he frowned. "I wasn't kidding, Chloe. I've wanted you from the minute I saw you that first day in class. I have never seen someone as beautiful as you."

My face burned and I looked away from him before he could see how much his words bothered me. He laughed as he put his fingers under my chin and pulled my face up to look at him.

"And I've never seen any other woman blush as much as you do."

I felt my face grow hotter at his words, but he still held my face up to his so that I couldn't turn away.

"Drake . . ."

"No, it's all right. I wouldn't ever try anything on you, especially now. Just go back to sleep, Chloe. I'll be here when you wake up."

He let go of my chin, but I couldn't look away. He was being so kind to me, and making me feel so special. I scooted up a little so I could lay my forehead against his.

"Thank you, Drake, for everything."

He gave me a tiny smile as he stared into my eyes. Without thinking, I leaned in just a few more inches and brushed my lips gently against his. He gasped as I pulled away and grabbed my face, pulling me back in. His lips found mine, and he kissed me like I had never been kissed before. There was so much force behind it that it scared me, but not in a bad way. The feeling of having his lips pressed against mine sent thrills throughout my body.

I leaned closer, hungry for more as I deepened the kiss and felt his piercing bite into my lip. It was the single most erotic feeling of my life. Suddenly, he pulled away from me, gasping for air.

"Chloe, please stop. I can't do this."

I dropped my gaze to the bedspread as shame and embarrassment took over. What had I been thinking, kissing him like that?

"I'm so sorry, I don't know what came over me. I'm so embarrassed."

He took a deep breath before he spoke. "Listen, it's not that I don't want to kiss you, I do. Badly. But I'm not going to take advantage of you tonight. You're vulnerable and not thinking clearly after what happened."

I nodded, still looking at the bed. "You're right, but I think it would be better if you went back to the couch, I'm okay now."

I glanced up at him and saw sadness in his eyes. "Yeah, that's probably a good idea. If you need me, you know where I am."

He stood and left the room, looking back as he shut the door behind him. I let out a breath I hadn't realized I'd been holding and fell back onto the pillows. What the hell had I been thinking? A shock went through my stomach as I thought about him saying he wanted to kiss me. Was he serious, or just trying to be kind and not hurt my already screwed-up feelings? I closed my eyes and eventually drifted off to sleep, my last thought being the feel of his lips on mine.

The next morning, I managed to crawl out of the bed and into the bathroom. Looking at myself in the mirror, I groaned. There was nothing like morning Chloe to make men run from the room screaming in terror. I rummaged through his vanity drawers, hoping to find a brush and hair tie. In the third drawer down, I found what I was looking for. Running the brush through my hair, I managed to get it tied back in a bun to contain most of it. Next, I grabbed the toothpaste and the unopened toothbrush he must have set out for me the night before and went to work on my morning breath.

Feeling slightly better about my appearance, I made my way from the bathroom into the living room. Drake was still asleep on the couch, and good Lord, he was only wearing a pair of basketball shorts. No shirt. I tried not to look at him, but it was impossible. Staring at him half-naked, I felt that familiar tingle between my legs I always seemed to get when he was around. I had been right about him being ripped.

He shifted on the couch and I noticed something glittering on his chest. My mouth dropped open as I realized he had both nipples pierced. It took every ounce of willpower I had not to walk over to him and run my hands across the hard muscles of his stomach, but not before gently tugging on those nipple rings. I quickly turned and walked into the kitchen before I made an idiot of myself. Glancing around, I decided to see if he had any food to make us breakfast with.

Surprisingly, he had actual food in his kitchen—unlike most guys. I pulled some eggs out of the fridge and started searching his cabinets for a pan. Finding one, I threw the eggs in and put a few slices of bread in the toaster. Once I had the eggs fried and the toast buttered, I started searching for glasses to put some orange juice in. Just as I reached up to open the cabinet above my head, I felt hands wrap around my hips, and I screamed and spun around, flailing my arms at whoever was touching me. My hand came in contact with skin and I heard a yelp of pain.

"Shit! Chloe, it's me! Ouch, damn it, stop!"

Drake grabbed my hands as I smacked at him again. My heart was racing and I looked up at him.

"Jesus, Drake! You scared the fuck out of me!"

He grinned down at me. "I had no idea, I just thought you liked being rough."

I rolled my eyes at his innuendo. "You're such a charmer. Seriously, tone it down, I can barely contain myself over here."

I turned back to the cabinet and pulled two glasses out. Turning back to him, I shoved them in his hands. "Go pour some juice into these. I made breakfast."

"Wow, breakfast for me? You shouldn't have."

I ignored him as I grabbed the plates and carried them to the table. I sat down in my chair as he brought the juice over and sat across from me.

"This looks great, Chloe. Thanks."

I glanced up from my plate to smile at him, but my mouth

froze as I noticed he still wasn't wearing a shirt. The piercings in his nipples glittered in the sunlight shining through the window, and I couldn't seem to remember how to move my eyeballs away from his chest. They had to be the sexiest things I had ever seen in my life, and I mentally fanned myself.

He cleared his throat, and my eyes shot up to his. They were sparkling with mischief and I knew I had been caught.

"What are you looking at, Chloe?'

I glanced down at my plate before meeting his gaze again. I gestured to his chest first, then at the piercings in his eyebrow and lip.

"Those piercings you have, they had to hurt."

"I'd be lying if I said they didn't hurt like a bitch, especially the ones in my nipples, but it attracts the girls, so in my opinion, they were totally worth it."

"You really only think with one part of your anatomy, don't you?"

His eyes brightened and he threw that sexy smirk at me. "Always."

We ate in silence for a few minutes before he spoke. "What about you?"

"What about me?"

"You ignored me before when I asked if you had anything else pierced besides your belly button that I should know about. So do you have any hidden piercings?"

I coughed into my orange juice as I noticed his eyes dropping to my chest.

"No, definitely not. I like being able to walk through metal detectors, thanks."

"What about ink? Surely you have something hidden away?"

I shook my head. "No, but I'd love to get a tattoo. I just don't think I'm brave enough. I don't handle pain well."

He rolled his eyes. "What a baby! The pain isn't even that bad, I was dozing off when I got this."

He pointed to his back. I stood and made my way around the table to stand behind him. The tattoos I had seen peeking out from under his sleeves were actually one large tattoo that extended from his upper arm, across his upper back, and down his other arm, stopping just above his elbows on both arms. I traced my finger over it and felt him tense. It was some type of abstract tribal tattoo with the initials *D* and *L* right at the center.

"Why did you get this?"

He shrugged his shoulders as I pulled my hand back and made my way back to my chair.

"I just felt like I needed something to impress the ladies with. I mean, who's in a rock band and doesn't have tattoos?"

He seemed uncomfortable, and I was sure he was lying to me, but I let it go. He was entitled to his secrets, and I wasn't about to push him. I glanced back up at him and noticed he was staring at me.

"What?"

He shook his head. "Nothing, just wondering if you have anything picked out if you ever man up and get one."

My insides clenched, and I debated on telling him the truth. He had, after all, just lied to me. Deciding it wouldn't really be telling him anything, I nodded.

"Nunquam amavit."

It came out as a whisper, and I quickly stood and took our plates to the sink, hoping to avoid his questions. I felt him come up behind me and place the glasses in the sink with the plates. His body radiated heat and I shivered at the sensation.

He leaned down, and I could feel his breath on my neck. "What does it mean?"

My stomach dropped at the question, and I closed my eyes to regain my composure.

"Never loved," I whispered.

I picked up a plate and started scrubbing as I prayed he'd leave it at that. As always, my luck was shit.

"Care to explain that to me?"

I shook my head and continued to scrub the already clean plate. "It's nothing really, I've had a shit life, but it's not something I broadcast."

He grabbed my shoulders and turned me to face him slowly. His fingers went under my chin, and he pulled my face up to look at him.

"You know I'm here for you, right? Just like Amber and Logan, you're my friend and you can talk to me."

I nodded my head as tears filled my eyes. "Thanks Drake, that means a lot to me. I don't really talk about it, but let's just say my mother won't be getting parent of the year anytime soon."

He pulled me into his chest and hugged me tight. "I understand. Like I said, if and when you're ready to talk about it with me, I'm here for you."

"I know. It's just complicated and really boring. Anyway, I better head home before Rachel sends out a search party for me. I never sleep anywhere besides our room and I'm sure she's freaking out."

I pulled away from him and made my way back to his bedroom to gather my stuff. After I had everything together I turned to leave and noticed him standing in the bedroom doorway.

"Listen, about last night . . ." he started, but I interrupted.

"I know what you're going to say, and seriously, it's fine. I was drunk and had a lot of stuff going through my head after everything at the bar. I know you don't feel that way, you don't have to lie, so let's just forget about it and go back to how we were before my stupidity took over."

He looked down at the pink carpet and nodded. "Okay, yeah. I'll try to forget you threw yourself at me like the skank you are."

I laughed at his teasing and walked across the room to punch him in the arm.

"Good to know where we stand, little man whore."

He looked up at me and grinned. "Now that we've got that settled I'm kicking your ass out." He motioned toward the door. "Hop to it, I've got things to do."

I glared at him as I stomped past him and to the door. I flipped him off as I opened it and threw a "Later, douche bag!" over my shoulder. I grinned as I made my way down his sidewalk and toward the bar, where my car was still parked.

CHAPTER EIGHT

SURPRISES

I barely remembered driving back to the dorm and walking up to my room as thoughts of Drake and everything that had happened in the last twenty-four hours swirled around inside my head. I had come so close to being raped it wasn't funny. If he hadn't followed us outside, my night and my life would have changed drastically. I would be forever thankful to him for what he had done, and I promised myself never to drink by myself with someone I didn't know again.

A chill went down my spine as I thought of what Nick had done to me, and I felt vomit rise in my throat. I suppressed a shudder and vowed never to let Amber, Rachel, and especially Logan know what had happened. Drake had promised to keep it between us, and I believed him. All I had to do was push it to the back of my head and pretend it was just a nightmare.

I straightened my back and plastered a smile on my face as I opened the door. As soon as I walked through, Rachel jumped from her bed and tackled me.

"Oh, thank heavens! Where the hell have you been and why didn't you answer your phone?"

I managed to push her off and smiled apologetically. "Sorry, my phone died and I didn't have a charger. I went to Starbucks and ended up stopping at the bar Drake was playing at. I got completely trashed and Drake lives like a block away from the bar, so he took me to his place to crash."

Her eyes popped at the mention of me staying with Drake all night. "Drake? As in the Drake of Breaking the Hunger?"

I nodded.

"You spent the night with Mr. Hot and Badass himself?" She squealed a bit before continuing. "What happened? Did you bump uglies with him? Please, for the love of all things holy, tell me you did."

I walked over to my bed and flopped down before laughing at her. "Sorry, no bumping uglies with him. He was a perfect gentleman. Besides, we are just friends."

She sighed dramatically. "After all the worrying you could have at least brought home a juicy story."

My mind instantly flipped to Nick, and my stomach dropped.

"Sorry, nothing even remotely juicy."

I pulled my phone out of my bag and plugged it into my charger before powering it on. I had several voice mails and over twenty texts. I clicked on the texts and saw most of them were from Logan.

Rachel peeked over my shoulder. "Oh yeah, you might want to call Logan and Amber. They are freaking out as well."

I glared at her. "You called Logan? You knew he would freak out!"

"Can you blame me? I come home and you're gone. You left a note about going to Starbucks, which is like twenty minutes round-trip, but you never came home. I called him and Amber to see if you were with them. Now call him before he starts busting heads around campus, you and I both know he'll do it."

I quickly dialed Logan's number, and he answered on the first ring.

"Chloe? Are you okay? Where are you?"

"I'm fine, Logan, calm down. My phone went dead, but I'm home now. I was with Drake last night."

Silence followed for several moments before Logan finally responded, "*With Drake?*" His voice was deathly quiet.

"Yeah, I drank too much and he helped me out."

I could almost hear the wheels turning in Logan's head. He stayed silent for a moment again before speaking. "I'll be at your place in ten."

Before I could respond, he had already hung up on me.

"Awesome. Just awesome." I fell back onto my bed and looked at Rachel. "He's coming over in a few minutes. This should be pleasant."

Rachel at least had the decency to look guilty. "Sorry, chick. I'm going to head out so you two can talk. I see lots of yelling in your future, so I'm out."

She grabbed her keys and shot out the door faster than I had ever seen her move.

"Traitor," I mumbled under my breath.

Just a few minutes after Rachel made her escape, a loud knock sounded on my door. I knew it had to be Logan, so I yelled from the bed for him to come in. As soon as he entered the room I knew I was in trouble. He slammed the door behind him and stomped over to my bed.

"What the fuck were you thinking, Chloe? Out drinking by yourself with some guy you barely know? And then staying the night with him?" he yelled, loud enough to make me jump.

Instantly, I got angry too.

"First off, I am a big girl, Logan! I can damn well take care of myself, I have been for years. You have absolutely no right to tell me what to do. We talked about you being overprotective before and you promised to try to control it! If I want to go get drunk and prance around naked with half the men on campus, you would have no say in it!"

Obviously this was the wrong thing to say, because his face turned bright red, and his eyes grew cold.

"So that's what you were doing with him? *Prancing around naked,* as you put it?" His voice was deathly quiet, and I had never seen him so mad at me.

I decided being nice might help my case a bit.

"Listen, Logan, I know you were worried, but you have got to get over this whole overprotective thing. I definitely did not get naked with him—he is my friend, just like you are."

I felt bad about lying to him, but if he knew I was secretly crushing on Drake it would only make things worse.

Logan's face twisted like he was in pain, but he remained silent.

I stood up from the bed and reached over to hug him. "I'm sorry I made you worry, okay? I love you more than life itself, Logan, and I don't want to fight with you. Please don't be mad at me." I looked up at him and gave him my best innocent face.

His lips twitched and his eyes softened. "Don't use that face on me, Chloe Marie. You know I can't handle it."

I grinned and leaned up to kiss him on the cheek. "That was the plan big man. Now come on, let's go get some lunch. Besides, I need to call Amber and let her know I'm still alive."

He frowned down at me as he followed me out the door. "Not even remotely funny."

After a quick call to Amber letting her know I was okay, and promising lots of details when Logan wasn't around, we went to a local Mexican place for lunch. Logan seemed to be back to his normal self as lunch went on, and I was glad. Logan and I rarely fought, and I hated it when we did. Without him, my life would have been ten times worse.

We finished up our lunch and went back to his room to work on a few assignments for class. Logan sat down on his bed and I took the desk next to it as I opened my book. Every time I glanced up at Logan, he would be watching me with a strange look on his face.

"What's that look for?" I asked after I caught him doing it the third time.

He shook his head, as if to clear his thoughts and smiled at me. "Nothing, just thinking how glad I am you're okay."

I smiled back at him and continued reading the chapter that had been assigned. Instead of seeing the words on the page, Drake's face flashed in front of my eyes. Kissing him had been an experience in itself. He had told me he wanted me, but if he was telling me the truth, he could have had his way with me last night. Instead, he had pushed me away. I had never been the girl to chase a guy, not that I had noticed any that sparked my interest before him to begin with, and I wasn't about to start now. I just had to accept the fact that we would always just be friends, even if that really sucked in my opinion.

I pushed Drake from my mind and went back to my reading. I only made it a few pages before my eyes grew heavy, and I decided to lay my head down for just a minute to rest. The next thing I knew, I felt myself being lifted from my chair. I peeked through my eyelids and saw Logan carrying me.

"What are you doing?" I mumbled, still half-asleep.

"Shhhh. I'm going to lay you down for a little bit so you can rest."

He sat down in the bed with me curled up into him. I snuggled closer and enjoyed his warmth, and his strong Logan scent. No one in this world could make me feel as safe as Logan did, although Drake was a close second. The last thing I remember before drifting off was Logan kissing my forehead and pulling me tighter against him.

I woke up groggy and disoriented. I felt someone pressed up against me and my heart started beating faster. I glanced over and saw Logan sleeping peacefully beside me. At the sight of him, my heart slowed down and my body relaxed. I watched him sleeping for a few minutes and smiled to myself, enjoying seeing Logan relaxed and peaceful. He was always wound so tight when he was awake, it was nice to see a different side to him.

I glanced at the clock on his night table and groaned. It was after midnight and I was in a male student's bed. If his roommate came home or anyone else caught us, we'd both be in some serious trouble. Even if this was a coed dorm, they had stressed to all of us that there was to be no fraternizing with the opposite sex. I tried to slide out from under him, but our legs had become tangled as we slept.

I was afraid to wake him, but I knew I had to leave, so I slowly slid his arm off me and sat up. Moving his legs was a lot harder and he groaned in his sleep before throwing his arm around my waist and pulling me back down. I sighed and pushed him back off me. Thankfully he rolled to his side, and I was free.

I stood slowly and started throwing my books into my bag as quietly as I could. Once I had all my stuff gathered up, I made my way back over to him and kissed his forehead.

He moaned in his sleep and then smiled. "Love you, my Chloe. So much."

I frowned at his words, now that I understood the true meaning behind them, as I made my way out of his room and back to my own.

. . .

I groaned and rolled over as my phone rang from the table beside me. I grabbed it and saw Amber was calling me.

"This had better be good. It's not even noon yet on a Sunday and I'm awake."

Amber laughed in my ear at my grouchiness. "Well, aren't you a ball of sunshine this morning? Get dressed and meet me at that little coffee shop we saw just off campus, I want to tell you all about my date! And I want to hear everything you've been avoiding telling me about Drake. Twenty minutes, bitch!"

She hung up before I could tell her she was insane. A Drake interrogation was not something I wanted to wake up to, especially when it was coming from Amber. My phone rang again as I stood up and I answered it without checking the caller ID.

"For the love of God, Amber, I'm up!"

I heard male chuckling on the line.

"Wow, you're in a good mood. But just so you know, I'm not Amber."

I sighed. "Apparently I'm popular today. What's up?"

"Can you meet me at my house today at around one o'clock? I want to take you somewhere, and before you ask, no I'm not telling you where we're going. It's a surprise."

His question caught me off guard. Drake didn't seem like the type to throw surprises out there and I was a bit leery of where he might be taking me.

"One question: you aren't going to take me out to the woods and murder me, right?"

He laughed. "No, not part of my plans. We won't be going into any secluded woods so that I can murder you, or have my way with you."

"All right, I'll bite. But if you are messing with me, I will cut off that part of your anatomy you seem to be so fond of."

"Deal. I'll see you later. Don't be late."

My mind was creating all kinds of different scenarios as to where he could possibly be taking me, but I came up with nothing. Since I was going to be seeing him later, I took a little extra time doing my makeup and even straightened my hair. By the time I arrived at the coffee shop to meet Amber, she had called me twice, telling me to hurry up.

I stepped into the cute little mom-and-pop-type shop and saw Amber sitting in a booth away from most of the other customers with two coffee cups sitting on the table. I grabbed a cup and starting sipping from it as I sat down across from her.

"Finally, you took forever." She looked me over and grinned. "What's up with you? You look all girly."

I rolled my eyes. "I'm allowed to look girly occasionally, but I'm meeting Drake after this so maybe I put a little extra effort into my appearance today."

"That explains it. So tell me all about him and start from the beginning. We haven't had any time alone to talk!"

I started when I first saw him and told her everything, only leaving out the part about Nick. As I spoke, her eyes grew wide and she squealed like a ten-year-old when I told her about dancing with him and my blundering kiss.

"Oh, Chloe! This is so great, I thought he was into you from how he acted around you, but hearing all of this I know for sure. He really likes you!"

I shook my head. "If he liked me, he wouldn't have pushed me away when I kissed him."

"You were drunk. If he had done anything else you would have been pissed off as soon as you sobered up. The fact that he didn't just makes him that much better. Plus, you know he's not just trying to get in your pants."

"I don't know, Amber. What about all the girls? I mean, the man had a drawer in his bedroom full of other girls' underwear for God's sake!"

"Well, I didn't say he was perfect, he obviously likes women, but maybe if you two got together he would stay away from them. You need to sit down and talk to him, tell him how you feel."

"No way am I putting myself out there like that. If he rejected me, it would be completely awkward."

She sighed. "Chloe, if you never put yourself out there, how is he supposed to know how you feel?"

She had a point. Look at how long Logan had kept his feelings from me and I had no clue. I bit my lip and stared at my almost empty coffee cup. "There's something else I haven't told you and I know you're going to be as shocked as I am."

Her eyebrows disappeared into her bangs. "What on earth could shock me after telling me all of that?"

"You remember the other night when Logan was drunk?"

She nodded. "Yeah, what about it?"

"Drake helped me get him to his room and then left us alone. I helped Logan get into bed and when I started to leave, he kissed me. I talked to him about it the next day and he admitted to having feelings for me, but he wasn't going to pressure me into anything. I've tried to ignore the whole thing, but it's eating at me. It's Logan, how could he have those kinds of feelings for me?"

Amber avoided my gaze as she played with a napkin in her hands.

"Amber? What is it?"

"I knew."

"What do you mean you knew? How could you know something like that and not tell me? What happened to the whole *I'll give you my favorite pair of Chucks if Chloe and Logan ever get together* speech you made to Drake the other day?"

She looked up at me and I saw anger in her eyes. "I've known for a while. I fell for Logan as soon as he started going to school with us, right before Chad and I started hanging out actually. I was drinking at a party one night when you were gone with your mom that summer and he gave me a ride home. I tried to kiss him, but he pushed me away and told me he wanted you. He made me promise to keep it to myself, not that I had ever planned on telling you after what happened that night."

I stared at her in disbelief. "I had no idea how you felt about him. Do you . . . Do you still have feelings for him?"

She shook her head. "No, I moved on. Logan is just my friend now. But that's beside the point. How do you feel about him?"

To be honest, I had no idea how I felt about him. It was all too new, and my mind was having a hard time viewing him as anything else but my best friend.

"I don't know, this is all so damn confusing. I know he wants more, even if he isn't pushing, but I'm not sure I can give it to him. Look at me, I am completely fucked-up and he deserves better than that."

She shook her head. "You are not fucked-up, Chloe. You've just had way more shit thrown at you than people twice our age. It made you grow up fast, and yes you are a bit jaded, but in no way are you fucked-up. You really need to think about this thing with Logan and with Drake. Both of them want you, there's no question about it in my mind, so you need to decide who you want and go for it."

There was no doubt about who I wanted. Drake. But if I started something with him, knowing what I did about how Logan felt, I knew Logan would take it as a personal insult.

"Maybe I should take your advice from before and just become a nun."

She laughed. "Yeah, you get right on that."

We sat in silence, both of us lost in our own thoughts. Finally she looked up at me and grinned. "Enough about you, I want to talk about my date with Alex."

I felt relief about the subject change and threw myself into the conversation as a distraction from my thoughts.

"Tell me all about it! Where did he take you?"

"It was so romantic! He took me to this quaint little Italian restaurant just across the state line. We sat there for a couple hours and just talked, and then he took me to the movies. He even watched a chick flick with me!"

"That's great, Amber. I'm really happy that you found someone who isn't an ass. Do you think there will be a second date?"

"I hope so. He told me he would call sometime next week. He's so different from Chad already. Chad was always good to me, but there were times that I wondered if he even wanted to be with me. When I was with Alex, he paid attention to everything I said, and we have so much in common. He even knows some of the small-time bands we both listen to."

"Well, that settles it for me—you need to marry him."

She laughed. "I figured you would say that. Speaking of bands, I really want to hear Drake play again sometime. I did a little asking around and everyone seems to love Breaking the Hunger. Why don't we go listen to him next weekend?"

I forced a smile on my face. She had no idea what had happened at the bar with Nick, and if I refused to go, she would know something was up with me.

"Yeah, that sounds fun. I'll let him know I'm bringing you. Maybe Logan will want to go with us too."

"Great, I'll ask Alex if he wants to go with us, then we can make a double date out of it." I frowned at her words, and she sighed. "Or we'll call it a date for Alex and me. And you can call it hanging out with your best friends."

"That sounds better. I don't want to put that label on it or it'll give Logan the wrong idea. I need time to figure this out before I start anything with either of them."

We each ordered another coffee and spent the next hour catching up about our classes. It felt nice just to have some uncomplicated girl time with Amber, and I soaked it up for as long as I could. Finally, she glanced at her watch before motioning me toward the door.

"You had better go if you don't want to be late. I'm sure Drake wouldn't appreciate being stood up."

I nodded, stood, and tossed my empty cup into the trash. "I still have no idea where we are going. If I'm not back by tomorrow afternoon, call the police. Oh, and you can have all my CDs."

She laughed. "Drake is a lot of things, but I don't think a serial killer is one of them."

"You never know, that boy is full of surprises."

I waved to her as I left the shop and walked to my car. Once I was inside, I just sat there debating whether or not just to go home and leave Drake hanging. I knew I was being a coward, but I couldn't help it. He was under my skin, and whenever I was around him my judgment always clouded over.

CHAPTER NINE

INKED

I decided to take a chance as I started my car and made my way across town to his house. When I passed the bar, a shiver ran up my spine. I had no idea how I was going to handle going back there. I pushed the thought to the back of my mind as I parked outside of Drake's house. He opened his door before I was even out of my car.

"About time, I thought you'd changed your mind." His eyes traveled up and down my body. "Wow, you look great."

I smiled to myself at his compliment. "Thanks, and no way—if I make plans to get murdered by some hot guy with tattoos and a bad attitude, I keep them."

"So you think I'm hot, do you?"

I mentally face palmed as I realized my slipup.

"You completely missed the whole getting murdered part didn't you?"

He walked over to me and slipped a hand around my waist as he led me to his car. I felt the tingles running down my back as he touched me.

"I always focus on the important things. Now get in."

He pushed me gently toward the passenger door before walking around to his side and getting in. I stood there debating whether I could still make a run for it when he rolled my window down.

"Get in. Don't think I won't throw you into this car. I'll even get on top of you to hold you down if it comes to that, not that I would mind."

I groaned as I opened the door and slid in, slamming it behind me.

"You're so bossy."

"Yeah, but you love it."

"Not really, it only adds to your annoying qualities."

He grinned at me as he pulled onto the road and started driving in the direction of the business district. "I wasn't aware that I had any annoying qualities, actually. Please enlighten me to what they could possibly be."

I looked at him in astonishment. "You seriously want me to list everything bad about you?"

He shrugged his shoulders as he weaved through traffic. "Sure, why not. Besides, none of the other girls I talk to have anything bad to say about me. Actually, they often yell how good I am, several times in a row."

I felt my face grow warm.

"I'm sure they do. All right, let's see if I can manage to name off all your bad qualities by the time we get to wherever we're going. This is going to take a while."

He grinned, but stayed silent, waiting for me to start.

"Well first, you're bossy. Then the fact that you refuse to tell me where we're going. You're also self-centered and arrogant. You walk around like you own the world and expect everyone just to bow to you."

He cut me off before I could continue. "I don't expect everyone to bow to me, just the female population. I mean, can you blame me though? You said it yourself, I'm smoking hot and I ooze sex appeal."

"I don't remember saying you ooze anything, hotshot."

"I read your mind and I know what you're thinking right now too. I bet you'd like either to rip my clothes or my head off."

"Try the second one," I grumbled as he pulled the car into a small lot. I glanced up and noticed we were at a tattoo shop. "What are we doing here?"

"This is your surprise, you're going to get that tattoo."

I shook my head as I looked at him in shock. "Not a chance, I told you I don't handle pain well."

"I'll be with you the whole time, and I'll even let you hold my hand if you want to."

I glanced up at the shop again as I bit my lip. "I don't know, Drake. What if he starts it and I can't handle it? I'll be stuck with half a tattoo for the rest of my life."

"You mean *she*."

"What?"

"You said, *What if he starts it*. My friend Katelynn is going to do it for you."

I raised my eyebrows at him. "So you think that having my tattoo done by one of your skanks is going to improve your chances of getting me in there? I might catch an STD from her or something."

He acted as if I had insulted him personally, which I guess I had.

"She isn't one of my skanks. She's someone I've known for a long time and she does good work. I called her and she came in on her day off to do this for you, so get your ass out of my car and let's go get inked."

"I'll go in, but I'm not promising you anything."

I opened my door and stepped out, my legs literally shaking with fear. I took a step and stumbled. Drake was beside me in a flash, catching me and holding me up.

"You weren't kidding about being clumsy, were you?"

"Bite me."

I pulled myself free from his grip and slowly walked to the shop. I had no idea why I was even out of the car; there was no way I could do this. I looked over at Drake. It was because of him, my decisions always had something to do with him. As we reached the shop, I pulled on the doors, but they were locked.

"Well, look at that, they're closed." I turned and started to walk back to the car, but he grabbed my arm and pulled me back.

"They are closed, but she came in to do this for us."

He knocked loudly on the doors and a moment later a tall woman with bright pink hair appeared. She unlocked the door and opened it, waving us in. As soon as we entered, she locked the door behind us and turned to Drake and me.

"Hi, you must be Chloe. I'm Katelynn."

She seemed nice enough, but I wasn't totally convinced.

"Nice to meet you. Listen, I'm not sure what Drake told you, but I don't want to get a tattoo."

She raised a pierced brow and glanced at Drake. "Really? Drake here acted like you were excited. Why don't I show you what I've got and if you still don't want it, I won't force you."

I nodded as she led us down a hallway covered in pictures of tattoos. Some of the pieces were truly amazing and had obviously taken hours to do. One stood out among the rest: it was a black-and-white portrait of a woman. The artist had been so detailed that if I reached out and touched her face. I almost expected her to be real.

"This is amazing."

Katelynn glanced back as she opened a door at the end of the hallway and motioned for us to enter. "Thanks, that's one of mine. The man who got it wanted it in memory of his fiancée. She died in a freak accident."

"Wow, that's so sad, but the piece is so beautiful."

She nodded as she pointed to a chair. "Take a seat by the desk and I'll show you what I drew up."

I sat down and glanced around the room. Like the hallway, there were several pictures of tattoos on the walls, and a photo album sat on the desk in front me. I opened it up and started looking through several pieces of flash work. I stopped on a page covered in different heart designs, and an idea popped into my head. I grinned up at Drake as Katelynn sat down next to me with a piece of paper in her hand.

"I'll make you a deal, Drake. I'll suck it up and get my tattoo if you get one with me. But I get to pick what you get and where you get it."

He raised his eyebrow and grinned. "Oh, really?"

"Absolutely, but you have to go first."

Katelynn was watching us with an amused look on her face. "Are you two together?"

I whipped my head around to her. "No! Why would you think that?"

"Sorry, it just seemed like you were."

"No, definitely not." I turned my gaze back to Drake. "Do we have a deal?"

He stared at me for a minute before answering, "All right, deal."

I grinned as I looked at Katelynn. "Good, now that that's settled, show me my new tattoo."

She held the paper in her hand out to me. I took it and stared down at the ink on the page. It was simple really, just my *Nunquam Amavit* in a beautiful flowing script with a small black silhouette of a bird beside it.

"I love it. Where should I put it?"

"Well, it depends on if you want to hide it or not."

I shook my head as I glanced at Drake. "No, I don't want to hide it, I want to remember this moment forever."

She gave me a knowing grin as she caught me looking at Drake. "Then I'd suggest your wrist or your neck. Whatever you feel comfortable with."

I thought for a moment as I looked at the drawing. "I think I want it on my wrist."

"Good choice. I made it small enough so that it should fit perfectly." She took the paper from my hand and held it up to my wrist. "Yeah, this will work perfect. Now what tattoo did you pick out for him?"

I grinned as I pointed to a tattoo on the page in front of me. "This one."

She burst out laughing as she looked down at the tattoo I had selected. It was of a butterfly landing on a flower shaped like a heart. Underneath that, the words *Pretty Lady* were written.

"I love it! Now, how big do you want it and where am I putting it?"

I glanced up at Drake, who was sitting across the room from us with an amused look on his face. "Don't you want to come see your new tattoo?"

"Nah, I'll look when it's done."

I gave him a devilish grin. "You're going to need a mirror."

"Really? And why is that?"

"Because it's going on your ass."

. . .

I sat in a chair next to Drake as she prepared both our tattoos. I glanced at him to see him watching me.

"Are you nervous?"

"Of course I am. I'm getting something permanently tattooed on my wrist and it's probably going to hurt and I'm going to cry like a baby."

He grinned and wrapped his arm around me, pulling me into his side. "I should be the one who's scared. I'm getting a tattoo, on my ass mind you, and I don't even know what it looks like. I wouldn't do this for just anyone you know."

I snuggled in tighter to him and took a deep breath. His scent assaulted me, and I took another deep breath as my body started reacting to being so close to him. He rested his chin on my head and starting running his fingertips up and down my spine. The movement distracted me as I focused on every brush of his fingers against me, and I felt my eyelids flutter and close as I rested my head against his chest.

It was moments like these that I truly appreciated the gentle side of him. He always pulled out the hard-ass card when others were around, but when it was just the two of us, he completely changed. Whether I wanted to admit it or not, I loved both sides of him, and that scared me. I was getting too close too fast, and I knew I'd have scars by the end of this.

Katelynn cleared her throat, and my eyes flew open to see her watching us with a secretive smile on her face.

"Come on over, Drake, you're up first."

He released me and stood, taking off his jacket and setting

it on the chair. As he walked over to where Katelynn stood, he slowly undid the buttons on his jeans and pulled them down so that I had a clear view of his ass. My mouth fell open as I dropped my gaze to the floor. He chuckled, and I glanced up to see him watching me.

"What's wrong, Chloe, see something you like?"

And there was cocky Drake back.

"Actually I had to avert my gaze because your ass is so blindingly white it hurt to look."

Katelynn giggled as she motioned for Drake to lie down. "I like this one, she's got spunk."

He glanced over at me. "Yeah, I kind of like her too."

I played with the rings on my hands as Katelynn applied the outline to his skin and picked up her gun.

"You ready?"

"Yes. Chloe, come over and watch. That way you'll know it's not so bad."

I rose slowly from my chair and went to stand behind Katelynn. The view from here was amazing and I tried to concentrate as Drake spoke, but my eyes were glued to him, and my brain was on leave.

I jumped as Drake yelled my name.

"Sorry, what?"

He smirked at me. "If you would stop staring at my ass you'd hear what I was saying. I told you to watch my face when she does it. That way you'll see that I'm not in any real pain."

I jumped again as the gun came to life. She held his skin taunt and slowly lowered her gun. Just as she touched his skin, Drake screamed out in agony. My hands flew to my face to control my own scream as Katelynn jerked back.

Drake's body started shaking with laughter.

"You guys are so easy."

I stomped over and smacked him across the back of the head.

"You jerk! That wasn't funny!"

He continued to chuckle. "Ouch, sorry. Go ahead, I'll try to control myself."

"Laugh now, but if I screw this up it's on your head, not mine," Katelynn said as she glared at him.

"I said I was sorry. Now ink me."

I smacked him again.

"What the hell was that for?"

"You're being bossy again, so lie there and shut up."

Katelynn slowly lowered the gun back down and went to work on outlining that tattoo. I watched his face as she worked and he showed no sign of pain, except an occasional twinge. In less than half an hour she was done. He stood slowly and walked to a mirror in the corner of the room. I expected him to start yelling at me as he turned and could see the image, but he just stood there in silence. He stayed that way for a few minutes, and finally I couldn't take the silence any longer.

"Drake, say something. How mad are you at me?"

He pulled his gaze away from his reflection to look at me. He walked silently across the room, his jeans still low on his hips, and stopped in front of me with a serious expression on his face.

"You want to know what I think?"

I nodded as he leaned in closer to me. I closed my eyes, waiting for him to start yelling at me.

"I think this is the funniest thing I have ever seen in my life."

I opened my eyes and peeked up at him.

"Come again?"

He started chuckling as he pulled away from me.

"I love it, and every time I stare at it I'll think of you."

I started laughing. "Um, exactly how often do you stare at your own ass?"

"I don't normally, but with this little piece of you back there, I might have to do it more often."

"Wow, like I said before—you're such a charmer."

He grinned as Katelynn came over and covered his new artwork with a bandage.

"You know the drill, leave the bandage on for a couple hours, and put petroleum jelly on it a couple times a day for about three days."

He nodded as he pulled his jeans back up and buttoned them. "Got it. It's your turn now, Chloe. Get your butt over there."

I walked past him and sat down in the chair as Katelynn cleaned up and started setting up for me. After she had everything ready, she applied the outline. I sucked in a deep breath as she powered up her gun and dipped it into the ink.

"You ready?"

I shook my head no and motioned for Drake to come over. He walked over to me and stood on the opposite side from her.

"Will you hold my hand while she does it?"

His eyes went soft, and he smiled. "Of course I will."

He pulled up a chair beside me and sat down as he laced our fingers together. I stared down at our entwined fingers and smiled as she began moving the gun across my skin. I tensed a bit at the stinging before relaxing.

"That's it?"

She looked up at me and smiled. "That's it. See, all that worrying for nothing."

I started to pull my hand away from Drake's, but he stopped me.

"I'm okay, you don't have to hold my hand."

"Well, you might decide you need it and it won't be there. I'll hold on to you just in case."

Katelynn finished mine a lot faster than she did Drake's, since there was a lot less detail to it. She applied the bandage and handed me a sheet with aftercare instructions.

"This will explain everything you need to know. If you have any problems, my phone number is on the bottom."

I stood up and threw my arms around her.

"Thank you so much for this."

She froze at first, then hugged me back gently.

"You're very welcome."

I pulled back and looked at Drake with a huge grin on my face. I walked over to him and threw my arms around his neck as well.

"And thank you for making me do this. I never would have been able to do it by myself."

He smiled as I pulled back. "Sure thing, sunshine. Let me pay her and we can get out of here."

My eyes widened. "No, you don't have to pay for it, I've got it. Actually, I'll pay for both, since I made you get one too."

"I know I don't have to, I want to." He turned to Katelynn. "How much do I owe you?"

She shook her head. "Nothing, this one's on me."

"You sure?"

"Yeah, now get out of here before I change my mind."

Drake hugged her briefly before putting his hand on the small of my back and leading us out of the shop to his car.

CHAPTER TEN

DEMONS

Drake took me back to his house, where we hung out for the rest of the afternoon, watching TV and talking about school, his band, and anything else we could think of as we sat together on his couch. It felt nice to spend time with him, just the two of us. After a couple hours I asked if I could take my bandage off to look at the tattoo. He nodded and helped me peel it off slowly.

When it was uncovered I felt tears start to sting my eyes. Those two little words represented everything that was my past—all the pain, the fear.

I looked up at Drake through my tears. "Thank you so much, you don't know what this means to me."

He raised his hand to my face and wiped my tears away.

"No thanks are necessary, I'm just glad I could do something for you. Will you tell me what it means?"

I looked at him confused. "I already did, it means *Never Loved*."

"I know what the words mean, but I want to know the meaning behind it."

I looked down at my wrist as my tears started flowing faster. "I told you before that my mother wasn't the best."

He nodded as I continued.

"She had me too young, and she resented me for it. She had to grow up to raise me. She managed to stop using drugs while she was pregnant and stayed sober for a while after, but she relapsed and went back to her partying ways. From the time I was little, she would either take me to parties with her and leave me there by myself or she'd just leave me alone at home for days at a time, and when she did come home she was usually stoned or drunk. I tried to stay out of her way, but she'd always find me and she was so angry. She would scream at me about how I ruined everything, how I ruined her life, and how she wished I was never born. It escalated a few times and she beat me. If she brought a boyfriend home with her, they would usually beat me too. There was this one guy, John, that she brought home when I was thirteen. Instead of beating me like the others, he just sat and watched my mother hit me. I was relieved that he wouldn't hurt me too. That night, after my mother passed out, he came into my room. He wasn't drunk or even stoned from what I could tell, but he crawled into bed with me and he started . . ." I bit back a sob. "He started trying to touch me. I woke up and realized what was happening so I started screaming."

I stopped and took a deep breath, but he spoke before I could.

"Chloe, did he hurt you? Did he rape you?"

I shook my head. "No, my screams must have woke up my mother and she came to see what was going on. She took one look at us in my bed and started screaming at me, calling me a whore. She didn't even say anything to him, but he stood up and left as she started beating me. The next morning, she was gone and I didn't see her for almost six months. I stayed with Amber most of the time while she was gone. When she came back, she seemed better and I hoped that things would change. Since it was summer, she even asked me to come along with her on her next trip. I spent the next three months with her, partying and getting stoned before we ended up at my aunt's. We stayed there for over a month before she disappeared again. My aunt helped me get home, and from then on out, I saw her maybe once or twice a year and she has only beat me a few times since then. I pretty much moved in with Amber and her parents, and then I came here to escape her. I never want to see her again, and I'm afraid of what she'd do to me if I did."

He pulled me into his arms as my body shook with sobs.

"Baby, I'm so sorry you had to go through all of that. If I had known you then, I would have protected you. You're far too precious for that."

I buried my face in his shirt as he spoke.

"Look at me."

I shook my head no, but he pulled away and cupped my face in his hands, pulling me up so that I was looking at him. His eyes were a mixture of emotions. Anger, worry, sorrow, and last but not least, pity.

"I don't want your pity, Drake."

He pulled my face to his and kissed me gently, taking me by surprise.

"It's not pity I'm feeling, it's blinding rage. I'd like to kill your mother for what she did to you. Thank you for telling me, I'm glad you know you can trust me."

I gave a weak smile as he pulled me back to him and kissed me again. Instead of pulling away like before, he deepened the kiss. I felt my body come alive as his tongue slid into my mouth to caress my own gently. Something hard flicked against my teeth, and I pulled back.

"Do you have your tongue pierced too?"

He grinned as he stuck his tongue out at me, and I noticed a silver barbell.

"Jesus, Drake, what don't you have pierced?"

His grin faded, and his eyes turned dark with lust.

"Why don't I show you what else I have pierced?"

My eyes widened. "Um, no thanks, I'll take your word for it."

He laughed as he leaned in and kissed me again before pulling back and relaxing into the couch.

"What are we doing, Chloe?"

"I don't know. I was hoping you could tell me."

He sighed and ran his hand through his hair. "I don't know either. We're friends, right?"

I nodded. "Yeah, we're friends who apparently kiss each other."

"I don't even know how to say this, so I'm just going to get it all out there. I like you, Chloe, and I'm attracted to you obviously, but I also consider you a friend. I really don't want to screw that up, and if we take this any further, that's exactly what's going to happen. I don't do relationships, but with you, sometimes I want to. Also, deny it all you want, but Logan has feelings for you. If something is going on between the two of you, I don't want to be in the middle of it."

I nodded as I let his words sink in. "I don't want to ruin our friendship either, but I do have feelings for you and I don't know what I'm supposed to do with that. Is it worth ruining our friendship to take a chance on something that might not work out? And you're right about Logan having feelings for me, he told me everything the other night. I don't know what I want from him, and my head is completely screwed up between the two of you."

I studied the swirling patterns on the couch as I waited for him to speak. The silence in the room was deafening.

"You should be with Logan. He loves you and he would take care of you. I'm not a good person and I don't pretend to be. I want you, but I can't have you," he said softly.

I nodded as tears welled up in my eyes again. "What if I don't want him? What if I want you?"

He leaned forward and pressed a kiss to my forehead. "You can't have me, not like that anyway."

I nodded as I stood. "You're right. We're great as friends, but anything else would be a disaster. I'm going to head home and take a nap, I'm beat."

He rose and walked me to the door.

"So I'll see you later?"

"Of course, Drake, we're friends—this conversation doesn't change that."

He kissed me on the cheek as I stepped outside to my car.

. . .

Tears streamed down my face all the way back to the dorm. I knew how Drake was, but hearing it directly from him hurt more than I was willing to admit to myself. I pulled into the parking lot and made my way up the stairs to my room, intending to take the world's longest nap. Logan was standing in front of my door as I reached the top of the stairs.

"Hey, I was just about to knock and see if you wanted to get something to eat." He took one look at me and ran to my side. "What's wrong? Why have you been crying?"

I shook my head as I raised my arms to wipe my tears away.

He caught my newly tattooed arm and pulled it up to look at it. "What's this?"

"Nothing, just a reminder of everything."

"What does it mean, Chloe?"

I looked down at my shoes. "Never loved."

He pulled me into his arms.

"Oh, baby girl, why do you do this to yourself? You have to let her go. What she did was horrible, but Chloe, you are loved. Amber loves you, and so do I."

He thought my tears were from all the painful memories from my past, and I wasn't about to correct him. If he knew they had everything to do with the present, with Drake, he would pull away. He leaned down and kissed me gently. I knew I shouldn't let him, but Drake didn't want me and Logan did. Drake was right—Logan would always be there for me, he would take care of me like he had been doing for years.

I kissed him back for a split second before pulling away. "Thanks, Logan. I don't know where I would be without you and Amber. Don't ever leave me."

"I wouldn't leave you, no matter what. Now dry your tears and let's get some dinner, I'm starving."

I gave him a weak smile as he led me back down the stairs and out to his car. He made small talk all the way to the restaurant, and he seemed genuinely excited when I told him about my new job.

"That's great, Chloe. I'm glad you found something."

As we drove, I laughed as he attempted to cheer me up with bad coffee jokes. I felt my heart lighten; being with Logan always felt so right. I watched him as he drove, studying him. He really was beautiful, but in a masculine way. I had always thought so, but now I was seeing him with new eyes. He was such a good person and he already knew everything about my past, knew that I was damaged.

He glanced over and saw me watching him. "What are you looking at?"

I turned my attention to the radio and started flipping channels until I found something good. "Nothing, you're just kinda beautiful."

He laughed. "Um, thanks, I think?"

"It was a compliment."

"Well, thanks then—you're kind of beautiful too."

I blushed as we pulled up in front of the restaurant.

The restaurant was almost empty when we entered and we were seated quickly. I sat staring at the menu, trying to decide what to get. "What are you getting? Everything looks good and I can't decide."

He pointed at the top of the menu. "Why don't we get their sausage burger? It's seriously huge, we can just share."

I agreed as a waitress appeared and took our order. She stayed a little longer than necessary, flirting shamelessly with Logan. I glared at her back as she went to the kitchen to place our order.

"Why are you giving her your trademark Chloe look of death?"

"She was flirting with you."

He shook his head and laughed. "No she wasn't."

I looked at him, shocked that he hadn't noticed.

"Logan, when a girl bats her eyelashes and twirls her hair like that, she's flirting. I'm a girl, I know these things."

His eyes turned serious. "Does it bother you when other girls flirt with me?"

I opened my mouth to tell him no, but stopped. Seeing her flirt with him had bothered me, and I wasn't sure why. Girls had flirted with him since we met, and it had never bothered me before. I had even pushed him to talk to that girl at the bar the other night.

"I . . . I guess it does."

He smiled as he reached across the table and placed his hand in mine.

"I would be lying if I said that didn't make me happy. Have you thought about what I said the other day?"

I lowered my gaze to our entwined hands as I spoke. "Yeah, I have, but I just don't know where I stand. What if we did try and it destroys us? I don't think I'd survive without you, Logan. I love you so much, I'm just not sure how I love you. Do you understand what I'm trying to say?"

He nodded. "I know exactly what you mean, and I've thought the same thing. Why do you think I waited so long to tell you?" He turned my hand over and gently ran his fingertips over my tattoo. "But I think it's worth it in the end to try if you're willing. We could be so great together."

I pulled my hand away and started playing with the straw in my drink. "Just give me some time to think about all of this. I don't want to rush into anything, especially right now."

He gave me a questioning look. "What do you mean, *especially right now*?"

I realized my blunder and quickly tried to think of an answer that didn't involve my feelings for Drake.

"Um, I just meant with us starting college. Everything is so new and I don't want to jump ahead of myself."

He smiled. "Of course. Like I told you before—no pressure, Chloe. When you're ready to give me an answer, I'll be here waiting."

The waitress appeared with our food, ending our discussion. I breathed a sigh of relief as I took a bite of my part of the sandwich.

"Holy crap, this is amazing! Good choice!"

"I ate here a couple days ago and the waitress suggested it. I was blown away too."

We sat in an easy silence as we ate, both enjoying our food too much to speak. When we finished, Logan paid for both of us, despite my protests.

"I've got it. It was my idea to come out anyway," he said as he led me back out to the car with his arm around my shoulders.

I snuggled into his side and enjoyed his warmth. "Thanks for tonight, I needed this."

. . .

The next morning, Drake dropped into his desk beside me as I pulled my things out of my bag for class and my stomach instantly clenched at the sight of him. I prayed he wouldn't mention anything about our conversation last night in front of Logan.

"Morning. How's the tattoo?"

I held out my arm to show him. "It's good, I put some of that cream on it. I thought it was supposed to itch though."

"It will, just give it a little while. When it does, do not scratch it, no matter how bad it annoys you, and don't mess with it once it starts to peel."

Logan turned to look at Drake. "How did you know she got a tattoo?"

Drake raised an eyebrow. "I'm the one who took her to get it."

I felt Logan watching me.

"Really? She left that part out."

I looked at Logan with an apologetic smile. "Sorry, must have slipped my mind."

Logan continued to stare between the two of us. "Did she tell you what it means?"

I glanced over at Drake, who had a smug look on his face.

"Yeah, she did. She told me everything."

Logan seemed upset over this news, but gave no further comment. I breathed a sigh of relief when class started. The rest of class felt tense in our little bubble, but I tried to ignore it as I took notes.

When class was dismissed, Drake turned to me.

"You want to help with that paper that's due tomorrow? We could meet at my house tonight."

I shook my head. "I can't, I start my new job at Starbucks tonight."

He nodded as he stood to leave. "Okay, I'll see if I can find someone else to do it for me." He glanced around and caught sight of one of the girls we had that class with. "Bingo. I've got stuff to do later, so I won't be at lunch. See ya."

I waved as he walked over to the girl and threw his arm around her. I refrained from growling since Logan was standing next to me, watching me closely.

"So you told him?" he asked as we walked together.

"Yeah."

He frowned. "I'm not trying to be a jerk, but can I ask why? I mean, you barely know him and you've never told anyone except for Amber and me."

I shrugged. "I don't know. I just trust him, I can't explain it."

My words seemed to bother him, and he frowned. "Is something going on between you guys?"

My stomach dropped, and I refused to meet his gaze. "No, we're just friends and that's all we'll ever be."

He seemed satisfied with my answer as he leaned down and kissed me on the cheek.

"Good to know. I just wanted to make sure I didn't have any competition."

"Never."

CHAPTER ELEVEN

IT'S COFFEE TIME

I stood in front of my mirror double-checking my appearance, making sure I looked okay for my first day on the job. Janet had told me to wear black pants and a white or black shirt. I had pulled my hair back into a sleek bun to keep it out of the way and applied a small amount of makeup. I was anxious as I pulled into the lot and walked inside.

Janet was standing behind the counter and greeted me with a smile. "You're early! Great, I have some paperwork for you to fill out."

She led me back to a small office and closed the door behind us. I sat in the chair across from her as she pulled a file folder out and handed me the papers inside.

"If you can fill these out for me, they're just basic emergency contact forms and tax information."

She sat quietly as I filled the forms out and handed them back to her. I had listed Logan as my emergency contact. She glanced down at the forms and stopped on his name.

"I don't mean to be rude, but you might not want to list a boyfriend as your contact."

I smiled. "He's my best friend."

"Good to know. I'm going to have you shadow Veronica tonight. If everything goes well, I'm going to schedule you for Monday, Tuesday, and Thursday from five p.m. to close. Does that work for you?"

"Sounds perfect. I really appreciate this job."

"Not a problem, we definitely need the help and since you've worked at another location before, we can skip making you take the training courses. Now come on, I'll introduce you to Veronica and you can get started."

I followed as she led me back to the counter. A pretty girl stood behind the register and smiled as we approached.

Janet gestured to me. "Veronica, this is Chloe. I want you to help her out tonight. Let her run the register and help keep things stocked while you and Anna make the drinks."

I smiled as I held out my hand to shake Veronica's. "Nice to meet you."

She was a few inches shorter than me, with dark brown hair. Her features and dark skin tone made me think she came from Hispanic descent. She motioned for me to come around the counter as Janet left us.

"I'm so glad you're here, our last girl just quit and left us hanging. Let me show you how to run the register, and then I'll show you where we keep all the supplies."

She took a few minutes to explain the register and watched as I rang up a few customers. She seemed impressed with how quickly I caught on.

"Not bad."

I gave her a smile. "Thanks. I worked at a Starbucks back home, so I know most of this stuff."

She nodded as she took me to the supply room in the back

next to Janet's office. "All the syrups are here. We keep the milk and whipped cream in the refrigerator over there, the coffees for the machines are here, and the bags we sell are on the shelves over there next to the refrigerator. The bakery items are brought in first thing in the morning, so you won't have to worry about that since you're on night shift."

I nodded, trying to keep up as she explained everything to me.

"All the bathroom and cleaning supplies are stocked over there, away from all the food obviously. If we're slow, you clean the tables and check the bathrooms. When we close, after you cash out, you need to wipe every table down, and restock all the syrups and coffee for the morning shift. Seem simple enough?"

"Yeah, I think I've got it."

"Good. Here's your apron. Let's get back out front before Anna has my head."

The next few hours flew by as I took orders while Veronica and Anna filled them. By the end of the night, my feet were killing me. I cashed out my register and took everything to Janet's office.

She smiled when I entered. "How did your first night go?"

"It was good, but now I'm beat."

She gave me a sympathetic smile. "Better get used to it again, we're always busy."

I waved good night as I walked back to the front and started wiping the tables down. Veronica and Anna restocked everything, and after I finished the tables, I cleaned the women's restroom while Anna tackled the men's. Once everything was finished, we split the tips, and I bade them good night as I walked to my car. I pulled my phone out of my pocket and switched it off vibrate. I had a new text from Drake.

Drake: I hope you're enjoying your night while I slave away over this paper.

I smiled as I typed my reply.

Me: Yes, I thoroughly enjoyed serving coffee to crazy customers all night, but my feet are dying a slow death. You shouldn't have waited until the last minute to finish your paper.

Drake: I guess you're right, I've just been distracted.

Me: I bet you have been. How's your butt?

Drake: Sore, thanks to you.

I laughed as another text came through.

Drake: That didn't come out right.

Me: No it didn't.

Drake: Shut up. I need to finish this, I'll talk to you tomorrow.

Me: Night.

The next few days passed by in a whirlwind of school, homework, and work. Tuesday night at work was much the same as Monday, with me taking orders while Anna and Veronica filled them. Thursday, Veronica decided I was ready to start tackling the drinks and put me with Anna while she took the orders. I had grown a bit rusty, and I messed up on a few orders. Apart from one man screaming at me about trying to kill him by putting milk in his coffee order, most of the customers were understanding.

I was getting along great with both Anna and Veronica. I really hadn't talked to Anna much while I was up front, but when I traded with Veronica, I spent the evening laughing with her. Whereas Veronica was all dark, Anna was the exact opposite—bright green eyes, pale skin, and blindingly white-blond hair. She was a bit too bubbly for me, but I could tell she had a good heart.

"So, what are you doing tomorrow night on your day off?" Veronica asked as we cleaned the machines after close.

"I'm going with my roommate and my friends to watch my friend Drake play with his band."

Rachel had heard Amber and me talking about the show the other night and asked if she could tag along to hear them play. Alex had something else to do, so Amber was going without him.

Veronica's mouth dropped open. "You mean the Drake who plays with Breaking the Hunger?

I nodded my head and she squealed. "You're friends with Drake Allen? How did I not know this? He's like a walking ball of sexual tension, and he's got the most amazing voice I've ever heard."

I laughed at her star-struck expression. "Don't let him hear you saying that, his already oversized head will swell."

"I'll help his head swell any day."

I burst out laughing at her dirty mind. "I never took you as a fan girl. Seriously though, he's a good friend, but he's crap to women."

She frowned. "Yeah that's what I heard. Too bad it's true. The things I'd like to do to that boy."

I smiled and waved as we made our way to our cars. I pulled my phone out and sent a quick text to Drake, reminding him we would be there tomorrow night. I had told him yesterday during class that we were planning on going, and he gave me a hard look, but wasn't able to say anything to me since Logan was with us. Before I could start my car, Drake called my phone.

"Hello?"

"Hey, I just got your text. Are you sure you'll be okay with going to the bar after what happened last time?"

My free hand gripped the steering wheel until my knuckles turned white. "I'll be fine. I will not let that asshole control my life."

I heard Drake's bed squeaking as he laid down.

"All right, but promise me you'll stay with Logan while I'm playing."

"I promise. I need to get home. I'll talk to you tomorrow, okay?"

"Good night, Chloe. Sweet dreams."

. . .

Drake wasn't in class the next morning, but he was sitting at our usual table with a girl on his lap I had never seen before when Logan and I walked into the cafeteria.

"You missed a bunch of notes this morning. Where were you?" I asked as I sat down across from him, ignoring the girl on his lap.

"I had some car trouble this morning so I had Adam drop me off late. I need to go to the library this afternoon after class, so if it's all right with you, I'll catch a ride with you guys to the bar."

I nodded as I stood to get in line for food. "That's fine. We're all riding together in my car, but I have enough room."

As I stood in line, I glanced back at the table and saw that the girl was gone, and that Logan was in deep conversation with Drake, their heads bent close together. When I approached the table, they both pulled away from each other and looked at me. While Logan had an easy smile on his face and seemed relaxed, Drake's body was coiled tight as he frowned up at me.

"What were you two talking about?"

Logan wrapped his arm around my shoulders and pulled me close while Drake followed our every move with his gaze.

"Nothing, just talking about watching him play tonight. I'm curious to see if he's as good as everyone says."

I looked at Drake, but he had lowered his gaze, his shoulders tight with tension. Somehow I didn't believe that's what they were talking about.

"I've seen them play, he's seriously amazing. You guys are going to go far, I can already tell."

Drake gave me a small smile, but it didn't quite reach his eyes. "Thanks, Adam has a tour set up for us over the summer once school is over. He's got us gigs in Virginia, Maryland, Pennsylvania, and even a couple small-time places in New York."

My smile brightened. "That's awesome, Drake! You watch, once summer is over you'll be a big-time rock star and you'll forget all about us little people."

"You don't have to worry about that, I don't think I'd ever be able to forget you."

Logan's hold on me tightened as I felt my cheeks warm.

"I bet you say that to all the girls."

He laughed as he pushed his chair back and stood. "You're right, I do. I've got to go make a few calls about my car. I'll see you guys tonight."

I felt Logan's grip relax as Drake left.

"I really don't like that guy sometimes."

I elbowed him in the ribs. "He's a good guy, he just likes to hide it."

"Still doesn't mean I have to like him." I glared at him and he laughed. "All right, I'll back off, I promised I would try to get along with him after all. So, after we leave the bar, I thought we could do a movie night in my room? My roommate won't be there like normal, so you can have his bed."

"I don't know, what if someone catches me in there?"

"Like I said, my roommate isn't going to be home and no one else is going to come to my room. Please, I feel like I haven't seen you in weeks."

I instantly felt bad; I had been neglecting Logan with everything else going on in my life. "Okay, but only if I get to pick the movie."

He smiled as he leaned down and kissed the top of my head. "Fair enough, it's a date."

I tensed at his words, but didn't respond at first. Maybe we could ease into this and see where it went instead of jumping in with both feet.

"It's a date."

CHAPTER TWELVE

EVERYTHING CHANGES

I sat on my bed with Logan, Amber, and Rachel, talking as we waited for Drake to show up. We had spent the last twenty minutes in my room, waiting for him to arrive, and so far the only thing he had done was make us wait. I glanced anxiously between the clock and a severely pissed-off Logan before deciding to call him.

"Hello?"

"Where are you? It's almost eight o'clock and you go on at nine."

"I'm finishing up at the library now. Can you come over and pick me up?"

I sighed. "Yeah, wait for us outside. We'll be there in a couple minutes." I hung up with him and turned to everyone. "Come on, we have to pick him up at the library."

Logan took my hand in his as we walked to my car. I caught Amber staring at us and gave her a weak smile. She chuckled and shook her head as she got in, but thankfully said nothing. We pulled up in front of the library a few minutes later to see

Drake waiting on us. I popped the trunk so he could stash his jacket and guitar inside.

Rachel scooted over closer to Amber with a star-struck look on her face as Drake sat down next to her. He glanced over at her and gave her that killer smile that made my knees weak.

"I don't think we've met. I'm Drake."

Rachel looked ready to pass out as she gazed up at him.

"I know who you are. I'm Rachel, Chloe's roommate."

My stomach tightened as they continued to flirt all the way to the bar. Drake had made his position with me clear, and yet I couldn't help but get jealous when he gave any girl attention.

I parked as far away as I could from the spot we had been in that night with Nick. Bile rose in my throat as I glanced in that direction, almost expecting him to still be lying there bleeding. I started shaking as we walked toward the doors. Drake, who had been watching me without my knowledge, was at my side instantly.

He wrapped his arm around me and pulled me into his side.

"It's all right, I'm here. He won't hurt you again, I promise."

My voice was stuck in my throat, so I couldn't reply. When we reached the entrance and caught up with our friends, he released me and stepped in first, giving me a minute to compose myself. I could feel his eyes on me as I pushed through the crowd to catch up, and I gave him a small nod to let him know I was okay.

Carrying his guitar, Drake led us to an empty table next to the stage.

"I had them save this one for you guys. I've got to go back and meet up with the guys and Jade."

Rachel watched his retreating figure with rapt attention, and my jealous side reared its ugly head.

"Earth to Rachel, come in Rachel," I said as I snapped my fingers in front of her face.

"What, oh sorry."

I shook my head as Logan chuckled.

"Don't go there, Rachel. If you have sex with him, you'll make it awkward for me when he kicks you to the curb."

Rachel frowned. "I wasn't planning on having sex with him."

I gave her an incredulous look. "Could've fooled me."

Amber jumped up before Rachel could reply.

"Chloe, why don't you come to the bar with me and help me get us drinks."

I stood and followed her to the bar. She spun around as soon as we were out of earshot.

"What the hell was that?"

I looked at her confused. "What are you talking about?"

"You know exactly what I'm talking about. You blew up at Rachel for no reason."

I shrugged as I ordered our beers. "No I didn't. I just saw the way she was looking at Drake. If they hook up, it'll make it awkward every time we're all together."

"Are you sure that's all it is? Because I saw the way you were looking at him. For God's sake, Chloe, get your act together. You were just holding hands with Logan earlier."

"You're imagining things. I'm over Drake, and I haven't given Logan an answer, we're taking things slow."

She shook her head. "I'm not blind, Chloe. You can lie to yourself, but you can't lie to me. You still care about Drake and you're stringing Logan along. Do you even have feelings for him or are you just trying to get over Drake?"

I grabbed the beers and turned to glare at her. "Yes, I do fucking care about Logan, I'm trying to get my shit together. I do want to give Logan a chance, but I'm afraid, okay? I don't want to lose him."

"Do you really think he would abandon you if things went south with him? He cares too much about you to let that happen. You need to get your head out of Drake's ass and see what's standing right in front of you."

"You think I don't know how amazing Logan is? Because I do, so stop trying to push me to him and let things happen!" I practically shouted as I walked back to the table. I set Logan's beer in front of him and forced a smile onto my face.

He pulled my chair closer to him and rested his hand on my thigh.

"What took you guys so long?"

I glanced at Amber, who was looking anywhere but at me. "We had to wait forever, sorry."

We sat and talked as we waited for Drake and the other members to take the stage. Logan barely touched his beer, but our waitress brought a couple over to me while we waited. Finally, the lights were lowered and the band came out of the side door and took the stage. I watched as Drake introduced them and then started into the first song. Just like before, I was mesmerized by his voice as the hairs on the back of my neck stood up. He just had a presence on stage that demanded you stop whatever you were doing and listen to him.

I bobbed my head with the music as they played a few fast songs. A group of girls appeared in front of Drake as he continued to sing. He would occasionally glance down at them and wink, causing them to scream out his name. I rolled my eyes at their attempts to get his attention.

He finished out the current song and waited for everyone to stop shouting out his name before he spoke. "All right, we're going to slow it down a bit with a new song. I wrote this earlier in the week, I hope you all enjoy it." He smiled at the women standing at his feet. "This one is for all the ladies in the room."

They started screaming as Jade started in with a slow beat, followed by Eric and Adam. Drake came in last with his guitar as he closed his eyes and started singing the most beautiful lyrics I had ever heard. I froze as his eyes opened and locked onto mine.

I've searched high and low for someone like you
Feeling like there was no one around
Until I saw you
You took my breath away, made me smile
Stole my heart and blinded me with your beauty
I'm raw when you're not around
Lost when you're gone you see, but that's how it has to be
Such beauty could never be wasted on me
I hope you'll understand why
I push you away and hide inside myself
I'll never be good enough, I'm caged inside myself
Please forgive me
Please forgive me.

My eyes stung with tears as I listened to him sing to me.

Logan nudged me and whispered in my ear, "You want to dance?"

I didn't, not while Drake stood on stage and bared his soul to me, but I nodded and let him lead me into the space where several other couples were already dancing.

He pulled me close and rested his hands on my hips as I watched Drake behind him. He was still staring at me with a look of pure pain on his face, and it broke my heart. If only things could have been different. Logan hugged me tight as we swayed back and forth and kissed me on the cheek. I looked away from Drake to Logan as I leaned in and gently kissed him on the lips. I had to move on, and Logan was standing right here in front of me, waiting on me, his eyes filled with love. I had to accept that I would never have Drake.

Logan returned my kiss eagerly before pulling back.

"What was that for?"

"It just felt right."

He smiled as Drake finished the song and told everyone good night. Logan and I grabbed a couple bottles of beer and returned to the table. The band packed up their instruments and followed Drake over to our table.

Jade smiled at me as she pulled a chair from a neighboring table and sat down next to me. "Hey, Chloe, good to see you again."

"Yeah, you too."

Everyone shifted around the table to give Drake, Eric, and Adam room to squeeze into our cramped space as Drake introduced the guys to us. This was the first time I had ever seen either one of them up close. Eric had his light brown hair styled in the same shaggy mess as Drake did, but he didn't have any of Drake's piercings. He looked surprisingly clean-cut for being in a rock band. He had a few tattoos scattered across his uncovered arms, but that was the extent of his body modification as far as I could see.

Adam, on the other hand, was an animal all his own. His hair was dyed an electric blue and was styled in a Mohawk that stood several inches high. His eyebrows were both pierced twice and he had a set of snakebites. He screamed *wild,* and I gave Amber a subtle kick under the table when I saw her watching him like he was a God.

We fell into an easy conversation as everyone settled themselves around the table. I refused to look at Drake as Jade and

I started talking, afraid of what I'd see if I looked into his eyes. We were interrupted when three girls came over and settled themselves in the male band member's laps. Jade was apparently used to this; she ignored them as she continued to ask questions about my classes and my job. I couldn't help but look up every time one of them would giggle at something that was said.

Drake sat with his hands running up and down a redhead's thigh, whispering into her ear. My stomach turned, and I looked around for our waitress, needing another drink. I finally caught her attention and signaled for two more beers.

"Don't you think you should slow down, Chloe? You've already had five," Logan asked, concerned.

"I want to have fun tonight, what's the big deal?"

He shook his head as he watched me down one of the beers the waitress brought me.

"Go ahead, but you're not driving us home."

I handed him my keys. "That's fine, you can drive."

Logan took my keys as I started in on the second beer. "Good idea."

As the night wore on, I felt the alcohol taking effect and caught myself constantly watching Drake and the redhead. Every time I looked at them, his hands were roaming over her body as she leaned into him. When I couldn't take it any longer, I stood and motioned for Logan to stand as well.

"I'm ready to go home if you are."

He glanced at Amber and Rachel, who were in deep conversation with Jade. "You guys ready?"

We told everyone good night as Logan led me out to the car, steadying me when I stumbled. The car ride home was loud as Amber and Rachel gushed about how amazing the band had been. I kept quiet and stared out the window as my head spun.

When we pulled in, Logan helped me out of the car. "You still on for movie night?"

I looked at him and smiled. "Of course."

. . .

Logan kept his word and let me pick the movie. I really didn't care, so I pulled a random action movie out and handed it to him. I sat down and kicked my shoes off as he put it into the DVD player and settled down beside me. He had taken his shirt off and changed into pajama pants when we arrived, and I felt his bare skin warm and soft against my cheek as I laid my head down on his chest, resting my hand on his stomach. My fingers drew circles over the tight muscles in his stomach as we watched the movie. When I started running my hands up and down the deep *V* of his abdomen he jumped up from the bed and walked across the room.

"I think I need a shot. You want one?"

"Sure," I mumbled as I sat up.

He pulled a bottle and two shot glasses out of his closet and poured us each one.

I took my shot and handed my glass back.

"Give me another one."

"You sure? You've already had a bunch to drink."

My mind was foggy as I looked at him through alcohol-glazed eyes. He really was beautiful, and I was lucky to have someone like him care so much about me.

"Yeah, I'm fine."

He poured me another shot and handed it to me, stashing the bottle back in his closet. I set the glass on the nightstand as he settled back down next to me, and I curled up around him. I started running my hands across his stomach again and felt his body tense.

"What are you doing, Chloe?"

I shook my head as I continued exploring his hard muscles. "I have no idea."

"You need to stop."

I raised my head to look at him. His eyes had glazed over with the lust he was trying to control.

"Why?" I whispered.

"Because if you don't, I'm not going to be able to control myself."

I smiled innocently as I brushed kisses across his chest. "Maybe I don't want you to."

His sucked in a breath as I flipped my tongue over his nipple. "Chloe, you're drunk and you'll regret this in the morning."

I rolled over until I was on top of him, straddling him. "I know exactly what I'm doing."

I was lying, but the alcohol had taken over, and I couldn't control what was happening. I leaned down and started kissing up his neck to his ear, before sucking on the sensitive spot behind his ear.

He groaned as he rolled over and pinned me to the bed beneath him. "Are you sure this is what you want? I told you I could wait, and I meant it."

I nodded as I raised my head to kiss him. "Yes, please, I need you."

My words were all it took to spring him into action. He raised me up and pulled my shirt over my head.

"You don't know how long I've wanted you. If you change your mind, just tell me and I'll stop. But if you don't, I have no intentions of stopping, I want you too much."

I whimpered as he unsnapped my bra and took both my breasts in his hands, kneading them gently. He bent his head forward and sucked my hard nipple into his mouth, biting on it.

His hands slid slowly down my stomach to the fastening on my jeans. He pulled them off before cupping me between my legs. His fingers found my entrance and entered slowly as he gently thrust them in and out, causing me to arch my body into his.

"You're so beautiful, Chloe, and you're mine."

I groaned and pushed myself up tighter against him. "Please, Dr— Logan, I need it harder."

My body tensed as I tried to cover my blunder. I had almost called him Drake in the heat of the moment. He didn't seem to notice as he obliged and thrust his fingers in harder before pulling away.

"What are you doing?"

"Tell me you're mine. I need to hear it." His fingers circled my entrance, driving me insane, but he refused to enter. "Let me hear you say it, Chloe."

"I'm yours. Now please."

He kissed me roughly before pulling his pajama pants off. He grabbed a condom out of the drawer and slowly lowered himself to push inside me. I hadn't had sex in a long time, and I felt a small twinge of pain at his size, but in my drunken haze, I immediately responded and pushed my hips up to meet each thrust. The pain quickly changed to pleasure, and I felt myself start to go over the edge as he slipped a hand between my legs and stroked my clit.

I ran my nails down his back, and his thrusts became harder and more erratic. My hands fisted in his hair as I came, and I heard him shout out at his own release. He pulled out slowly and threw the condom away before settling back in behind me and pulling me close.

"That was amazing, Chloe. You were amazing."

He kissed my head before falling asleep quickly. I laid there curled up in his arms as a single tear slipped down my cheek.

CHAPTER THIRTEEN

THE CHEAT

I woke to fingers gently running up and down my spine, confused as to where I was. Thoughts of the previous night slammed into me, and I feigned sleep as I tried to pull myself together. I had slept with Logan and, in one night, changed everything about us.

His breath tickled my ear as he spoke. "Wake up, sleepy head."

I stayed still for a few moments before stretching and rolling over to look at him. I had never seen him look so happy, his skin was practically glowing, and his perfect blue eyes were sparkling. I gave him a weak smile as he brushed his lips across mine.

"Morning, beautiful. Did you sleep well?"

I nodded as I rolled back over and glanced at the clock. "It's not even eight a.m. yet, why did you wake me up?"

He stood, and I quickly looked away from his nakedness as he pulled a pair of boxers on.

He laughed as he watched me. "Don't act all shy on me now." He bent down and kissed me deeply. "Last night was incredible, the best night of my life."

He pulled back and grabbed some jeans and a shirt out of his closet.

"I thought we could go grab some breakfast, but you can go back to sleep if you want to."

I sat up and grabbed my head as pain shot through it. "Ouch, holy hangover."

He laughed as he grabbed me a couple of Tylenol and handed them to me with a glass of water. "Here, take these— they'll help."

I quickly swallowed them as I started searching his room for my clothes. I pulled my bra and thong back on and was fighting with my jeans when my phone started ringing from the desk beside Logan. He picked it up and after glancing at the screen, answered it with a smug look on his face.

"Hello?" He was silent for a moment. "This is Logan, Chloe is busy."

I gave him a questioning look, but he just smiled at me.

"Hold on a minute, she's putting her clothes on."

My eyes widened in surprise over him telling someone that.

He walked across the room and handed my phone to me. "It's for you."

"Well duh, it is my phone." I held the phone up to my ear. "Hello?" Silence followed and I thought whoever it was had hung up. "Hello? Is anyone there?"

"Sorry, I didn't mean to interrupt anything. I just wanted to see how you were feeling this morning, you were a bit drunk last night."

My heart stopped as I heard Drake's voice. That's why Logan had made sure to mention that I was getting dressed with him there. I cleared my throat before sending a glare toward Logan. "I'm all right, just a headache. Logan gave me some pills to help me though."

He was silent for a moment before he spoke. "Did you sleep with him, Chloe?"

I glanced up at Logan and noticed him watching me closely. "Does it matter?"

"No it doesn't, but for some reason I want to know."

I sighed and rubbed my throbbing temples. "Yes."

I heard him take a deep breath before speaking. "I'd better go, I'll talk to you later."

I set my phone on the bed and pulled my shirt over my head, avoiding Logan's gaze.

"What was that about?"

I picked up my purse and threw it over my shoulder. "Nothing, he just wanted to see how I was feeling after drinking so much last night."

"Does he make it a habit to call you so early in the morning?"

I turned to glare at him. "No, he doesn't. Is this how we're going to be now? You jealous over every male friend I have?"

He walked across the room and pulled me into a hug. "No, he just makes me nervous. And we really haven't talked about where we're going to go from here. I don't know if you feel like last night was a mistake or not, if you want me."

I pulled back as I cupped his cheek in my hand. "Last night wasn't a mistake, Logan. I assumed you knew that. I want to give this a try and see where it takes us."

A huge smile spread across his face. "I want that too, you have no idea how much." He pulled me to him and kissed me roughly.

"I need to take a shower before we get some breakfast. Meet me downstairs in an hour?"

He nodded as I closed the door and walked to my room.

I took longer in the shower than necessary as I tried to wash away all my mixed emotions. Drake had no right to call me and act like that. He had pushed me away, had told me to go to Logan, and that's what I had done. My decision was made, and I wasn't about to change it now. I would get over him as I focused my attention on Logan. It was only fair to Logan that we started our relationship without any conflicting emotions on my part, and that's what I intended to do. If it meant losing the friendship that I had with Drake, then so be it—he wasn't a priority any longer.

I dressed quickly and met Logan by his car. He pulled me tight against him and kissed me deeply. It felt nice, but none of the fireworks I saw when Drake kissed me appeared. I pushed the thoughts away as I pulled back and smiled up at him. "What was that for?"

He smacked me lightly on my bottom before walking to the driver's side and getting in. I slid in next to him and fastened my seat belt. "I just wanted to kiss you. There've been so many times I've held back, and now I have every intention of kissing you as much as possible."

I smiled at his sweet words, and I leaned across the console to give him a peck on the cheek.

"Okay, what was that for?"

I giggled as he pulled out of the lot. "Because you're so sweet. I could get used to this whole romantic side of you."

"You'd better get used to it, because you're going to be seeing a whole lot of it."

After breakfast, Logan and I spent the morning out shopping at the local mall and watching a movie. We stopped by my work on our way home to grab some coffee. When Veronica saw us, her eyes widened as she took a long look at Logan. "Who's your friend, Chloe, and where have you been hiding him?"

Logan's face broke out in a huge smile as I introduced him as my boyfriend.

"What the hell, woman? You're friends with Drake and now you come walking in here with this guy? I think I officially hate you."

I laughed as we paid for our drinks and left.

We went back to Logan's room and spent the rest of the day in bed together, cuddling and kissing. I could tell Logan wanted more, but he didn't push, and I appreciated his thoughtfulness. I told him so as we lay tangled in his sheets.

"I won't push you, Chloe, you know that. Last night was amazing, but I understand why you're holding back." He kissed my head as I snuggled deeper into his chest and slept.

Logan and I walked into class the next morning together, holding hands. He slapped Drake on the back as he took his seat. "Morning, Drake, beautiful day isn't it?" He pulled me to him and kissed me full on the lips.

I felt my face warm as I looked over at Drake, who was staring at us with cold indifference.

"Yeah, I guess it is."

I pulled my eyes away from him and cornered Logan with a glare.

"What?" he asked with an innocent smile.

"You know, if you wanted to mark your territory, all you had to do was pee on my leg."

He laughed as he leaned back in his chair. "Good idea, I'll have to remember that for next time."

I rolled my eyes as I started pulling things out of my bag. Drake ignored us for the rest of class, and disappeared as soon as class ended. He was nowhere to be seen at lunch either. By the time I arrived at work that evening, I was getting seriously pissed at him for ignoring me. If he didn't want anything to do with me, that was fine. But he didn't have to be a jerk about it. My night quickly went from bad to worse. I was so focused on being mad at Drake, I constantly messed up drink orders until Veronica forced me to run register.

"What is wrong with you tonight?" she asked as I threw yet another messed-up order in the garbage and walked up to the register to start taking orders.

"Nothing."

She waited until I finished punching in a customer's order before starting in on me again. "Obviously something is bothering you since you've destroyed every drink you've made tonight and you almost broke the register you were pushing buttons so hard."

"Honest, it's nothing. Just a bad day."

She rolled her eyes, but let it go. I managed to get through the rest of the night without breaking the machine or ripping any annoying customer's head off and breathed a sigh of relief as we closed up and I walked to my car. My relief was short-lived when I saw someone leaning against my car. I approached slowly and pulled a can of pepper spray out of my bag. "Can I help you?"

My body relaxed as the figure turned and I saw that it was Drake. He grinned as I approached and leaned back onto my door.

"You scared the fuck out of me!" I yelled as I reached the car.

He glanced down at the pepper spray in my hand and smirked. "Were you really going to pepper spray me?"

"It crossed my mind. Now move or I will," I said as I tried to shove him away from my door. He refused to budge.

"What's got your panties in a bunch tonight? Trouble in paradise already?"

"No, not that it's any of your business, now move!" He just gave me a smile, not moving an inch. I threw my hands in the air. "Why are you here?"

"Can't I just come visit you at work?"

I glanced at my phone. "You do realize it's after midnight and we're standing in a dark parking lot, right?"

"Come with me, I want to go for a drive."

I shook my head. "I need to get home, just tell me what you want."

He pushed himself off my car to stand in front of me, lifting his hand to brush it down my cheek. "Please?"

I sucked in a ragged breath at the contact and stepped away. "I don't think that's such a good idea."

"I'll keep my hands to myself, promise."

I bit my lip as I debated. Finally, I nodded, and we made our way across the lot to his car. We were silent as he drove down Mileground Road and merged onto the interstate.

"Where are we going?" I asked as we weaved through traffic.

"Someplace I go when I need to think or to write music, depending on my mood."

I stayed silent as he took an exit and pulled onto a side road I hadn't even noticed. After a few minutes of silence I glanced over at him. "I thought we already had this discussion. I do not want to go deep into the West Virginia wilderness to be murdered."

He grinned. "I'm not going to murder you. We'll be there in a minute."

The trees began to thin until they opened up into a clearing.

He pulled up to an embankment and shut off the car. My breath caught as I stared out at a lake in front of us. "Where are we?"

He got out of the car and grabbed a blanket out of the backseat, throwing it over the hood of the car. He jumped up on the hood and turned to grin at me. "This is my secret place and this," he gestured at the water in front of me, "is the Cheat Lake. Now get out here."

I stepped out of the car and sat down next to him. "It's beautiful."

And it was. The moon was shining brightly, reflecting off the surface. There weren't any lights for miles around and the whole scene brought about a sense of peace in me. I scooted up so I could rest my back on the windshield and looked at him as he spoke. "Yeah, it is. I like to just come out here and get away from everything."

We sat in silence for a few minutes, both enjoying the view and the peace that came with it. "Why did you bring me out here, Drake?" I asked softly.

He turned to me and gave me a small smile. "I don't know. I couldn't sleep and I decided to come out here. How I ended up in that parking lot I'll never know."

I reached over and gave his hand a small squeeze before pulling away. "Why did you ignore me all day? And don't say you didn't, I know when someone is purposely avoiding me."

He slid back and settled down next to me, staring up at the moon. The ring in his lip caught the moonlight, and I had to force myself to look away from his full lips.

"I was avoiding you, I won't lie."

I sat in silence as I waited for him to continue.

"You threw me for a loop yesterday morning. I told you to be with Logan, but I didn't think you'd dive into it like that."

I sat up and glared at him. "So you're avoiding me because I had sex with someone? That's just stupid. If our roles were reversed, I'd never be able to talk to you again with all the women you're with."

"You're different. I have no morals, you're better than that."

"So now I'm a slut for sleeping with one guy? You're such a fucking hypocrite!"

I started to slide down the hood to get away from him, but he caught my arm and pulled me back. "That's not what I meant. I know you're not a slut, I just didn't expect you to go have sex with someone without even being in a relationship with them."

I sat fuming, speechless.

"Don't be mad at me, Chloe. I'm just looking out for you."

"I'm not mad, Drake, I'm livid. None of this is your business, so I wish you'd just butt out!"

He sat up as he grabbed my face and pulled me to him, our noses almost touching. "You'll always be my business, Chloe. I care a lot about you." He released me and slumped back down against the windshield as I sat speechless, staring at him. "So are you guys together now or was it just a one-time thing?"

I smacked him in the stomach and he laughed.

"What? I'm just asking."

"Yeah, we're together now."

He nodded as he turned his attention back to the water. "I'm happy for you then." He sat up and slid down the hood, holding his hand out to me. "I'd better get you home, it's late."

I took his hand and let him help me down. Once I was safely on the ground, he released me and grabbed the blanket. He threw it in the backseat as I opened my door and slid silently into the car. Drake got in and started the car, taking us back to the interstate and to my car. We were still silent as he pulled his car next to mine.

I glanced back at him as I opened the door. "We good?"

He gave me a sad smile. "Yeah, Chloe, we're good."

I turned and pulled him into a tight hug, shocking him. He was stiff at first, but he relaxed and hugged me back. "I'm glad, Drake. You're important to me and I don't want to lose you."

He kissed me lightly on the cheek as I pulled away and got out. "You won't lose me, Chloe. I'll see you tomorrow, okay?"

I smiled as I got in my car and drove home, feeling lighter than I had all day.

CHAPTER FOURTEEN

THE GREATEST MISTAKE

The next couple of months seemed to pass in a blur as I fell into a frenzied routine of work and school. Classes were getting harder the closer we got to midterms, and I spent most of my free time working on assignments or studying. Anytime I wasn't doing any of the above, I spent my time with Logan, Amber, Rachel, and Drake.

After the night out at the lake, Drake and I had fallen back into our easy friendship, often seeing who could annoy the other one the most. The whole gang would always make it to Drake's performances every Friday night at Gold's and it quickly became our favorite hangout spot. Jade and the guys fit right in with us instantly and would join our table after their performances more often than not.

Amber and Alex broke up a couple weeks after their first date, and I noticed her watching Adam closely on more than one occasion. This worried me, seeing as he was a bigger player than Drake—if that was possible. She didn't need another broken heart. The groupies continued to flock to our table, and I tried not to let it bother me, but it did, especially on the nights

I had to watch Drake leave with one or even sometimes two of them.

Logan and I spent most of our evenings in his bed, studying or cuddling, and I was happy with how things were progressing between us. We still hadn't had sex again, and I started to feel guilty, but I pushed the thoughts aside. When I felt comfortable, we would. Preferably when I was sober. The only thing that was bothering me about him was his overly affectionate tendencies when Drake was around. When we were with him, I could barely keep his hands off of me. Drake didn't say anything about it, but I would catch him watching us with an angry or annoyed look on his face.

Drake and I had made plans to study together the evening before a huge test that counted for a quarter of our grade. Logan hadn't seemed happy with the idea, but he grudgingly agreed after I told him, yet again, that he had nothing to worry about. He even seemed relaxed about it after he had made a big show of kissing me breathless at lunch in front of Drake before leaving.

I sighed as I pulled in front of Drake's house, thinking about the spectacle that Logan had made. I pushed the thought back as I knocked on Drake's door and let myself in.

"Hello? Anybody home?" I yelled. There was no response, but I heard HELLYEAH blaring from the stereo in his bedroom. I walked quietly to his door and knocked, afraid of what I'd see when I opened it. No response came, so I pushed the door open slightly, peering through the crack. I felt a rush of relief as I saw Drake on his bed alone. I pushed the door open and walked in.

He was lying on the bed in just his boxers with his eyes closed and I took a moment to just stare at his body. The muscles in his arms and stomach were hard and defined; he was pure male perfection, and I felt myself become aroused at just the sight of him. Pulling myself out of my lust-filled trance, I walked over to him and poked him in the stomach. His body jerked as his eyes flew open and he came up swinging. I quickly backed away, barely missing a fist to the face. He caught sight of me and stopped.

"Jesus Christ, woman. Don't fucking sneak up on me," he yelled as he sat up and turned the music down to a low hum.

"Sorry, I knocked and yelled."

He rose from the bed and moved past me to the living room, still in his boxers. "It's a good way to get yourself knocked out. Don't do it again."

I glared at him. "Don't give me attitude; you knew I was coming over tonight. It's not my fault you had the music loud enough to drown out a train if it came barreling through your house."

He sat down on the couch. "Whatever, let's get this over with."

I sat down in the chair across from him. "What's with the attitude?"

"I don't have an attitude, I just want to get this shit out of the way."

I rolled my eyes as he opened the book and looked at me. "Fine by me, but can you put some clothes on first?"

He grinned for the first time since I entered the house. "Why, is it going to be a distraction for you?"

"Drake, I'm a woman. Yes, it's going to be a distraction for me."

He smirked as he stood up and walked back to the bedroom, returning a few minutes later fully clothed. "Better?"

"Much, thank you. Now let's get started."

We spent the next hour studying. Or rather, I spent it studying, he spent it staring off into space with a pissed-off look on his face. I finally gave up and slammed my book shut as I glared at him. "That's it! What's wrong with you today? You've been crankier than normal ever since I got here."

"Nothing's wrong with me. Just back off, okay?"

I continued to glare up at him as he tried to walk past me and out of the room. I caught his arm and dug my nails into the hard muscle. "No, I will not just back off. Tell me what the hell is bothering you."

He jerked his arm out of my grip and backed away. "You don't want to know the answer to that. Just leave it alone, Chloe."

I threw my hands up in the air and stomped my foot. "Tell me what your fucking problem is, Drake. I'm not letting it go until you do."

He spun around to face me. "Fine, you want to know what my problem is? I can't fucking stand to watch you with him every single day, watching him hug you, kiss you, when it should be me!" he yelled as I stood frozen on the spot.

"What are you talking about? You were the one who told me I couldn't have you, who told me to be with Logan even when I wasn't sure! You don't want me, Drake, you just want to fuck me!"

He walked to me and shoved me up against the wall. "You're right, I do want to fuck you. I want to pick you up and carry you to my room and slam into you until you scream my name over and over again as you shatter to pieces underneath me, but I can't. I won't do that to Logan. I'm an asshole, but I won't be that guy." He punched the wall beside my head and I jumped.

"I don't know what you want me to say. I made myself clear before and you pushed me to him."

"I know I did, and I've been living with it ever since that day. I want you so bad, Chloe, I just gravitate to you," he whispered quietly as he rested his forehead against mine. "I don't understand any of this, I just know I have to have you or I'll never be able to let go."

The words slipped out of my mouth before I could stop them. "Then take me."

He pulled back and looked me in the eye. "What?"

I leaned forward to wrap my arms around his neck and pulled him back down to me, not sure what I was doing, but unable to stop myself. "If you want me, take me. If this is what it takes for us to get each other out of our systems, then we'll do it and move on."

He hesitated. "What about Logan?"

I closed my eyes as guilt took over. "I can't move on with him until I can stop thinking about you. Please, Drake. I need this, give it to me." My lips went to his, and I kissed him hungrily.

He responded immediately with a groan as he kissed me back. "God, Chloe, you always taste so good." He went back to kissing me as he lifted me off the ground and I wrapped my legs around his waist, feeling him already hard against me. He moaned as I shifted my hips to rub myself against him.

Walking backward, he carried me to his bedroom and threw me on the bed before climbing on top of me. His lips sought out mine again as his hand slipped under my shirt. I sighed and threw my head back as his fingers went to my nipple and started rolling it gently between his thumb and fingers. I arched my back up so that I could press myself closer to him as he slipped his tongue into my mouth. Now that I knew about his tongue ring, I was ready for it as I sucked on his tongue, the metal hitting against my teeth.

He groaned again and pressed into me. "I need you naked. Now."

He lifted me up long enough to rip my shirt off and unclasp my bra before unbuttoning my jeans and pulling them and my underwear off together. I reached for his shirt, but he took it off before I even touched it. My hands fumbled with his jeans as he threw the shirt across the room. As soon as I had the buttons undone, I slipped my hand inside and wrapped my fingers around his length.

He shuddered. "Chloe, you have to stop or I'm going to blow before I even get inside you."

I continued to run my hand up and down his shaft and he started panting. He grabbed both my hands and pulled them above my head. "I'm not kidding, I'm about to blow and I've barely even touched you yet." He kicked his jeans off and crawled up over me so that he was staring directly into my eyes. "Move your hands and I'll tie them to the bedposts."

My body shuddered in delight at the thought of Drake tying me up and having his way with me. "I'll be good, I promise."

He lowered his head and slowly kissed my lips, then moved to my neck. He nibbled a path from my neck down to by breasts—sucking first one, and then the other into his mouth and swirling his tongue ring around them.

"Oh God, don't stop," I moaned as I arched my back.

He released them and slowly licked his way down my stomach, stopping at my hips to suck on them too. My body convulsed, and I felt my orgasm building. He grabbed my legs and threw them over his shoulders as his tongue flicked across my throbbing clit over and over, his tongue ring adding to the sensation. He slid a finger inside me as he continued to lick, and I felt my body tensing around him.

"Drake. Oh God, please."

"Shhh, come for me baby. I want to feel it."

His words were all it took to send me over the edge. I screamed out his name as my legs clenched around him, holding his mouth tight against me as he continued to lick, prolonging my orgasm.

Finally the waves settled and I groaned. "That was amazing."

"I'm glad you liked it, but I'm not done yet."

I raised my head off the bed to look at him. "I've never . . . I don't think I can go again."

He smiled wickedly. "I don't think I'll have any problem getting you there again." He kissed his way back up my body before positioning himself between my legs. "You're on some kind of birth control, right?"

I nodded, but stopped him before he could penetrate me by rolling him over until I was straddling him. I started kissing my way down his body, stopping at each nipple ring to flick my tongue across them. He ran his hands down my back as I dipped my head lower, but something caught my eye, and I pulled back.

"You really weren't kidding about being pierced everywhere."

His laugh was cut short as I lowered my head and ran my tongue up and down his length several times, causing him to jump. "Stop teasing me, woman, and get on with it!"

I laughed. "Impatient much?"

"Ver— Fuck me!" he shouted as I wrapped my lips around

him and took him as deep as I could without gagging. I began sucking on him gently, rolling my tongue over the tip of him, enjoying the taste as he moaned. Suddenly, he pulled me off of him and flipped me on my back before positioning himself at my entrance again.

"Enough of that. Are you ready for me, baby?"

I nodded as he slowly slid into me, inch by excruciating inch. Once he was fully inside me, he stopped for a moment to give my body time to adjust to his size.

"Dear God, Drake, you're huge."

He chuckled as he slid out and slammed back into me repeatedly, his piercing rubbing against me in a way that made me scream.

"Drake, please . . ."

"Please what, baby? Tell me what you want."

I threw my head back against the pillow as he continued to slam into me. "Fuck me harder, Drake, please! I need it harder!"

He quickly pulled out and flipped me over. Raising my hips, he slammed into me from behind. "God, you're so fucking tight, so fucking hot, Chloe!"

My fingers grabbed the sheets as I threw my hips back, trying to take him deeper. I felt myself building again.

"Are you ready, baby? I want to go together," Drake asked as he continued pumping into me.

"Yes, please don't stop."

He reached down between my legs and flicked my clit, sending me over the edge. I screamed out his name as I came, and I felt him explode inside me.

Drake collapsed on top of me and stayed there for a minute as we tried to control our breathing. Finally, he pulled out and walked to the bathroom to clean himself up. I rolled to my back as he returned to the room and lay down beside me.

"You're amazing, Chloe."

I closed my eyes as I curled into him, resting my head on his chest, enjoying his warmth.

He wrapped his arms around me and kissed the top of my head. "You should probably go."

My body tensed at his words as what we had just done finally sunk in. I pulled away and started throwing my clothes on as quickly as I could. "You're right, I'm glad we got that out of our systems."

Drake sat up, the sheet falling down around his waist. "Chloe, that's not what I . . ."

"Save it, Drake. I know what you meant." I all but ran from the room and out to my car, tears streaming down my face as I drove away.

I didn't return to my dorm. Instead I drove around the city, pulling into an empty parking lot as guilt and anguish crippled me. I rested my head against the steering wheel and let loose a torrent of tears. After a few minutes, I managed to pull myself together enough to sit up. I'm not sure how long I sat there watching the passing traffic, hiccupping and shaking. I had really screwed things up this time. Instead of getting Drake out of my system, having sex had only amplified my feelings tenfold. Obviously it hadn't had the same effect on him, seeing how he tossed me out of his bed the minute we were done. I closed my eyes and let my head fall back onto the seat. Things were ruined between us and I knew it.

It was my fault after all. He had tried to push me away, and I had thrown myself at him. I knew from the beginning that the only thing I would get from Drake was a broken heart, and

I had walked blindly into it. Logan's face crept into my thoughts, and I started crying again. How could I face him after this? I had cheated on him. He was too good for me, and I knew it, this just drove my point home. I'm not sure how long I sat there wallowing in my thoughts before my phone went off with a new text message. I grabbed it, secretly praying it was Drake. Instead, a message from Logan was waiting for me.

Logan: **Hey babe, you still with Drake?**

I took a deep breath, debating on telling him the truth. Instead, like a coward, I pushed my guilt away.

Me: **I am, but I'm leaving now. I'll see you in a few. Xoxo**

Logan: **Okay, stop by my room. I ordered us Chinese.**

Me: **Will do.**

I wiped my eyes as I started my car and made my way home.

CHAPTER FIFTEEN

ESCAPE

The next few weeks passed in a haze. Drake was back to avoiding me at all costs, and I was only speaking to him in the class we shared with Logan so that he wouldn't become suspicious. I was depressed and hurt over how my life seemed to be spinning out of my control. When Logan asked what was bothering me, I gave him a vague excuse about classes and my job draining me. He didn't seem completely convinced, but he left me alone about it after a while.

Drake stopped sitting with us at lunch, and I was relieved until I started seeing him with other women again. Every time I saw him, he was always with a different woman, and I knew just how little I meant to him. I picked up the Friday night shift at work just so I could have a valid excuse as to why I had stopped showing up at Drake's shows and spent almost all of my free evenings immersed in my studies, avoiding everyone as much as possible.

Logan had finally managed to find a job at a local repair shop, doing tune-ups and tire rotations. It meant that we saw each other even less than before, and secretly I was glad. I could barely look at him without the guilt of what I had done eating me alive. I knew I should tell him what had happened, but I couldn't bring myself to do it. I was well aware of the fact that I was a horrible person, and I felt like I needed to suffer by myself, or maybe I was simply a coward. I knew that once I told Logan about Drake there was no going back from all of this, and I would not only lose my boyfriend, but my best friend as well, and I wasn't ready to give him up yet, regardless of how selfish that made me.

The only bright spot in all of this mess was the fact that I had spent so much time holed up in my room and in the library studying that, when finals came, I knew I had passed every single one of them with flying colors.

Winter break was upon us and I decided to go home with Amber to her parents' house to spend Christmas. Janet was actually pretty cool about me missing so much work when I asked her for the time off. She explained that with most of the college students leaving, business would slow down, and the rest of the employees would be able to handle it with no problem.

The night before we departed, I had all of the things that I was taking with me packed up and loaded into Amber's car, as well as the presents I had bought for her and her parents, Dave and Emma. Since Logan had just started his job, he decided to stay in Morgantown over break to pick up extra hours even though his boss told him it wasn't necessary. I was slightly disappointed by this, despite the fact that I had been trying to avoid him. It was our first Christmas together as a couple and the first Christmas since I had met him that we wouldn't be spending together. It seemed like an omen of our future: being together would be what kept us apart.

Since Logan had to work the night that Amber and I left,

we had spent the previous evening together exchanging gifts and saying our good-byes. I bought him a new video game that he had been eyeing every time we went out for the past month, and he bought me a gift card for Amazon so that I could buy more books for my Kindle, which Emma had given to me for Christmas last year. After he managed to beat almost half his game in two hours, we spent the rest of the evening cuddled up together before saying our farewells.

I decided to go to bed early since we were leaving at dawn, but after an hour of tossing and turning with sleep nowhere in sight, I got dressed and grabbed my keys. I drove around Morgantown and the surrounding area before finding myself taking the same exit Drake had taken that night that felt like so many years ago now. I passed the hidden road twice before finally spotting it.

I drove for what seemed like hours and began to wonder if I had somehow gotten turned around, when I entered the clearing. Parking in the same spot Drake had, I got out and found my way to the edge of the bank. I felt that sense of peace I had before as I watched the water gently churn. I looked around and noticed a small path that led to the water's edge and made my way down carefully, slipping and sliding as I went.

When I finally reached the water, I sat on a rotting log and took my shoes off, dipping my feet in the water. Winter was fast approaching and the night was cold, the water freezing. I pulled my jacket tighter around me as I let the water numb my feet and my thoughts. It felt nice just to let everything go for a while, not to have the dark cloud of regret and guilt hovering just over my head like a storm cloud.

The worst part of it was that while I felt regret over hurting Logan, I didn't feel the regret I should about actually sleeping with Drake. Despite the horrible ending, the night had been one of the best I could remember in my life, and despite everything that was happening, I would do it all over again. I shivered as I remembered the way Drake's body had felt against mine, and desire began pooling at my center.

I shook my head to clear my thoughts as I stood and pulled my pant legs up. I waded into the frigid water until it was up to my knees, then to my waist, completely soaking the pants I had just rolled up. I took another step just as someone grabbed me from behind and pulled me out. I screamed into the night, slicing through the silence.

"What the fuck are you doing, trying to get pneumonia?"

I felt my knees give way, and I fell to the ground in a heap as I was released. I looked up to see Drake standing above me, looking angry. I tried to stand, but I was shivering too hard and I fell back to the ground. "Whaaa—What are yoooou doooing here?" I tried to ask as my body convulsed with chills.

He bent down and scooped me up into his arms before carrying me up the hill. He sat me on his still-warm hood as he opened his trunk and pulled out a blanket and a bag.

"Jesus Christ, Chloe, you're fucking freezing," he growled as he threw the blanket over me and started taking things out of the bag until he found what he was looking for. He grabbed a pair of sweatpants out and handed them to me. "You need to change, put these on."

"Fiiiiine, but tuuurn arounnnd."

He rolled his eyes, but turned to give me privacy as I slipped off the hood and started fighting with the buttons on my soaked pants. My fingers were numb and I was shaking too hard to make any progress. I sighed as I turned to him, dreading asking him for help. "Can you heeelp meee?"

He turned to me and had my pants off in seconds before helping me into his. They were far too big for me, but I instantly felt warmer. He grabbed me in the blanket and threw me into the front seat of his car before getting in himself and starting it, turning the heat up as high as it would go. I pointed the vents to me and held my hands over them as I felt the warmth start flowing through my body. We sat in silence for several minutes until I was warm enough to function properly.

"Want to tell me what you were doing out there besides trying to freeze yourself to death?"

I stared at my hands, but didn't respond. Now that I could think again, I wanted to be anywhere but in this car with him. Being this close to him was physically painful, and my chest began to hurt. I crossed my arms over my chest, trying to hold myself together as I felt him staring at me. I would not fall apart in front of this man, I couldn't. Besides saving me from my own stupidity, he didn't care about me, and I wasn't going to let him see how bad I was hurting because of him.

He sighed, and I glanced over at him as he ran his hands through his hair, something I had noticed he did when he was agitated or upset. "Are we ever going to talk about this?"

I shook my head as I stared out at the water in front of us.

"Damn it, Chloe, fucking talk to me! Why were you here? Why were you out in the water like that?"

I took a deep breath before turning to him. "I just wanted to find peace. I walked out there because I wanted to be numb—I didn't want to feel, even just for a little while."

"You could have found a better way than that to do it. Besides, you shouldn't be out here alone this late at night. Anyone could have stumbled across you and you would have been defenseless against them."

"I can take care of myself. I have been for a long time."

"What are you running from, Chloe?"

I felt tears slip down my cheeks as I turned to look at him. "You. I'm running from you, and I can't even escape you here."

I threw the blanket at him and was out of the car in a flash. I heard him shouting my name as I ran to my car, but I peeled out of the clearing before he could reach me. I'd never find the peace I was looking for, not even here.

. . .

Amber and I were on our way back to Charleston before dawn the next morning. I remained quiet the first part of the ride as I thought about last night. Seeing Drake had been a shock to my already fragile heart. I realized that even though I hated him, I still cared about him so much that it hurt. Having my heart out there for him to crush made me feel vulnerable and that vulnerability scared me more than the feelings I had for him.

Amber seemed to blame my quietness on the early morning hours and left me alone as the miles slipped away in silence. We stopped at the halfway point to grab something to eat, use the restroom, and fill the car back up with gas. My mood was greatly improved when we went to the restroom. Amber refused ever to sit on any public toilet seat, especially one as disgusting as this one was. The walls were covered with stains that I didn't even want to contemplate, and the stalls were covered in more graffiti than a train car.

She was in the stall beside me, holding on to the walls like a monkey when I heard a commotion followed by a splash and a few choice words. I stifled my laughter as the curses continued.

"Do I even want to know?"

"Shut up! I just fell in this god-awful, bacteria-infested toilet! I think I'm going to vomit!"

I couldn't contain my laughter as she came out of the stall, the back of her T-shirt soaking wet. Tears streamed down my cheeks as I bent over, clutching my stomach. "Oh my God, Amber, I'm dying right now. I. Can't. Breathe!" I managed to gasp out between fits of laughter.

Amber shot me a death glare as she washed her hands and walked back to the car. She pulled a shirt out of one of her bags in the backseat, cursing as she went. She took her shirt off right in the parking lot and threw the clean one on.

"I need a shower, pronto."

I was still chuckling as we made our way up the entrance ramp and into the congested traffic. I pulled one of my favorite CDs out and threw it into the stereo. We spent the rest of the drive head banging and singing off-key.

Emma ran out to meet us as soon as we pulled into the driveway, Dave right behind her. She grabbed us as soon as we were out of the car and pulled us into a rib-crushing hug. "My babies!"

I laughed as I pulled away and rubbed my now tender ribs. "I missed you too, Em."

She kissed my cheek as Dave started grabbing our bags and taking them into the house. I grabbed a few to help him and made my way up the sidewalk to the massive house. Although I had pretty much lived here during my high school years, I was still dazzled by the size and beauty of their home.

It was a two-story colonial red-brick home with white windows and trimmings. Two large, white pillars sat in front to support the roof of the massive porch, which had several hanging baskets of flowers spaced across it. The yard and flower garden in front were well tended. Around the back of the house, I knew there was a full tennis court and an in-ground pool that took up most of the space.

Emma was an emergency physician at the local hospital, while Dave ran his own law firm. Needless to say, they were rolling in dough, but for all the grandeur of their home, I had never met two people who were more down-to-earth. I stepped into the spacious marble-floored foyer and glanced around to see if anything had changed. Everything remained the same, except for a few pictures of us at college hanging on the wall, which Amber had sent home. My heart clenched at the one of me standing between Drake and Logan at the bar one night, all of us smiling and happy.

To my left was the kitchen, where Emma was making sandwiches for us. It was bright and cheery, designed with beautiful pastel colors and white, tiled floors, the appliances all black and state of the art. The dining room opened up across from it. A polished oak table sat directly in the center of the room, large enough to seat ten guests.

To my right was the living room. The leather couch sat against the far wall, facing a massive seventy-two-inch television and an impressive sound system. There were several chairs spaced throughout the rest of the room, all matching the couch. Directly in front of me was the staircase leading up to our rooms.

I sat my bags down by the door as Amber walked in, and we made a mad rush for the sandwiches Emma was holding out to us. We sat and all but inhaled our sandwiches as Emma smiled at us and yelled for us to slow down. After draining the glass of water she handed me, I grabbed my bags and lugged them up the stairs to my room. I spent the next half hour unpacking everything before stretching across the bed to relax. My eyelids fluttered shut and I slept.

. . .

I woke to the feel of someone gently rubbing my hip as soft lips made butterfly kisses down my neck. I opened my eyes and sat up to see Drake standing above me with a sexy smirk on his full lips. I glanced around the room and confirmed that I was still at Emma and Dave's house before turning my attention back to him. "Drake? What are you doing here?"

He pressed a finger over my lips as he bent down and started nibbling on my ear. "Shhhh. That's not important. I'm here, that's what matters."

I fell against the pillow as he moved onto the bed and straddled me. His mouth took mine in a hungry kiss, and I felt myself already growing wet. I ran my hands down his back and realized he wasn't wearing a shirt. My nails ran across his naked flesh as he pulled my shirt and bra off, and started kissing a trail down my neck, to my collarbone, and finally to my breasts. He ran his tongue around the outside of my nipples, without actually touching them. This drove me mad with desire, and I tried shoving his head down.

He chuckled as he pulled back slightly. "No need to be so impatient, we have all night."

I moaned as he suddenly sucked my nipple into his mouth and started nibbling on it. "That feels so good."

My hands went to his head, and I ran my fingers through his soft hair as he switched and started giving my other breast the same attention. He released it with a pop and started kissing down my stomach to the top of my jeans. He undid the snaps and ran his tongue underneath them, making me shudder in delight before pulling them down my hips and off of me. His shorts quickly joined them in the growing pile of clothes on the floor.

I groaned as I felt a finger, then two, slip inside my heat. He began pushing them in and out in a fast rhythm as his thumb found my clit and started making slow circles around it. My breath turned to gasps as he finger fucked me, and I felt myself go crashing over the edge, calling out his name. My breathing was still ragged when I came down from my high, and I smiled at him. "You're so good with your hands, and not just with a guitar."

He laughed as he started kissing up my body. "And you're always so responsive, you have no idea what a turn-on that is."

I smiled as I rolled him onto his back and began running my hands across his stomach and chest. I felt him shudder when I gently tugged on his nipple rings. "Does that feel good?"

"You have no idea."

I grinned as I bent down and ran my tongue up the hard ridges of his stomach to his nipple and began making small circles around it before flicking it with my tongue. I turned my attention to the other one as I ran my fingertips down his stomach to grip him. I began stroking him gently and he groaned. "Suck me."

I shook my head as I continued to stroke him. "Not until you ask nicely." I gripped him harder, and his body arched off the bed.

"Chloe, you don't want to test me."

I leaned down and swiped my tongue across the head. "You don't want to test me. Now, ask nicely."

He groaned, this time in aggravation, before speaking. "Chloe, will you please suck me?" His tone was sarcastic, but

I obliged, sliding my mouth slowly over him until the tip was touching the back of my throat.

I pulled back and looked at him. "Is that what you wanted?"

He growled in response, and I smiled as I took him back in my mouth and starting sucking gently. I ran my tongue over his piercing, and he grabbed my hair to pull me back.

"Change of plans. Get on me before I lose it."

I climbed on top of him before slowing sinking down onto him. I sat up and started working my way up and down slowly, driving both of us mad.

"Faster, Chloe."

I refused, not wanting this to end too quickly. He growled again before flipping us over so that I was underneath him, with him still inside me. He began thrusting hard and fast, so hard that the bed started knocking against the wall.

"Oh yes, God yes!" I yelled as he rammed into me over and over. The knocking sound changed, and I realized someone was at the door. "Drake, someone . . ."

"Don't worry about it."

I glanced back at the door as it swung open, Logan standing there, staring at us with a look of horror on his face. "Chloe! How could you?"

. . .

I sat up, gasping and stared around the room. It had only been a dream, but a very real one. I still felt the throbbing between my legs as I realized the knocking at the door hadn't stopped, and I yelled for whoever it was to come in while I tried to get my body under control. The door opened and Emma peeked her head in. "Sorry if I woke you, but dinner is ready."

"No problem. How long have I been asleep?"

"Most of the afternoon. We didn't want to bug you, you girls had a long drive." She closed the door and walked across the room to sit at the foot of the bed. "Chloe, there's something we need to talk about. I didn't want to say anything in front of Amber and scare her, but you need to know."

My heart started beating faster as I watched her play with a string on the quilt. "What's wrong? Are you and Dave okay?"

"No, honey, it's nothing like that. It's about your mother. She came here a couple weeks ago looking for you."

My eyes widened. My mother had never come here before, and I wasn't even sure how she knew where Amber's parents lived. "What did she want?"

She shook her head, lost in thought. "I don't know, she wouldn't tell us anything. Only demanded to speak with you and when we told her you weren't here she tried to get us to tell her where you were."

"You didn't tell her did you?"

"No, I told her I hadn't seen you in months and I wasn't sure where you were. Which was true, I had no idea exactly where you were at that moment in time."

She gave me a devious smile as she spoke, and I laughed. "You're the best, Emma!"

She chuckled before clearing her throat to speak again. "I'm pretty sure she was on drugs, Chloe. She was so aggressive and confrontational. She thought we were lying to her about you being here and tried to force her way into the house. Luckily, Dave was here too so we managed to keep her out. She finally left after we threatened to call the police. I don't know what she wants from you, but she's determined to find you. I'm scared for you."

I scooted down to sit next to her and pulled her into a tight hug. "Don't worry about me. The chances of her finding me almost six hours away are slim to none. Besides, I have nothing to give her if she did."

She nodded as I pulled away. "Just be careful, honey. You might not realize it, but I consider you my daughter too. Dave and I even discussed trying to adopt you before, but we didn't want to bring her back here to you."

I felt tears sting my eyes at her words. "Thank you for everything you have ever done for me. As far as I'm concerned, you're my mother and I love you."

We sat together, sharing both happy and sad tears together for a few minutes before Emma wiped hers away and gave me a watery smile. "So what have you been up to? I've barely heard from you since you started at WVU! Amber told me you and Logan are finally together. I have to say, it took you long enough."

I glanced up at her. "You knew?"

"Of course I did, anyone with eyes could see the way that boy looked at you. Well, everyone but you it seems."

I gave her a weak smile. "I'm always the last to know."

"You've always lived in your own head. I'm surprised he didn't have to get a flashing neon sign and hold it in front of you."

I chuckled. "That would have helped."

We sat in silence for a moment before she bumped my shoulder with hers. "So, tell me all about it. How are you two doing together?"

I shrugged. "We're okay, I guess."

She raised her eyebrows. "Uh oh, just okay?"

I started playing with the same string she had earlier. "No, we're great."

"Chloe, you know you can tell me anything, right?"

I looked up at her and choked on the lies I was about to spew. This woman loved me, I could see it shining in her eyes now that I knew to look for it. I couldn't tell Amber my problems because she was friends with both of us, and that would put her directly in the middle of us. If she told him, she'd betray me; if she didn't, she'd betray him. I wouldn't put her in that position.

But could I tell Emma without her passing it on, even by accident? I had to tell someone, this was eating me alive and I couldn't take it anymore. I couldn't handle being the only one who knew.

"I did something really stupid. I'm a horrible person and I don't deserve Logan. He's such a great guy and I'm nothing more than trash."

She placed her hand on my shoulders and starting rubbing circles gently. "It can't be that bad, honey."

I shook my head. "It is, Emma. I don't know how I can live with myself. I cheated on him, I cheated on the most amazing friend I've ever had."

Her hand stilled on my shoulder, and I waited for her to start yelling at me. I deserved nothing less.

"Oh, Chloe, what happened?"

"His name's Drake and I fell for him the minute I saw him. He's gorgeous and even though he has a rough exterior, he has the biggest heart I've ever known. Or at least I thought he did."

She listened as I poured my heart out and told her everything that had happened since I met Drake, asking questions from time to time. When I finished, I had tears streaming down my face again as she pulled me into a tight hug.

"You've really made a mess out of everything, haven't you?"

I nodded as I buried my head in her neck.

"I know you're going to hate me for saying this, but you really do need to tell Logan. Yes, you might lose him, but you can't keep living like this. And from what you've told me about Drake, I can't say that I agree with your opinion on his feelings. He obviously has issues since he goes through so many women, but that doesn't mean he isn't hurting too. You have to talk to both of them before this spins even more out of control."

I nodded as I pulled back. "I know. And thank you for listening to my sob story, but please don't say anything to Amber. I don't want her in the middle of this."

She nodded. "Your secret is safe with me. Now go wash up so we can eat dinner. Dave and Amber are waiting for us."

She stood and left the room, leaving me with my thoughts. It felt like a weight had been lifted off my shoulders by telling her. I knew she was right. I had to tell Logan, but I didn't know how. I couldn't just walk up to him and say, *Oh by the way, I slept with Drake. It didn't mean anything to him, but it broke my heart. Just thought you should know.* Yeah, that would go over real well.

I went to the guest bathroom and washed up, scrubbing my face as well to try to hide the evidence of my tears. By the time I made my way downstairs, everyone was already at the table. I sat down beside Amber, and she looked over at me with a worried expression.

"You okay? You look like you've been crying."

"I'm fine, it must be because I just woke up."

We spent the rest of dinner catching up on each other's lives. I pushed the conversation with Emma away as I sat and laughed with Amber's family. With my family. Maybe I wasn't quite as alone as I had always thought.

CHAPTER SIXTEEN

CLEANING OUT MY . . . CAR?

Amber and I spent most of our winter break out and about—shopping, going to the movies, and even to a few parties that our former classmates had invited us to when they saw that we were back in town. I even let her drag me to a salon to have my hair done, her early Christmas present to me.

I hadn't so much as had my hair trimmed since months before we moved to Morgantown, and it was so long it reached my waist. Amber and the lady she took me to convinced me to cut it, but I refused to go any shorter than my ribs. I ended up with low lights and a few purple streaks spread throughout my hair by the time they finished with me. I had to admit I loved it, and Amber said it only accented what she called my rocker-chick look. I had always laughed at her description, but even I had to agree with her assessment with my hair like this.

Christmas came quickly and brought me yet another Amazon gift card from Amber and a savings account with ten thousand dollars in it from Dave and Emma. I nearly collapsed when Dave handed me the piece of paper and I saw the balance.

"I can't accept this!"

David rolled his eyes. "Of course you can. You don't have to spend it, just let it grow and add money to it when you can."

I had thrown my arms around both of them, sobbing uncontrollably at their kindness.

Logan called me every few days, and we rang in the New Year's together over the phone. My stomach was in knots every time I spoke with him, but I refused to let it get to me. I would have to tell him the truth soon, I knew that, but I wasn't going to let it ruin my time away from everything.

The days following New Year's flew by, and soon Amber and I were packing our things and saying our good-byes. Emma hugged me tight as we stood in the driveway. "You need anything—anything at all—you call me, okay?"

I nodded as I got in the car and we were off. We had gone no further than the end of the driveway when Amber turned to me.

"Want to tell me what that was about?"

I tried playing dumb. "What was what?"

She rolled her eyes as she turned her attention back to the road. "Don't play me, Chloe. I heard what Mom said and I know you were crying that night she was in your room, so spill."

I bit my lip as I debated what to tell her. I decided to go with the lesser of the two evils. "My mom is trying to find me. She came to your house searching for me. It wasn't exactly a happy occasion."

"Why didn't you tell me? What did she want?"

"I have no idea, she wouldn't tell them. She just wanted to know where I was, and we didn't tell you because I know how you worry when it comes to her."

She sighed. "You're right, I do worry about that crazy bitch after everything she put you through. But that doesn't mean I don't want to know what's happening with you. You know I care about you, right?"

"Yeah, I know. I'm sorry I didn't tell you. I just didn't want to bother you with it."

"Chloe, you're such a dummy. You can bother me with anything. Except your sex life with Logan . . . I draw the line there."

I laughed as she merged onto the interstate. "Or my nonexistent sex life with Logan you mean."

Her head spun around in my direction. "*What?* You mean you two haven't done the deed yet?"

"No, we have, but it was when we got together. We haven't done anything since, it just doesn't feel right."

"How can sex with Logan not feel right? He's my friend, but I'm not afraid to say he's smoking hot. I bet he's great in bed! Is he? Tell me! Oh wait, don't tell me. Ahhh, I have to know."

I laughed as Amber fought with herself. "You done yet?"

She giggled. "I can't help it! I want to know, but then he's my friend too so I don't want to know. Oh, I give up! Just spill it already!"

"It was . . . it was nice."

She raised an eyebrow. "Just *nice*? Oh God, he's bad in bed, isn't he?"

I shook my head. Being with Logan had been nice, but he wasn't Drake. Truthfully, I didn't think anyone could top him, not that I had much experience in the matter, but still even I knew Drake was amazing. "No, he's not bad, honest."

She was silent for a minute. Just as I leaned back in the seat to relax, she spoke again.

"Chloe, is everything okay with you guys? You barely mentioned him over break and you seem less than enthused with this conversation."

I mentally smacked myself for letting the conversation get this far. Amber had always been a pro at gauging my emotions, and now was no different. "We're fine. But that's the problem, everything about him is just fine. I love him, but I don't know if I share his feelings or if I'm mistaking friendship for something more because that's what I'm supposed to do."

"Don't you think you should have figured that out before you decided to get into a relationship with him? Actually, I distinctly remember telling you to get your shit together."

"Yeah, I know. I'm a dumbass. Point made."

She gave me a sympathetic smile. "Sorry, but you've got to figure this out. It's not fair to string him along like this if you aren't sure."

I groaned and sunk further back into my seat. "Trust me, I know. You have no idea how much I know."

We made it back to Morgantown in record time, mostly due to Amber's crazy driving. She had been fine on the drive to her parents', but on the way home I had asked her what the hell the rush was as she weaved in and out of traffic. People blew their horns at us, and I had more than one middle finger pointed at me when I was brave enough to glance at them. When we pulled up outside our dorm, I nearly fell to my knees and kissed the ground.

"What. The. Hell?" I yelled as she stepped out of the car and opened the trunk to start pulling our bags out.

She threw my bags at me and grinned. "What's your problem?"

"My . . . wha—*You tried to kill us!*"

"You're such a baby! I was just trying to make it back in time for Drake's show with the guys. And since you're off, you can go too! You haven't been to one in forever!"

My stomach plummeted to the ground I was currently worshipping as I tried to come up with a valid excuse not to go. "Um, I can't. I have to go pick up my work schedule and get all this stuff put away."

She rolled her eyes as we walked inside our dorm. "You can do that tomorrow. Tonight, we party! Let's meet down here in two hours, and I will hunt you down if you try to get out of it!"

With that, she turned and walked down the hallway to her room. I groaned as I carried my things up the stairs to my room. There was no way I was getting out of seeing Drake tonight, and I knew it. When Amber set her mind on something, you might as well just go along with it and save yourself the time and aggravation.

I threw my bags on the ground and fell onto the bed. Rachel wasn't back yet, so I was left with nothing more than my thoughts and silence. I was back here with both Logan and Drake, and I had to deal with my demons. They were staring me straight in the face now, and I couldn't ignore them or push them away any longer. I vowed to tell Logan everything that had happened when the time felt right. Who was I kidding? That time would never come, so I settled for next week after we were adjusted to our new classes.

I rose from the bed and sent Logan a quick text letting him know we made it home mostly intact and that I would be at the bar for the rest of the evening before I started getting ready for what was sure to be a miserable evening. I knew Amber would go for a sexy, knock-the-boys-to-their-knees look since Adam was going to be there, and so I decided to do the same. As I thought about the looks Amber gave him, I would've bet my whole music collection that he was the reason for the newly acquired mad driving skills.

I pulled a short black dress that barely covered my legs or my breasts out of the back of my closet and pulled it on. I left my hair down and decided actually to wear makeup for once. I used dark-colored eye shadow and a bit more mascara than was necessary to pull off the look I was going for, but I wanted to look amazing. I checked myself out in the mirror before slipping out of my room and down the stairs to meet Amber.

She was already there waiting for me and glanced up as I stepped out of the stairwell. "It's about damn ti— Whoa! Holy shit, Chloe, you look amazing!"

I glanced down at her super short miniskirt and ripped stockings. "You don't look too bad yourself. You ready?"

We chatted all the way to the bar, both of us full of nervous energy. "What's got you so wound up tonight, Amber? Let me guess. . . . Does it start with an *A* and end with an *M*?"

She giggled like she was fifteen. "Shut up! It does not. Well, maybe a little bit. Do you think he'll notice me in this outfit?"

I gave her a bewildered look. "Are you kidding me? Every male in the whole damn place will be begging at your feet. He'd have to be blind not to notice those legs."

She smiled like the cat that got the canary. "I hope so, he's barely even glanced my way."

I hesitated before I spoke. From what I knew of Adam, he wasn't a one-woman kind of guy, and I was afraid Amber would get hurt. "Amber, I'm only saying this because I love you. I have no doubt he will notice you, but he's not the type to stick with one girl. I just don't want you to get your hopes up for something that is pretty much impossible."

She snorted as she pulled the car into the parking lot and maneuvered into a space far too small. "You think I don't know that? I don't want to marry the guy. Have some fun? Sure, why not. I'm done with relationships for a while, I just want to have a good time!"

I nodded as I tried to get out of the car without hitting the massive truck that was parked way too close to us. "All right then, that changes things. Go get him!"

We linked arms and giggled as we made our way into the bar. Heads turned as soon as we walked in, and I felt a smug grin curve my lips. Breaking the Hunger was already playing as we made our way to our usual table. Despite our absence the last couple of weeks during break, it was still empty, waiting on us. The heat of a hundred male stares engulfed my body as I took a seat and looked up at the band playing on stage.

I felt my heart constrict at the sight of Drake standing there in all of his rock-god glory. He wore a black pair of jeans and a black shirt that clung to his body, showing every ridge of muscle that I knew was underneath. His hair was stuck to his sweaty forehead as he belted out a heavy rock number, and I just wanted to run my hands through it.

Drake hadn't noticed us yet since his eyes were closed as he threw himself mentally and physically into the song. I took full advantage of this time just to watch him. After watching him play so many times, he still amazed me with his presence on the stage. He sang one note, and the world stopped for anyone who was lucky enough to hear it.

He finished out the final line of the song with a scream before opening his eyes and smiling at the crowd. "All right guys, one more song and you get to pick. Tell me what you want!"

The crowd went wild as people began shouting song titles up at him. Before I could stop myself, I stood up and walked to the front of the stage. Drake's eyes snapped to me instantly and almost bulged out of his head as he took in my dress. *Eat your heart out, buddy.*

"I have a request!" I shouted over the crowd, who had quieted slightly when they noticed the looks he was giving me.

He walked over and leaned down until we were eye level. "And what would that be?"

I gave him a seductive smile, knowing I was playing with fire. "'Gentleman,' by Theory of a Deadman. You know that one, right?"

His eyebrows disappeared into his hair as the women in the crowd started whistling. "Sure do, I'm a pro at it." He walked back to the center of the stage and motioned for the band to start.

I sat back down with Amber as he started into the chorus and smiled to myself. Let him take what he wanted from this! Let him know how much of an asshole I thought he was. He constantly glanced at our table with a strange expression as he sang, and I couldn't help but feel like I had won this battle.

The band finished their set and made their way to our table, fighting women as they went. Drake leaned down and whispered in my ear as he passed, "You think you're hilarious don't you?"

I grinned and gave him a look of complete innocence. "I have no idea what you're talking about."

He chuckled as he sat down across from me. "I'm sure you don't."

The rest of the band sat down around us, and Adam ended up in the chair next to Amber. I could almost hear her squeal of excitement as he turned to stare at her. "Amber, right?"

"Yeah, and you're Eric?"

Eric, who had just sat down next to Jade and Drake, choked

on his beer. "Dude, you just got burned. You've been sitting at the same table as her, drooling in her lap for months and she doesn't even know your name!"

I laughed at Amber's mind games as Adam flipped Eric off. He turned back to Amber and smiled. "Nah, that douche over there is Eric. I'm Adam."

Amber gave him the fakest embarrassed smile I had ever seen. "Whoops. Sorry, Adam."

"It's all right. Let me buy you a beer?"

She nodded as he motioned for the waitress to bring a round over to our table. Since we were with the band, they appeared in front of us almost instantly. I glanced at Drake to notice him glaring at something behind me. I turned slightly and noticed a group of guys watching me from a couple of tables away. I gave them a small smile before turning away and taking a sip of my beer.

Drake gave a small growl as one of the men sat down in the empty chair beside me. He gave me his most charming smile.

"Hey, I'm Chris."

I gave him a small smile. "Hi, Chris. I'm Chloe."

The guy was attractive, no doubt about it. His hair was a light brown, and he had amazing green eyes. He was built bigger than Drake or Logan, with muscles bulging out of his tight, white shirt.

"Can I buy you drink?"

I shook my head and held up the half-empty bottle in my hand. "No thanks, I'm good."

He seemed disappointed, but I didn't feel the least bit guilty. I had enough guy problems as it was, no need to give this guy the wrong idea and myself a headache.

"Come on, that one's almost empty. Just one."

Before I could speak, Drake broke into the conversation. "She said no, buddy. Why don't you take the hint and go back to your table?"

Chris glared up at Drake. "I don't remember asking your opinion, *buddy*."

"Well, you got it. Move along."

Chris glanced back at me. "You with this asshole?"

Shock crossed my face as I shook my head. "No, definitely not."

Chris turned to give Drake a smug smile. "Looks like you don't have any say then."

Drake clenched his fist on the table before pointing to the door. "You need to leave, now. Or I'm going to help you leave."

Chris laughed as he threw his arm around my shoulders. "I'd like to see you try."

Everyone at the table was deathly quiet as Drake stood so fast he knocked his chair over. I quickly removed myself out from underneath Chris's arm. "Guys, chill out. Drake, sit back down. Chris, thank you for the offer, but no thanks. I have a boyfriend who isn't him." I pointed at Drake, who was still standing and shooting murderous glares across the table at us.

Chris frowned, but stood to leave. "That's too bad. I'll be over there if you change your mind." He gave Drake one last glare as he walked back to his table.

"Asshole," Drake muttered as he picked his chair up and sat back down.

Everyone was staring at him as Eric started laughing hysterically. "I have seen it all. Drake Allen just took up for a girl."

I rolled my eyes as everyone started laughing with him. "Shush. And you," I turned my gaze to Drake, "I don't need you to take up for me. I can fight my own battles."

His eyes turned hard as they met mine. "Sure you can. Sorry, it won't happen again."

The rest of the night was tense as everyone sensed the anger rolling off of both of us. Everyone but Amber and Adam that is: they were in their own little world talking quietly together. A few girls came to the table and attempted to flirt with Drake, but he brushed them away. Finally, I decided it was time to leave. I poked Amber in the ribs and motioned to the door. "You ready?"

She glanced back and forth between Adam and me. "Actually, I was going to hang out here with Adam a little longer." She pulled her keys out of her purse and handed them to me. "Take my car. I'll catch a ride back with someone."

I winked at her and told everyone else good night. Drake completely ignored me as he nursed his beer. I walked out, making sure to avoid Chris's table as I went. Once I made it to my car, I took a deep breath. How dare he defend me like that? He was more of an asshole than that guy could ever be, and I didn't want or need his help with anything. Seeing a nicer side of him only confused me more, and right now, I didn't think I could handle any more.

. . .

I woke up the next morning with a text Amber had sent in the middle of the night, telling me that she was staying the night with Adam. I laughed as I rolled out of bed and found some comfortable clothes to wear for the day. I was happy for her, I just hoped she meant what she said in the car the night before.

Since Logan had to work all day yet again, I spent most of the afternoon running errands, picking up my schedule for work the next week, and unpacking my stuff from over break.

Once I finished unpacking, I grabbed one of those industrial-sized garbage bags that you could hide a dead body in and made my way out to the parking lot to clean out my car. January in West Virginia was usually pretty cold, but today was actually warm enough to go outside without a jacket.

Since I hadn't cleaned out my car in months and it was starting to look like an advertisement for every fast-food chain known to man, I took full advantage of the pretty weather to clean it out. I groaned as I opened the back door and stared inside. Maybe I should have brought two bags out. I spent the next hour throwing away all the garbage and throwing anything important into the front seat while In This Moment was blaring from the speakers of my car. I chuckled as I received several glares for my loud music from people walking by. Some people had no taste in music.

I finally finished the inside of the car and opened the trunk. I hadn't been back here in forever, and God only knew what I'd find. I sucked in a breath as I noticed Drake's jacket sitting inside from that night all those months ago. I set it carefully aside as I started rummaging through the rest of the contents, debating on what to do with it. I could just give it away. It's not like he'd missed it after all this time.

I sighed as I finished cleaning and hauled the garbage bag to the nearby dumpster and carried his jacket back to my room. I set it on my bed and went to shower, still debating on what to do with it. It was still sitting there when I returned. I had hoped someone would break in and steal it while I was in the shower and take care of the problem for me, but no such luck. I grumbled to myself as I pulled on a pretty blue jean skirt and a long-sleeved shirt. I decided I would just stop by the bar and give it to Jade or one of the guys. Since it was Saturday, they wouldn't have a show and hopefully Drake would be anyplace else in the world besides that bar.

I took a deep breath before stepping into the bar, holding Drake's jacket to my chest like a shield. I could do this—just walk up to Jade, drop it off, and leave. Glancing around the room I spotted the band sitting at our normal table, but Drake wasn't with them. Hoping luck was with me for once and that he hadn't just stepped away for a minute, I headed for the table. Jade glanced up and smiled at me. Figuring she was the safest one, I sat down in the chair next to her. "Hey, lady, is Drake here?"

She shook her head. "No, he decided to stay home tonight."

"Oh, well, can you give him his jacket for me when you see him then? I'm sure you'll see him before I do."

She frowned and shook her head again. "Actually, I'm headed home to my parents' house first thing in the morning since we don't have any more shows this weekend so I won't see him until next week sometime. You know, his house is just around the block and I'm sure he's home—just drop it off."

Warning bells went off in my head. This was so not a good idea. I had been avoiding him like the plague ever since that night, and I was not about to go knock on his door. "Um, that's okay. I'm sure I'll see him next week sometime."

Jade raised her eyebrows at me. "What's up with you two? You were practically attached at the hip before you started dating Logan, and now you'll barely even look at each other. And what was that last night with that Chris guy? I've never seen Drake get so pissed off over something like that."

As soon as she finished speaking, her mouth popped open as the situation clicked in her head. "Oh. My. God. You didn't! Oh God, I can see it in your eyes—you did. Chloe! How the hell did this happen?"

I glanced around at the guys at the table, but most of them had their attention on the girl or girls in their laps, even Adam. I would have to mention that to Amber later. "Will you be quiet, Jade? Yes? Okay, yes. But it was a mistake, and not one I intend to do again. Please don't say anything. I can't let Logan find out, not like this!"

She nodded, her eyes still wide. "This is insane, woman! Pure insanity! I mean, I noticed you two together a lot, but oh I don't know . . . Just a shock I guess, but your secret is safe with me."

I hugged her tightly. "Thanks, Jade, but you see why I can't take his jacket back to him. It would be all awkward and embarrassing, and possibly angry. I miss him, but he hates me."

She pulled back from my hug with a frown on her beautiful face. "Sweetie, that boy could never hate you. Why don't you take the jacket back to him as an excuse, and then talk about everything with him while you're there. I know for a fact he misses you, he's been so down since you quit hanging around."

I thought her words over. "I guess I could try. It's not like things can get any worse."

CHAPTER SEVENTEEN

IT GETS WORSE

I gently knocked on Drake's front door, hoping he wouldn't hear me so I could sneak away claiming I had tried. Unfortunately, the front lights flipped on, and the door opened. Drake starred at me with a look of disbelief. He quickly masked it with a look of indifference. Even with his face void of emotion, seeing him took my breath away. He wore only a pair of faded blue jeans low on his hips and a white T-shirt that looked like it had been painted onto this body. The sight made me shiver with desire.

"Chloe, what a surprise."

I glanced down at my shoes before looking back up at him. "Yeah, sorry to bother you. I just wanted to drop your jacket off. I was cleaning out my car and found it. I figured you might want it back."

I held out his jacket, and he took it, slowly looking me over as he did so. "Well, thanks. Anything else I can help you with tonight? My bed is only a few feet away."

I felt heat rush up into my cheeks at the suggestion in his words. I had been safe last night with all of our friends around, but now it was just the two of us, and the gloves were off. "Well, uh, no. I better go." I turned and started walking down the path before stopping and spinning around to face him again. "Actually, yes, there is something else."

I stomped my way back up to him. "Can I come in so we can talk? Please, Drake. I don't like things being like this between us."

"I tried to talk to you before you left. You didn't seem interested."

"I know, I was an ass and I'm sorry. But we've both got to get over whatever this shit is between us."

I figured he would close the door in my face, but instead he stepped back, allowing me access into his house. I made my way into the living room and sat down on the couch as he followed silently, sitting in the chair across from me. Great, he couldn't even stand to be on the same couch as me.

"Look, I screwed up. I know it, you know it, and your bed knows it. I cheated on Logan, I hurt you, and I just all around fucked up, okay? But I am so sorry, and God, Drake, I just miss you. I miss how close we were. I felt we had something special, and I want to get it back. Can you ever forgive me?" I said the words in a rush, hoping to get them all out at once so I wouldn't have to say them again.

He studied me silently for a minute before speaking. "Sure, Chloe, I can forgive you, but first I need to know which part I'm supposed to forgive. The fact that you cheated on your boyfriend with me, or the fact that you fucked me, or the fact that you just ran after said fucking. Or maybe for the fact that you ignored me when I tried to talk to you about all of this. Or—"

I stopped him midsentence. "Okay, I get it, Drake. I just miss you. You and I were a mistake, one that I will regret for the rest of my life because I cheated on Logan, and obviously hurt you at the same time whether I realized it or not. I didn't mean for it to happen, I just want my friend back. I want you back."

Tears stung my eyes as I poured my heart out to him, but I refused to look away from him. His eyes hardened at my words, and he quickly stood and walked over to me.

Kneeling down in front of me, he caught me with a murderous glare. "For someone who misses me so much, you sure seem to regret everything about me. What was I to you, Chloe? One of those *I'm bored and he's here* fucks? Or just a typical *I've had a long day and need to blow off some steam* fuck? Well, I've got news for you: I don't regret it at all. Feeling your skin pressed up against mine, being inside you, hearing you cry out—that was one of the best nights of my life until you fucked it up with all your guilt. I miss you too, but things aren't going to go back to the way they were, Chloe. I've felt you, tasted you, and now all I want is more."

His words stunned me and turned me on all at once. "Drake—"

"No, don't even say anything, Chloe. When you talk everything gets so screwed up. I want you, and I know you want me too."

I shook my head at his words. "I can't, Drake. I'm with Logan. I won't hurt him."

He leaned in until he was inches from my face. "You mean hurt him *again*, because you already did once, whether he knows it or not. You want me and I want you—don't even deny it, Chloe. You've wanted me since the beginning, and I was too damn stubborn and proud to take it when you offered. Please, Chloe."

He leaned in to kiss me, but I shoved him away. "I don't want you, Drake! Damn it! Damn it all! I want my friend back."

I stood and turned for the door, but he caught my arm and spun me around to face him. "You want me, Chloe, and I'm going to show you just how much." Before I could respond, he pulled me against his chest and was kissing me hard.

His lips pressed against mine roughly, his lip ring cutting into my skin, our teeth hitting together with the force of it. I tried pushing against his chest, fighting him, but his kiss quickly took over. Before I knew what I was doing, I was kissing him back with as much ferocity as he was giving me. I wrapped my arms around his neck and pulled him closer until I felt his hard body everywhere.

He shoved me up against the wall as his hands slipped under my shirt to run his fingers across my stomach and my ribs, until he was cupping my breast through my silk bra, pinching my nipple roughly. He let go of me only long enough to pull my shirt up and over my head. As soon as I was free of my shirt, he pressed back up against me and resumed kissing me with so much force and passion I thought I would explode.

My hands ran down his chest and stomach to the bottom of his shirt, and with some tugging, I lifted it from him and threw it across the room. My legs wrapped back around his waist as he lifted me up, and I felt his hardness push up against me. I groaned into his mouth, and I felt him smile.

"Do you like that?"

I mumbled something that resembled a *yes* as his hands moved from my waist to my bra, unhooking it and pulling it down my arms and away from us. Bare chest to bare chest, I felt my nipples rub against him, and I moaned again. No one could make me feel passion like this man did, no one could make me feel so alive. I quickly undid the buttons on his jeans and pushed them and his boxers down. I grabbed his hard dick and ran my hand over it fast and hard.

"Oh God, Chloe, that feels so good," he groaned into my mouth as his hand slid under my skirt and pushed my thong to the side. I felt his thumb rub over my clit roughly, before thrusting two fingers into me. "Thank God you're wearing a skirt."

There was nothing sweet or loving about this—he was being rough with me, and I certainly wasn't being gentle with him. I moaned and arched my back, trying to take his fingers deeper inside of me.

"What do you want, Chloe? Tell me what you want and it's yours," he whispered into my ear, licking as he went.

"Fuck me, Drake, please. Fuck me hard and fast."

He groaned at my words and positioned me over him before thrusting hard and deep into me. I cried out at the feeling of him inside me as he pushed me up against the wall harder, driving into me over and over, harder every time. His mouth caught first one nipple, then the other in his mouth and sucked and bit until I was moaning over and over.

I felt myself tightening and before I knew it, I went over the edge. I had never been very vocal during sex, but with him I screamed his name over and over as I came. With a few final thrusts I felt him shudder as he cried out at his own release.

He dropped his head onto my shoulder as he stood there trying to catch his breath. "That was amazing, Chloe. Seriously." He slowly pulled out, and I instantly felt empty without him. He set me on the ground and stepped back, eyeing me the whole time.

All at once, what we had just done hit me. I had cheated on Logan yet again, without so much as a thought to how this would affect him. I slid down the wall until I was sitting on the floor and covered my face with my hands. "Oh my God, what have I done?" I sobbed.

Drake kneeled down in front of me. "Look at me."

I ignored him as I continued to sob.

"Damn it, woman, look at me."

I shook my head, refusing to move my hands from my face. If I didn't look at him, this wouldn't be real, but if I looked him in the eye, I would have to face this, whatever it was. He gently wrapped his fingers around my wrists and pulled my hands to my sides. "Please don't cry, Chloe. I'm so sorry, I shouldn't have done that. This one is all me, I just want you so damn bad and I can't control myself around you. I care so much about you. Why can't you see that?"

"Why now, Drake? Before when I tried, you shoved me away. If you had said yes, I would have been yours. Now we've royally screwed everything up yet again. Why did you have to wait until I was with him?" I sobbed.

He let go of my wrists, gently cupping my face and pulling it up until I was looking at him. "Because, before we hadn't known each other very long and you had just told me everything you had to deal with growing up. I knew I was a royal fuckup and I didn't want to hurt you anymore than you had already been hurt. I've got my own demons, my own past, Chloe. I knew what they would do to you if you knew, but I felt connected to you from the beginning. I knew if we slept together right away, you would be just another woman to me. I wanted to get to know you better, and I wasn't about to throw it all away for one night of rolling around in my bed.

And I was right about you, we got to know each other and I fell in love with you. That's what this is to me: I've fallen in love with you, and if you would just give me a chance I could prove it to you."

My heart stopped at his words. He was in love with me? What did that mean for me, for us? I knew I felt something strong for him, but was it love? Was it worth losing Logan for the bad boy in the band? I knew better than even to ask myself that question. Drake had become far more to me than the dangerous, tattooed, and pierced bad boy I had seen in him before. He was someone special to me, and Lord help me, I knew I was falling in love with him too.

So where did that leave Logan and our relationship? He had been my best friend most of my life and now so much more to me. Was it possible that I could be in love with both of them at the same time, or were my feelings for Logan nothing more than friendship wrapped up in a relationship? Regardless of what I felt, I had to tell Logan what I had done, what a mess I had made of everything.

"I need to get out of here." I stood and walked across the room to where he had managed to throw my shirt and bra, quickly putting both on and adjusting my skirt.

"Don't leave, Chloe. Stay here and talk to me," he pleaded as I made my way past him.

"I just need time, Drake. I have to figure things out. Just give me time."

He grabbed my wrist as I reached for the front door. "Take all the time you need, just know I'm here and I'm waiting for you. We can make this work, you just have to give me a chance, let me prove that I'm serious about you, about us." He leaned down and brushed his lips gently over mine. "I love you, Chloe."

He released my wrist and stepped back, letting me open the door. I bolted out and down the walk to my car as fast as my legs would carry me.

. . .

The next morning I felt like hell. I had driven home the night before and cowered in my bed, crying myself to sleep. As my alarm went off, I slowly pulled myself off the bed and grabbed my bathroom bag. Luckily, I was one of the first people up, so I had the entire bathroom to myself.

After I had showered and dressed for the day, I grabbed the books I would need for tomorrow and threw them into my bag. Logan sent me a text asking if I wanted to meet him for lunch since he didn't have to work today. I still hadn't seen him since I'd returned, and after last night, I debated on crawling back into my bed and never coming out. I quickly shook the thought away. I couldn't spend the rest of my life hiding from him.

I had made a mistake, and I needed to face it. I made my way up to his room a couple of hours later and knocked. He opened the door almost instantly, a huge smile on his face.

"Chloe! I missed you!" He pulled me into the room, slamming the door behind me before throwing me on the bed and kissing me senseless.

He finally came up for air, and I gasped, trying to catch my breath. "Wow, what a welcome! I missed you too."

I stared up at him, and my stomach started to hurt. How could I be such a slut when I had someone who cared about me as much as Logan did? I should tell him everything right now, clear the air and get it all out, but as I looked at him so happy to see me, I couldn't do it.

I forced a smile on my face as I sat up on the side of the bed. "So where are we going for lunch?"

He bent down and kissed me gently on the lips. "I thought we could go over to Gold's. I'm dying for one of their burgers."

My body tensed, and he seemed to notice. "What's wrong? We don't have to go there if you don't want to."

I knew that if I said no, I would have to explain why. "No, it's fine. I can see if Amber wants to go with us."

"Sure, sounds great. Come on, we can take my car and you can text her on the way there."

I sent Amber a text asking her to meet us there, but she declined, saying she had plans with Adam. I raised my eyebrows at that, but didn't ask any more questions. I silently cursed as we pulled into the bar's parking lot and I noticed Drake's car parked near the door. This should be interesting to say the least. I hoped he wouldn't bring up last night with Logan around, but with Drake there were no guarantees.

We walked across the parking lot slowly, since Logan was walking backward while he told me a funny story about one of the guys from his work. I glanced up behind him as we reached the door and saw Drake coming out. His eyes sought out mine instantly, and I stopped walking. The barely controlled look of rage on his face told me everything I needed to know about how he felt seeing me with Logan.

I couldn't keep doing this to either of them. I had to tell Logan what had happened, even though I knew it would break him and destroy any friendship we had ever had. I had no idea where that would leave me with either of them, but decided to push that particularly painful thought back until the time came as I focused on the fact that I had both of them here within mere feet of each other.

"So he got out from underneath the car and . . . Whoa!" Logan spun around as he bumped into Drake. "What the—? Oh, sorry, Drake. Didn't see you, man." He smiled and slapped Drake on the back. "You leaving?"

Drake's eyes were still on me as he shook his head. "No, came out for a smoke break. Gotta love the smoking ban in bars."

Logan nodded. "You at our usual table?"

"Yeah, Jade's in there too."

Logan smiled as we made our way around him. "Cool, we'll see you inside then." He threw his arm over my shoulder as we walked inside and went to the table. Jade gave me a questioning look as she noticed Logan's arm around me, but didn't say anything as we sat down.

"Hey, Jade, mind if we join you?"

She gave Logan a genuine smile. "Not at all. We were just working on some new material. I could use a break."

The waitress came over and took our orders as Drake sat down at the table in the chair next to me. I wanted to beat my head against the table. How was I supposed to sit through lunch with one of them on each side of me? Thankfully, Drake made no move to talk to me. Instead, he turned to Jade and started showing her something on the piece of paper between them. Logan pulled me closer to him and gave me a kiss on my forehead. "I feel like I haven't seen you in years. Break really sucked without you."

"I missed you too, but I'm sure the guys at the shop gave you plenty of entertainment from the story you were telling me earlier."

He laughed. "Yeah, they're great. But I'd much rather look at you sweaty and covered in grease than at them."

I felt my face start to burn. Drake was sitting close enough to hear what Logan had just said. The waitress appeared with our food and saved me from replying. I dug into my food as I glanced over at the paper Drake was holding. "What's that?"

He continued to study the paper for a minute before replying. "Working on some new stuff to use for when we tour this summer."

"Oh yeah, I forgot about that. Everything lined up?"

"Yeah, we'll be on the road until right before school starts back."

For some reason I felt depressed about him being gone for almost three months. I would probably be going back to Charleston over the summer anyway, so I had no reason to be disappointed. Maybe it was the fact that I was afraid someone in the industry would notice their band and sign them, and I would never see him again. The thought of never seeing him again scared me.

"I bet you're excited to get out of here."

He stared at me for a moment, searching my eyes for what, I don't know. "I'm excited to tour, but there are things I will miss here. Things I'd always come back for."

I glanced down at my plate as Logan snorted. "What could you possibly miss here? Sure it's nice, but it doesn't compare to the bigger cities. Besides, we aren't exactly known for our love of rock. Most people prefer country around here."

Drake laughed. "Yeah, you're right. Somehow I feel like we'd be more popular if I played a banjo or a fiddle."

I grinned. "Hey, listen here! Some of us would rather cut our ears off than listen to country! I'd choose rock any day."

Logan shook his head. "I wouldn't call some of that screaming shit you listen to rock, more along the lines of headache-inducing crap."

Logan and I had never seen eye to eye on music. While we

both enjoyed rock, my tendency to love metal while he preferred country often left us at ends.

"Better than that crap you listen to about cheating and broken hearts!"

As soon as the words were out of my mouth I regretted them. I glanced at Drake to see him studying the music he was working on like it was the most interesting thing in the world. Logan seemed oblivious to my unease. "Whatever. At least you can understand what I listen to."

I was silent as I finished my burger while Jade defended metal. "You can understand it! You just have to listen!"

I laughed as they bickered back and forth. They finally gave up and agreed to disagree. We spent the rest of lunch in an uneasy silence with me refusing to look in Drake's direction. My head snapped up as Jade cursed rather colorfully. She pointed to the doorway, and I turned to see Chris approaching our table.

"What?" Logan asked, but before anyone could answer Chris was standing behind me.

"Hey, Chloe," he greeted me as I turned to look at him.

"Hey, Chris, how are you?"

"Good. Mind if I join you guys?"

I shook my head. "Um, actually we were just leaving."

He frowned. "That's too bad. Can I at least get your number this time?"

I glanced over at Logan, who was looking more and more pissed off by the minute. "I don't think that's a good idea. I told you before I had a boyfriend." I motioned to Logan. "This would be him. Logan, this is Chris."

Chris sized Logan up before smirking. "Well, when you get bored with this guy let me know." He pulled out a pen and wrote his number on my napkin.

I was shocked at his attitude. "Chris, that isn't going to happen."

He just smiled and turned away. "Whatever you say."

I turned to look at Logan, but he was glaring at Chris from across the room.

"Who the fuck was that guy?" he yelled as he looked at me.

"No one. He tried to buy me a beer the other night, but Drake ran him off."

Logan looked to Drake, who was watching us with amusement. "Apparently you didn't do a very good job since he came back."

Drake's face clouded over, and he sent a glare at Logan. "I didn't see you jumping in to defend her. Maybe you're not too worried about defending what you've got. Maybe you don't appreciate it."

I felt the challenge in his words as the air around us crackled with electricity.

"He never gave me a chance. And don't ever question my relationship with Chloe. You think I haven't seen the way you and other guys look at her? I'm just not worried because she's with me and not you. She chose me. She's too good of a person to leave me for someone like you."

"Someone like me? Just what type of person am I, Logan?" Drake challenged with a growl.

"You use women. Everyone sees it, including Chloe. She wouldn't waste her time with someone like that. She's not stupid."

Drake glanced between the two of us, and I was terrified of what was going to come out of his mouth. Logan couldn't find out like this, not in a bar full of people from someone other than me.

Jade interrupted before Drake could reply. "Both of you

guys shut up. This isn't the time or the place for this bullshit. You're both important to her, so put the testosterone away before you both screw up."

I shot her a grateful glance as Logan stood. "You're right. I'm sorry, Jade. Come on, Chloe. I need to get out of here before I do something stupid."

I grabbed my purse and stood, refusing to look at either of them. We walked back out to his car and got in, Logan slamming his door with so much force that I was afraid he was going to break the window. "That's it. I've kept quiet about your friendship with that asshole, but not anymore. I don't want you around him again."

I instantly bristled at his command. "You don't control me, Logan. I can talk to whoever I want."

He slammed his fists into the steering wheel and I jumped. "Damn it, Chloe! Can you not see how he looks at you? I just called him out in there, right in front of you and he didn't deny it. He has feelings for you."

I threw my purse on the floor and turned to glare at him. "You're being stupid, Logan!"

"No, I'm not. Promise me you'll stop talking to him!"

"I'm not promising you anything! You're being ridiculous and I refuse to talk to you until you get your shit together! Now take me home!"

"You're so fucking impossible, Chloe!"

I ignored him as he started the car and peeled out of the lot. We spent the ride home in silence, and as soon as he parked the car I was out and running. I didn't stop until I had slammed my dorm room door behind me. Rachel was on her side of the room unpacking, but stopped what she was doing to stare at me. "Um, hi?"

I growled as I stomped to my bed and sat down.

"What's wrong with you?"

I growled again. "Logan! He's such an asshole. I told him from the beginning he couldn't control me or who my friends were, but yet here we are."

I fell back on my bed as Rachel frowned. "Uh oh, lovers' quarrel?"

I shot a glare in her direction. "Yeah, you could say that."

My phone started ringing in my pocket, and I groaned as I pulled it out. It was Logan, of course. I hit ignore and threw it on the bed beside me. It rang again, but I ignored it. A few minutes later someone started pounding on the door. I made no move to answer it, so Rachel sighed and walked over to open it. She just barely cracked it open, but I could see Logan standing there.

"Can I talk to Chloe?"

Rachel glanced over to me, but I shook my head no.

"Logan, I don't think right now is a good time. Let her cool off, okay?"

He groaned. "Fine. But tell her I'm sorry, okay?"

She nodded before shutting the door in his face.

"Thank you, thank you, thank you."

She gave me a small smile as she walked back to her bed to start grabbing clothes to put away. "You owe me. I feel like I should get a free drink when I come to visit you at work."

"Done," I answered instantly and she laughed.

"Well, that was easy. Maybe I should have thought this out a little better before making my demands."

"Sorry, you already set your price. No take backs."

I ducked and laughed as she threw a shoe at me. "Fine, be that way!"

CHAPTER EIGHTEEN

MOMMY DEAREST

I spent the rest of the day in my room with Rachel, dodging calls from Logan. The next morning I left early to go to class, hoping to avoid him. Unfortunately, he was standing in the lobby waiting for me. I slowed as I approached, and he grinned at me as he held out a cup of coffee.

"Peace offering? I'm sorry if I acted like a jerk yesterday. I just get so crazy when it comes to that guy."

I took the coffee from him and started sipping carefully. "You were a jerk." I started walking toward the door, and he followed close behind.

"Yeah, I know I was, but I want to make up for it if you'll let me."

I stared at the ground as we walked. I felt guilty for being angry with him since he was spot-on with his observations about Drake. But how could I tell him that without the entire truth coming out? "I don't know, Logan. Everything is so messed up right now."

He frowned as he pulled me into a hug. "I know. We haven't spent any time together lately, and when we do I go and pull this crap. Just let me make it up to you. I promise things will get better between us. I don't want to lose you, Chloe. I love you."

My heart squeezed painfully as I heard the words *I love you* come out of his mouth. I couldn't think of anyone who was less deserving of them.

"Give me a couple days to cool down, okay?"

He nodded as we reached my building. "Fair enough. Find me when you're ready." He kissed me gently and then walked away, his shoulders slumping.

I turned and walked into the building. My eyes landed on Drake the minute I stepped inside the classroom. My stomach was in knots as I stared at him. He felt the heat of my gaze and turned to look at me. I gave him a small smile before taking a seat a couple rows away from him. He frowned and stood to walk over to me. He sat down in the seat next to me and set his book on the desk. "Hey."

"Hey," I mumbled back, feeling uncomfortable.

"So are we back to ignoring each other?" he asked as he stared at me.

"No, just figured it was best to stay away until I got things figured out, you know?"

He ran his hands through his hair, looking agitated. "Look, I'm sorry for yesterday with Logan. I shouldn't have said what I did, but it's the truth. He has no clue what he's got with you. He doesn't appreciate you."

I instantly came to Logan's defense. "Like you would? Where would you find the time between all the women you're with? I'm not stupid, Drake. You wouldn't give all that up for me."

"Are you serious right now? Of course I would give it up.

Have you seen me with anyone lately? I've stopped it all, for you. I wish you would take me seriously, but obviously you've already decided what you think of me."

I thought about what he said. I hadn't seen him with anyone for a while. Even when those women had come to our table Friday, he had pushed them away. I thought at the time it was because he was so mad at me, but maybe that wasn't the case.

"I'm sorry, Drake. I'm not being fair to you, but it's hard to see you as anything different. You've been with so many women though, what do you expect? You can't change overnight."

"Before you tripped right into my life I would have said the same thing. But there's something different about you. I don't know what it is, but it makes me want to change every bad thing about myself."

I glanced around the room and noticed the professor enter. What could I say to something like that? Drake had me in knots from the moment I laid eyes on him, I couldn't deny that. Things could have been so different if he hadn't pushed me away before, we could have been happy right now. Instead I was in the biggest mess of my life. All because of him.

"That doesn't change anything, Drake. We're both so screwed up on our own, but together we're a whirlwind. Nothing survives that gets in our path."

He opened his mouth to speak, but the professor started introducing himself at the front of the room, effectively ending our conversation. The rest of class passed in a blur, my mind was so far gone that I couldn't even begin to tell anyone what we had talked about. Once we were dismissed, I grabbed my things and flew out the door, hoping Drake wouldn't approach me. I made it halfway across campus before looking behind me.

Drake was behind me, but there were several students between us, and he was making no attempt to catch up.

I breathed a sigh of relief as my phone started ringing. Expecting it to be Logan again, I was confused when **Blocked Number** showed across my phone.

"Hello?" I answered cautiously. There was no reply so I spoke again. "Is anyone there? This isn't funny." I could hear breathing on the other end of the line, but still no one spoke. "Fine, whatever. Be a creep."

I started to pull the phone away from my ear to hang up, but I stopped as I heard a voice on the other side that made my blood run cold.

"Chloe? Is that you?"

I stepped off the path and leaned against a tree as I listened to my mother's voice.

"Mom?" I felt someone come up next to me, but I ignored them as I waited for her to speak.

"Yeah, it's me. You're a hard person to find."

"What do you want? I told you the last time I saw you to stay away from me." I felt a hand on my shoulder, and I turned to see Drake watching me with concern.

"Oh, stop being a spoiled brat. Spending all that time in that nice house with the rich doctor and lawyer spoiled you. Made you think you're better than you are. You're nothing more than the trash you always were, Chloe."

My heart stopped as I listened to her speak to me as she always had, like I was beneath her. "You can't talk to me that way anymore. Tell me what you want or I'm hanging up."

She gave a high-pitched laugh. "I'm your mother, whether I want to be or not, so I'll talk to you however I want. Now, where are you? We have some things to discuss."

I shook my head back and forth viciously, even though she couldn't see me. "I'm not telling you where I am. Leave me alone!"

"I found your number, didn't I? It's only a matter of time before I figure out where you are. I need your help with something."

My knees started trembling as she spoke, and Drake wrapped his arm around me to help support my weight. He grabbed the phone out of my hand before I could react and started yelling at my mother. "Who the fuck is this?"

His eyes took on a coldness as he listened to her talk. "No, you listen to me, you bitch, you leave Chloe alone. I mean it. You come after her and you'll have to go through me. Don't call again." He hung up on her while she was in the middle of a rant and threw the phone in his pocket. It started ringing again almost instantly, but he ignored it as he pulled me tighter against him.

"Wow, she was pleasant. Glad you didn't get your personality from her."

I gave a small laugh as my mind raced over what she said. She needed my help with something, but I had no clue as to what she was talking about. I had nothing to give her, not that I would even if I did.

"I don't know why she's so determined to get to me now. I spent most of my childhood trying to stay out of her way, hiding from her, and now I'm back to doing the exact same thing. I'm terrified of her, Drake. Terrified."

He hugged me tight before pulling back. "You don't have to be afraid of her anymore. I'm here and I'm not letting her get anywhere near you."

"Drake, if she wants to find me, she will. No one will stop

her, especially if she's still on drugs. You have no idea what they do to her. She's mean when she's sober, but under the influence she'd kill me as soon as she'd look at me." I pulled back and held out my hand for the phone in his pocket. "Can I have my phone back?"

He shook his head. "Not a chance. You'll answer if she calls again and I'm not letting you deal with that."

I gave him a pleading look. I had to call Logan, I needed him right now. He was always there when my mother went crazy. "Please. I need to call Logan. He always takes care of me when she's around."

His eyes turned cold as he pulled the phone out of his pocket and slapped it into my hand. "Of course, I forgot about pretty boy."

"Drake, it's not that. It's just that he's been through this with her before. He always knows what to do. How to protect me."

His gaze turned murderous. "And I don't? I could help you, Chloe, if you'd let me. Instead, you go running back to him. Just forget about it, okay? I'm second best and always will be. I'm out of here." He turned and stormed away, his body tight with anger. I called his name over and over, but he never turned to look at me.

Passing students watched me curiously as I slid down the tree and slumped to the ground. I wrapped my arms around my knees and cried. Cried harder than I had in a long time. Sure, this mess with Logan and Drake was horrible, but my mother was a whole other ball game. I had no idea what she wanted, but she wouldn't stop until she had it. She was dangerous, and I would have to keep my guard up at all times.

I tried to control my tears as I dialed Logan's number. He answered almost instantly. "Chloe! I was hoping you'd call me. I've been driving myself nuts worrying about us."

I started sobbing louder at the sound of his voice, and he stopped talking.

"Chloe, what's wrong?"

"It's my mom. She just called me. I'm so scared, Logan."

I heard muffled cursing on the line as I rested my head on my knees. "Shhh, it's all right. Tell me where you are."

I told him where to find me, and he promised to be there in just a few minutes. I was still crying when he found me and carried me back to his room. He laid me down on the bed and got in beside me, pulling me tight against his chest. I buried my face in his neck as he soothed me.

"It's all right, baby girl. I've got you, she won't get near you."

"You don't understand. She always finds me, Logan. Why won't she leave me alone? I just want to be left alone!" I screamed into his chest as I let my anger pour out.

"Chloe, if I could take everything bad she did to you back I would. No one deserves to grow up with what you did. You're such a good person, nothing like her." He pushed me back gently and grasped my chin in his hand, pulling my face up so that I was looking into his eyes. "She will never touch you again. I promise you that. I won't let her. Until we figure this out, I don't want you answering any of her calls, and I want someone with you at all times. We won't give her the chance to get to you. Okay?"

I nodded as he pulled my face up to his, kissing me gently. "I love you, Chloe. I'd die for you."

I deepened the kiss, needing to feel his protectiveness, his love. He groaned as he rolled me onto my back and started trailing kisses along my jaw line. My body instantly responded to his touch, and I ran my hands under his shirt to his back and pulled him down on top of me. His arousal was apparent through his jeans, and I groaned as I pushed myself up closer to him.

"I need you, Logan. I need you so much."

Tears ran down my face as he slid my shirt over my head and gently kneaded my breasts. "I need you too, baby girl."

I knew I was only setting myself up for more heartache, but I couldn't stop myself as I pulled his shirt off and started working on the button and zipper of his jeans. They sprang open, and I pushed my hand inside the tight space, grabbing his shaft and running my hand along it roughly. His body convulsed at my touch. He pulled my hand away long enough to get rid of his jeans and boxers before lying back down on his back. I kissed down his chest and stomach, feeling the muscles quiver underneath my touch.

I ran my tongue over his shaft gently before pulling him into my mouth and sucking. I found a fast hard rhythm as he moaned and thrust his hips up to let me take him deeper. "God, Chloe, you're amazing with your mouth."

I pulled back, grinning at his words. "Care to return the favor?"

He laughed as he flipped me on my back. "Hell yeah, I will!"

He sucked and nibbled on my nipples first, until they were tender and swollen with want, before using his tongue to slowly glide down my stomach to my core. I melted into the bed as I felt his tongue flick over my swollen clit. He pushed two fingers inside me, and I moaned at the sensations that were running through my body. His tongue quickly replaced his fingers, and my body jerked up off the bed at the feeling as he tongue fucked me.

"Logan!" I screamed as I fell apart beneath him. Before I had time to recover, he was inside me, thrusting hard and fast. I felt myself building again as I clung to him, my nails leaving marks across his shoulders as he pounded into me. His thrusting became erratic, and I felt him shudder as he exploded inside me, taking me with him. He collapsed on top of me as I tried to catch my breath.

"That was so worth waiting all these months for. You're as incredible as I remember," he whispered in my ear as he slowly pulled out and collapsed in the bed beside me. He pulled me tight against him and nuzzled my neck. "I'll always keep you safe. I'll never let you go, I promise."

We lay together for several minutes as I let the guilt slowly start to wash over me, realizing the position I had just put myself in. The feeling that I was betraying Drake by sleeping with Logan soaked deep into my skin until I felt like I was drowning in it. I knew that technically I had done nothing wrong. Logan was my boyfriend and this was what was supposed to happen, but my heart told me a different story. It was screaming for Drake, and I couldn't deny it.

The worst part was that it took having sex with Logan again to come to my senses.

I rolled to face Logan, my heart in my throat as I opened my mouth to tell him everything. "Logan, can we talk?"

He kissed my nose and smiled before standing. "Yeah, but can it wait? I have to be at work soon."

I nodded as relief took over my body. I didn't have to tell him just yet, I could wait. I felt guilty for not pushing the issue, but I couldn't really lay everything out for him twenty minutes before he had to be at work.

Logan pulled me into a hug before pulling his clothes on. "You working tonight?"

"Yeah, until close and the same thing tomorrow. I won't have a free evening until Wednesday night."

He grabbed his keys off the stand and turned to smile at me. "Okay, we'll talk Wednesday then."

CHAPTER NINETEEN

AND WE ALL FALL APART

Wednesday never came. Veronica had some kind of plans and begged me to trade my Friday shift with her. I agreed, but I wasn't happy with it. Not only was I forced to wait to talk to Logan yet again, but I had a Friday off and no excuse not to go to Drake's show if Amber asked me. Luckily for me, Amber was so wrapped up in Adam that she had barely even texted me throughout the week, and I was let off the hook.

When Friday evening rolled around, Logan was curled up with me in my bed, helping me to study for a test I had the following Monday. He was an excellent tutor, since he'd already taken the class last semester.

"I swear if I look at one more page, my head is going to explode," I groaned.

We had been at it for over two hours, and my brain was passed the fried mark for the week. He gently took the book from my hands and set it on the floor before pulling me into his arms.

"Let's take a break for a few."

He leaned down and kissed me with such gentleness

my heart melted. He and Drake were so different from each other—Logan so gentle and caring, Drake with raw passion and danger. Why was I lying here kissing Logan, yet all my thoughts were comparing him to Drake?

He deepened the kiss and started slowly sliding his hand under my shirt and up my stomach. I froze at the touch and pulled away.

"What's wrong, babe? If we're going too fast just tell me. I thought after the other day . . ." he looked at me with concern in his eyes. I couldn't do this to him any longer.

"Logan, remember how I wanted to talk to you the other day?"

He nodded, but stayed silent.

"Well, there's something I need to tell you." I closed my eyes and took a deep breath before opening them to look at him again. "Something happened between Drake and me. Right after we got together I went over to his house to hang out and study for a couple of our classes. Neither of us intended anything to happen, but we ended up having sex. I am so sorry I didn't tell you, I just couldn't stand the thought of hurting you. It was an accident."

He froze as he looked down at me. "*An accident?* What, you just accidentally fell on his dick?" he yelled, his face turning a violent shade of red I had never witnessed on him before. He took a deep breath, trying to calm himself before continuing. "Why are you telling me this now? Why wait all these months and then dump this on me?"

"I don't know. I guess I just couldn't take the guilt anymore. I don't want to keep lying to you." I stared into his eyes as I spoke, and I could see the storm raging behind them even though he was attempting to stay calm.

"I'm glad you told me, Chloe. I want you to be honest with me. I don't really know what to say, but I'm trying to understand here. You said this was right after we got together?"

I nodded, feeling more guilt cripple me.

"Okay, well as long as it was just the once I am willing to look past it. I know how confused you were about us then." He pulled me into a hug as I burst into tears. "What's wrong, Chloe? I forgive you, baby girl, I forgive you."

I continued to sob as I managed to gasp out the few words that would seal our fate. "It wasn't just then. It happened again a couple weeks ago. I went to his house to try to work things out, because we hadn't really talked since it happened, and things got carried away."

I felt his arms stiffen around me. "You had sex with him two weeks ago? What the fuck, Chloe?" He quickly dropped his arms from around me and stood. I was still crying as he continued yelling. "That son of a bitch! He knew you were mine, and he still went after you. Twice! Unfuckingbelievable! I'm going to kill him!" He stormed across the room to the door and threw it open.

I jumped off the bed to go after him. "Logan! Logan, stop! Where are you going?"

He glanced over his shoulder at me as he headed for the stairs. "I'm going to teach that bastard a lesson. I knew something was up between you two, I just never thought he would pull that. I never thought you would do this to me! How could you, Chloe?" He continued to yell as I chased him down the stairs. All around us, students stopped dead in the hallway and stairs to stare at us as we passed.

"I'm so sorry, Logan, but please just stop." I reached for his arm, but he threw my hand away.

"Stay away from me, Chloe, or God help me, I won't be responsible for my actions."

We had made it down the stairs and out into the parking lot, and he quickly unlocked his car and jumped in. I tried to open the passenger door, but he kept it locked as he put the car in drive and left black marks as he screeched out of the parking lot. Sobbing uncontrollably, I ran for my own car and quickly tore after him. He went straight to the bar, knowing Drake would be playing on a Friday night. As soon as I shut my car off, I jumped out and ran after him into the building.

Drake was up on stage playing with the band when we entered. Logan headed straight for the stage with me on his heels. Before I could stop him, he jumped up onto the stage and punched Drake in the face. I screamed as I watched Drake's head jerk back with the force of it and blood start trickling down onto his lips from his nose. The crowd started screaming and the other band members quickly grabbed Logan as he lunged for Drake again.

"What the fuck?" Drake yelled glaring at Logan.

He glanced up and went pale at the sight of me standing in front of them crying and shaking as Logan started screaming at him.

"You stupid son of a bitch! Did you think I wouldn't find out you'd been fucking Chloe behind my back?" He lunged again and Adam was caught off guard, letting him go. Drake saw him coming and jumped back before landing a punch of his own in Logan's stomach. Logan grunted and dropped before jumping up and going at Drake again.

"Come on, pretty boy. I'm standing right here, come get me," Drake taunted him.

Logan threw another punch that Drake wasn't quick

enough to dodge, and it landed in his rib cage. Logan threw himself at Drake while he was distracted by the pain, and they flew backward into the drums, sending them flying. I screamed out as they continued to throw punches before Adam and Eric could pull them apart.

Eric pried Drake off of Logan and held him tight as Adam twisted Logan's arm behind his back and held him in a death grip.

Jade, who had been standing on the end of the stage the entire time, put her fingers in her mouth and whistled. "That's it! Grow the fuck up, boys, or at least take it outside!"

Logan looked at Drake with pure hatred in his eyes. "How could you, Drake? I asked you that day at lunch if there was anything between the two of you before I went for her. You told me nothing was going on and nothing would. You promised me you would leave her alone and look what happened. You fucked her not once, but twice behind my back."

Drake glared right back at him. "Yeah, I did fuck her. Twice because once just wasn't enough for me and I'd do it again if I could."

Logan tried to lunge for him, but Adam was prepared this time and held tight.

"All right guys, both of you outside now," Adam growled as he held Logan back. He marched him off stage and across the bar to the door, Eric following closely behind still holding on to Drake. Jade and I followed behind them at a distance with her arms wrapped around me, hugging me tight.

When I stepped out into the cool night air, I breathed deeply. How had my life come to this? I was almost certain I had already lost Logan, not only as a boyfriend, but as my friend too. And Drake, well, I never knew where I stood with him from day one. My insides trembled as Eric and Adam released Logan and Drake and stepped back.

"All right, you want to kick the shit out of each other, be my guest. We're not going to stop you, but you guys need to get your shit together. Fighting over a girl is fucking ridiculous and you know it. So do what you want, just get it out and over with before our drums suffer anymore," Eric growled as he and Adam made their way over to where Jade and I stood.

Logan and Drake stood facing each other, and suddenly I was afraid they would start hitting each other again. I stepped forward until I stood between them.

"Listen to me, both of you. This is so stupid, like Eric said. This is all my fault and the two of you beating the shit out of each other isn't going to fix anything. I fucked up, not you two. So if you want to take your anger out on someone, take it out on me. I ruined everything." Tears ran down my face as I looked at both of them. "You both mean so much to me, and I will never forgive myself for what I have done to you."

I quickly turned from them and headed across the parking lot to my car. As I got in, I glanced up and saw both of them staring at me with identical looks of pain and rage on their faces.

. . .

The texts started a couple hours after I made it home. First from Drake, checking on me, then from both of them, apologizing for what had happened at the bar. I couldn't really face either of them at this point, not because of what had happened tonight, but because I was ashamed of myself and what I had done to both of them, so I ignored the texts. They were both better than this whole situation, better than I was, and neither of them deserved to be stuck with me.

Rachel had forgotten some of her stuff at home when she came back from break, so she had gone home to see her parents and grab her things for the weekend, which meant I had the entire room to myself as I moped and refused to answer their text messages as my phone continued to ding. I grabbed a bottle of vodka from our minifridge and poured a shot straight. Gulping it down, I poured another and drank it too. If I was going to be miserable, I might as well do it right.

A few shots later, I was lying on my bed staring at the ceiling as it gently swayed back and forth. I giggled at the stupid ceiling. *Life wasn't so bad,* I thought as the ceiling continued to sway. I'm not sure how long I lay there laughing at the ceiling before I heard a knock on my door. Giggling like a fool, I stumbled from my bed and slowly made my way to the door. Swinging it open, I saw both Logan and Drake standing in front of me.

I smiled at the sight of these two gorgeous men who had come to visit me. "Heeeey, guys! How are you?" I giggled again as I spoke. "Actually, never mind. You're both pretty damn fine like always." I turned and made my way back to my bed and fell on top of it. I glanced back at Logan and Drake when neither of them said a word. They were both staring at each other with concern before turning their gazes to me.

"Are you all right, Chloe?" Logan asked, stepping into the room ahead of Drake.

"I'm great! I had a couple shots and now I'm all set." I smiled brightly at them. "What are you guys doing here? Wait, you're together, and there's no blood!"

Both of them continued to stare at me. Logan leaned down beside my bed and looked into my eyes. "Just how many shots have you had, love?"

I rolled my eyes at the concern in his voice. Why did he seem so worried, when everything was just fine.

"Only a couple," I motioned to the bottle on my nightstand. "See, it's still full. I just opened it tonight."

Drake glanced at the stand before looking back at me. "Uh, Chloe, the bottle is empty."

I stared at the bottle, noticing he was right. I slapped my hand across my face before laughing. "Whoops! Guess it's a good thing it's the cheap stuff, otherwise I'd be seriously drunk right now."

They both exchanged looks with each other again, their facing growing more concerned.

"Chloe, honey, you *are* drunk. Excessively drunk actually," Logan stated from beside me.

I rolled my eyes again. "Seriously guys, I'm fine. Why are you here?" The world tipped as I spoke, and I was glad I was lying on my bed.

Drake spoke up from his spot in front of my bed. "Look, Chloe, you're trashed so I don't think right now is a good time to talk like we planned. We'll come back tomorrow." He glanced at the bottle again. "Or the day after. I'm pretty sure you aren't going to be up to any talking tomorrow."

They were both really annoying me at this point. "I said I was fine!" I sat up as I spoke, and the world spun around me. My stomach churned, and I grabbed the garbage can beside the bed and threw up violently into it. Logan jumped back a couple feet as I continued to throw up. It seemed like hours passed as I kept my head in the can. Finally, there seemed to be nothing left in my stomach, and I rolled back onto my bed groaning, "Fuck. Maybe I am drunk."

Drake chuckled quietly. "No shit, Chloe."

I glared at him. "Just say what you came here to say, asshole."

My insult didn't seem to faze him as he continued to stare down at me. "We came to tell you to decide who you want. Both of us want you, but what you want is what really matters. Whoever you don't chose will back off. No questions asked."

I could see the pain in his eyes as he spoke. The last thing I remember doing before darkness took over was muttering the only truth I knew at that moment. "What if I want both of you?"

. . .

The next morning, the world exploded inside my head as I opened my eyes.

"Holy crap! How much did I drink last night?" I yelled. Pain tore into my head with renewed vengeance at the sound. Grabbing my head, I moaned and rolled onto my stomach. Finding the pillow, I quickly pulled it over my head to shield myself from the sun shining cheerfully into the room.

I lay there, willing my stomach and head to cooperate with me. After a few minutes of pleading and self-loathing, I gave up and slowly slid out from under the pillow. Still clutching my head, I made my way to the desk and grabbed a bottle of water and a couple of pills to help my headache. I stood motionlessly for a few minutes before grabbing my bathroom bag and shuffled down the hall toward the showers. I slowly undressed, fearing the pain any sudden movement would cause. After taking the longest shower on record, I made my way back to my room and fell back onto my bed.

As I lay there, images of the previous night started flashing through my mind. Studying with Logan and telling him the truth, the fight, and finally both of them coming here to see me.

What if I want you both? My heart seized as the memory surfaced from my cloudy mind. Had I really told them that? Of course I had, my idiocy really knew no bounds. I shot straight up in bed, and my head protested. I ignored the pain as I grabbed my keys and ran from the room.

. . .

Knocking on Drake's door was probably the hardest thing I had ever done in my life. I stood frozen as he opened the door and raised his eyebrows at the sight of me.

"Wow. I didn't expect you to show up today." He gave me a thoughtful look. "Or be conscious, to be honest."

"Can we talk about last night, please?" I almost hoped he would say no to my request, that he would tell me to come back later. Instead, he nodded and stood aside, allowing me entrance. I moved swiftly past him and walked to the couch. I was beginning really to hate this couch, every bad thing between us had started on it.

Unlike last time, he sat down beside me and took my hand into his own. I looked down at our joined hands, and such a simple sight took my breath away. How was I going to do this to either of them? At the end of this, all three of us would walk away shattered, utterly broken.

The truth was that I loved Drake, more than breathing, more than anything, but I knew in my heart that I loved Logan too, just in a different way. I couldn't imagine surviving what I was about to do, but I had to do it. I had to set both of them free. Neither of them deserved the pain I had caused them, and I was going to make this right.

I looked up into his eyes, memorizing them before finally speaking. "I love you, Drake." His eyes lit up with such joy I almost stopped there. "But I love Logan too." The light in his eyes faded, and he looked away from me.

"I'm so sorry that I hurt you, and if I could, I would take it all back." My eyes burned as tears threatened to spill over. I took a deep breath before finishing my death sentence. "I'll always care about you, but I think it's best if we stay away from each other. All I do is cause you pain, and I can't stand the thought of you hurting because of me."

I reached up and gripped his chin, pulling his face back to me. The haunting look in his eyes nearly killed me. "Good-bye, Drake."

I started to stand, but stopped myself. If this was the end, I wanted closure. Still holding his chin, I pulled him to me and kissed him softly on the lips as my tears finally made their way down my cheeks. Without another word, I walked out the door.

· · ·

I was still crying as I pulled into the parking lot of my dorm and shut off the car. I sat there trying to compose myself before I faced Logan. It took a lot longer than I had expected, but finally my tears dried, and I stepped out of the car and into the building. Before I knew it, I was standing in front of Logan's door. I knocked softly and prepared myself for what was to come.

My heart had already broken once today, and after this visit was over, I wasn't sure there would be anything left. With Drake I had lost love, but when it came to Logan, I was losing more than just love. I was losing years with my best friend. As much as it hurt, I knew I was doing the right thing. My stomach twisted as he slowly opened the door and started at me.

Without a word, he turned back into the room and sat on

his bed. I walked in, closing the door behind me. The look on his face said it all. He looked totally and utterly defeated.

He sighed before glancing up at me. "I lost, didn't I?"

I looked at the floor. "Not really. I'm so tired of hurting both of you, Logan. I love you both, just in different ways. I'm not choosing him, but I'm not choosing you either."

What was left of my heart shattered with my words, but I stood my ground. He stood and crossed the room to stand in front of me.

"I understand, and I accept your decision."

Tears started falling from my eyes again. "I'm so sorry, Logan. I ruined everything we ever had. I didn't just lose my boyfriend, I lost my best friend in all of this mess."

He pulled me into a tight hug. "You haven't lost me as a friend, Chloe, but I need some time before I can go back to the way things were. Just don't give up on our friendship. I promise I won't leave you."

I hugged him back as hard as I could. "I understand. Thanks, Logan." I pulled away and made my way to the door. I opened the door to leave. "When you're ready, you know where to find me." I closed the door behind me as I left my heart lying on the floor.

CHAPTER TWENTY

PICKING UP THE PIECES

The following weeks were absolute torture. Rachel, and to my surprise Jade, tried to cheer me up with unholy amounts of ice cream and girl time. I tried to act cheerful around them, but I felt utterly broken inside. Amber, who hadn't been at the bar that night for some reason and had heard everything from Adam, refused to speak to me, and I understood why. She loved Logan as much as I did, and I had hurt him beyond repair. I missed her as much as I did Logan, but if I was truthful with myself, I missed Drake more than anything in my life. Every time I would see him around campus, my heart would start fluttering like a hummingbird in my chest, and I would feel dizzy. I would catch him staring at me from time to time in class, where he had taken his old seat several rows away from me, but he never approached me.

I tried to keep myself busy at all times so I didn't think of either of them, but they always snuck into my thoughts at the most unexpected moments—in the shower, when I was folding my laundry, even at work. My work was suffering miserably, and I knew I was going to be called out on it. Finally, one evening Janet pulled me into her office.

"Listen, Chloe, I don't know what's going on with you, but you need to get your head on straight or I'm going to have to fire you. I don't want to, but I've had so many complaints over the last few weeks that there is no way I can keep letting this go on."

I slumped into my chair and nodded. "I'm so sorry, Janet. I promise I'll start trying harder. I've just had a lot of personal stuff going on, but that isn't an excuse."

She nodded and smiled at me. "I really do like you, Chloe. Listen, take a week off to figure stuff out, and then come back in the Monday after next."

I nodded and stood to leave. "When I come back, I promise things will be better."

"I hope so, Chloe. If you need someone, you know where to find me."

As I closed the door behind me, tears formed in my eyes. I had cried more in the last few months than I ever had in my life. Even with my mom always being so shitty, I never cried this much. I waved good-bye to Veronica as I left, leaving her with a questioning look on her face.

Speaking of my mother, I had thought I was safe after the phone call that Drake had witnessed. Unfortunately, she had decided that now was the perfect time to torture me. The calls had started coming through again this past week. I received as many as ten a day, sometimes in the middle of the night. I knew she was playing a game with me, but I refused to be part of whatever she was planning. My mother was a conniving and cruel-hearted bitch, and I was better off completely ignoring her.

My phone rang again on the way home, making it the sixth—or was it seventh—call of the day. When I arrived back at the dorm, I checked my phone, and sure enough, another blocked number. I powered off my phone and walked up to my room. Rachel was lying in bed reading when I came in.

"You're home early. What's up?"

I threw my bag on the table and sat at the edge of her bed. "My boss kicked me out."

Her eyes widened. "Oh no! Did you get fired?"

I shook my head. "No, she told me to take a week off and get my shit together. Don't worry, I know I still owe you that free cup of coffee. I'll make sure you get it before I get fired."

She laughed and hit me over the head with a pillow. "You're so dumb, Chloe. I wasn't worried about my coffee." She looked thoughtful for a moment. "Actually, I am. I'll stop by the day you go back just in case."

I laughed as I grabbed the pillow she was about to launch at my head again and quickly hit her back, right in the face. What ensued after that can only be described as the most epic battle of pillow fights, known to man. By the time we were finished, feathers littered the floor, and we were both in desperate need of new pillows.

"Oops," Rachel giggled as we fell back onto the bed.

"Yeah, that would be a good description of what just went down. And now we have to clean up this mess."

We spent the next twenty minutes picking feathers up off the floor, the bed, and out of our hair. I was grabbing a stray out from under my bed when a knock sounded at the door. Seeing as no one but Rachel and Jade wanted anything to do with me and Jade was at a show tonight, I let Rachel answer it. Whoever it was, they were obviously looking for her. I slowly made my way out from under the bed, careful not to hit my head as she opened the door.

Her startled gasp had me spinning around to see who was

at the door. The garbage bag I had been holding slipped from my grasp and feathers went everywhere as I took in the sight of Logan standing in the doorway. His gaze dropped to the mess at my feet, and he chuckled. "Do I even want to ask?"

"Pillow fight," I whispered as I took in the sight of him. I hadn't seen him in weeks, not up close at least. He was still my Logan, except he had a ragged edge to him, and his eyes held a sadness within them. He looked like he was sleeping about as much as I was.

"Mind if I come in to talk?" he asked quietly.

Rachel held the door open the rest of the way for him as he entered, making his way to stand in front of me. Rachel stood by the doorway like a deer caught in the headlights of an oncoming semi.

"I'm . . . Yeah . . . I'm going to go. Call me when you're done." She gave me a hopeful smile as she grabbed her keys and made a hasty retreat out the door.

Logan and I were silent as we stared at each other. Needing something to do, I quickly bent down and started scooping the escaped feathers back into the bag. I watched out of the corner of my eye as he kneeled down beside me and started helping.

"How have you been?" he asked once we finished searching for feathers.

"Fine. You?"

I stood up quickly and set the bag by the door, trying to avoid all eye contact with him. I had no idea what he was doing here, and frankly I was afraid to ask.

"Not so good. I've missed you a lot, Chloe. I don't like how things are between us." He shifted weight from one foot to the other as he spoke. "I tried calling you first to see if it was okay if

I came by, but it went straight to voice mail. I wasn't sure if you were avoiding me or had it shut off."

I shook my head as I walked over and held up my phone. "It's off. I wouldn't ever ignore you, Logan. I've missed you too."

His forehead crinkled in confusion. "Why is your phone off? What if someone needed to get ahold of you?"

I snorted in a very unladylike manor. "Like who? Besides Rachel and Jade, no one ever speaks to me."

"Has anyone been giving you a hard time since . . . since everything happened?"

I shook my head as I set my phone back down. "No, everyone has left me alone. Even Amber." I looked away as understanding and pity filled his eyes.

"I see. I'll talk to Amber tomorrow. She doesn't need to ignore you because of me. You've been friends far too long to let me get in the way. But that doesn't answer my question. If no one was bothering you, why did you shut your phone off?"

I gave him a weak smile as I sat down on my bed. "Um, my mom has been calling me a lot lately. I shut if off so I didn't have to hear it ring all night."

I watched as his body went rigid. "She's still bothering you?"

I nodded. "Yeah, but it's not a big deal. I just ignore it."

He sat down next to me and started to hug me, but stopped himself. "Why didn't you tell me? Have you been talking to her?"

I scooted across the bed a bit to get away from him. "No, I haven't spoken with her since that day I called you. Drake got on the phone with her then and I think we scared her off for a while, but she's back with a vengeance."

His body went stiff at the mention of Drake.

"And I never told you because it's only been happening for

the last week or so and we haven't exactly been on speaking terms. I couldn't just run to you about it like I did before."

He took a deep breath before turning to look at me. "Chloe, you can always come to me about this stuff, no matter what's happening between us. Just because things ended the way they did between us doesn't mean that I don't care about you anymore. You're still my best friend and always will be. That's actually what I came here tonight to talk to you about. I miss you, Chloe. I know that there's nothing left between us romantically, but I don't want to lose you completely. You've always been such a big part of my life. These past few weeks have been hell without you."

Tears broke free from my eyes and started rolling down my cheeks as he spoke. I threw myself into his arms and hugged him as tightly as I could manage. "Oh, Logan! I've missed you so much, you have no idea. I was so sure you'd never speak to me again after everything. I thought I'd lost you!"

I sobbed into his chest as he rubbed my back. "I told you I just needed time, Chloe. I could never leave you for long. You're too important to me for that. I've felt like I've had a hole in my chest."

I pulled back to look at his beautiful face. "I have too. The world's not the same without you in it."

We sat together on my bed for hours, just talking. I told him everything that had happened from the beginning, and he listened quietly as I spilled every regret, every loss, every happy moment. When I finished we were both shaken and tearful.

"I wish you would have told me everything from the beginning, Chloe. Things could have been so much different for all of us."

I nodded as I wiped my tears away. "I know that now, but I figured that out too late. I was too deep in with you and I didn't want to hurt you."

"I know you didn't, baby girl, but you did. What's in the past is exactly where it needs to be—behind us. From today on we'll start over—no more looking back at our mistakes, only to the future. I'm not about to lose you again."

I hugged him tightly as a smile spread across my face. "I'm not going to let you go again either. Logan and Chloe, partners in crime until the end."

. . .

Things began to return to normal in the days following my talk with Logan. Amber had burst into my room the next morning, sobbing like a baby. I had held her in my arms for a full five minutes until she could make a coherent sentence.

"I . . . I missed you so damn much, Chloe! This has been killing me inside."

I hugged her tightly as I laughed. "I missed you too, Amber, but I got what I deserved. What I did was wrong and I needed to pay for it."

"I'm sorry I was such a bitch to you. I was so mad at you for what you did, and for not telling me. I had to find out from Adam after the fact. I thought you trusted me more than that!"

"I did trust you, I just couldn't put you in the middle of all this. Logan is your friend too and if I had told you, it would have torn you guys apart. I didn't want to do that to you."

She nodded as she wiped under her eyes to get rid of the smudged mascara. "I guess I understand why, but it doesn't make me feel any better about the whole thing."

I stood up and looked out my window at the campus below. "I know it's a crappy excuse, but it's all I've got. I was so confused and I made some really bad choices. But I paid for it in the end. I nearly lost Logan and I did lose Drake."

"Have you talked to him any since all of this happened? I've been to some of the band's shows. He seems as depressed as you are."

I turned away from the window to see her watching me closely. My shoulders slumped as I thought of how I had hurt Drake, how I was still hurting him. "No, I haven't. I thought it was best to cut ties with both of them. We all needed time to heal from all of this. I want him, but I don't even know how he feels about me now. Besides, I don't think it would be fair to Logan if I caused all of this and then skipped merrily off into the sunset to live my happily ever after."

Amber snorted. "Yeah, you've been living your happily ever after all right. Do you really think Logan would want you to go on like this? He wants you to be happy, Chloe. That's all he ever wanted."

I sighed as I started gathering up clothes to wash. "I don't know. I just know I hurt him and I don't deserve to be happy. I'm sure Drake has moved on by now anyway."

Amber picked up a dirty sock and threw it at me. "Did you listen to anything I just said? Drake is as miserable as you are, and he's definitely not moved on. You have no idea how many girls I've watched him practically throw off of him at the bar. That boy is in mope mode, trust me."

I growled as I shoved the dirty sock in the laundry basket with the rest of the clothes. "I can't, Amber. I just can't. If he rejects me I'll never survive it."

. . .

With Amber and Logan back at my side, I was beginning to feel whole again, despite missing Drake. He had left a gaping hole in my chest that I wasn't sure anyone would be able to fill.

I saw him around campus a few times and in class. When he would look at me, I gave him a cautious smile, but he never returned it. I started back at work and threw myself into it with a vengeance to make up for lost time. Janet seemed impressed with my transformation and told me so. I was glad things were starting to look up in my life.

My mother had continued to call my phone until I was forced to change my number. I was upset, afraid Drake would decide to call me only to find the disconnected number and think I did it because of him. I knew it was a long shot, but I was still worried. I told Amber, and she offered to pass on my new number to him, but I refused. I didn't want to appear desperate in his eyes.

I had been doing such an amazing job at work that Janet told me to go home early Friday night. "You've been working yourself to the bone since you came back. Go out and have some fun with your friends tonight."

I thanked her as I grabbed my bag and made my way out to the almost empty parking lot. I sent Amber a quick text asking if she wanted to hang out, only to get a reply from her telling me she was at the bar. I groaned as she sent another text asking me to come. I really didn't think that would be a good idea. I told her I was tired and going home. My phone started ringing as soon as I sent the text.

I smiled at Amber's determination. "Yes?"

"Don't *yes* me, Chloe Marie! Get your butt over here. They're playing a bunch of new stuff tonight and it's a great show. You can leave before they finish if you want to. It's not like I'm asking you to have a heart-to-heart with him, just come watch them play."

I could make out shouting in the background as someone played a solo on the guitar.

"All right, I'm across the street so I'll be there in a minute." I hung up, still debating on just going home and hiding. I knew she'd never let me live it down if I did, so I slowly pulled across traffic and into the bar's parking lot. There was literally no place to park, so I pulled in next to the back door and made my way inside. It took me several minutes to push through the massive crowd to get to our table. After several elbows to the face and all of my toes being stepped on at least twice, the crowd cleared enough for me to reach the table.

I was out of breath as I sat down in a chair next to Rachel. She and Amber both broke out in giggles at the sight of me.

"What happened to you?"

I pointed over my shoulder to the crowd of rowdy bar patrons. "It's a damn mosh pit back there. I'm lucky I made it here with all my limbs intact!"

They continued to laugh as a waitress brought me a beer. I gave them a dirty look as I took a sip and let my eyes fall on the stage in front of us. My heart skipped a beat as I looked up to see Drake staring at me. I gave him a small smile and chugged my beer. I was going to need more than beer to survive this night.

I motioned for the waitress to bring me another one, but Amber shook her head. "No way are you getting wasted and making an ass out of yourself. Just watch the music and enjoy."

I groaned as I laid my head down on the table. "You're killing me, Amber, slowly and painfully. I hope you know that."

She slapped me on the back as the band finished their song. "I do know. I'm thoroughly enjoying myself right now. If you won't man up and talk to him, someone has to push you into it."

I opened my mouth and gasped at her. "This was a setup, wasn't it? You can forget about it, Amber, I'll be long gone by the time they finish. Actually, I think I'm going to leave now before you can try anything else on me." I stood and turned to leave just as Drake's amplified voice filled the bar.

"Thanks to everyone who came out tonight. We've got one more song for you guys before we're done. It's another new one and we hope you like it."

His eyes locked on mine as I stood there staring at him in a trance. This was the closest I had been to him in weeks, and the sight of him standing there in all of his bad-boy glory made my knees weak. He was wearing a sleeveless shirt that showed off more of his tattoo than I had ever seen him show at a performance before. The stage lights hit off his eyebrow and lip rings, making them sparkle brilliantly.

But it was his eyes that truly caught my attention. Standing this close to him, I could see all the despair and regret swirling within them.

I felt tears spring to my eyes as he spoke. "This one, well this one is for anyone who's had their heart ripped out. For anyone who thought they found love, only to have it ripped away viciously and without any regard to your feelings." He raised his hand above his head and shouted, "To all of us who are empty inside!"

With that, Jade started into the song slowly, with Adam and Eric following closely behind. As Drake started singing, I could see every bit of hurt I had caused radiating out from him, engulfing me and the audience. I stood rooted to the floor as he sang directly to me.

> *I wasn't sure what it was,*
> *What you did to me,*
> *I felt myself change,*
> *Something shifted when I looked into your eyes,*

Engulfing me in flames,
Burning me to the core,
But it wasn't meant to be,
You see, you and I,
We're a whirlwind,
Destroying everything in our path,
But isn't that what love does,
It makes us weak, far from free
I gave you everything and you turned it back on me,
You turned it back on me

He whispered the last line, and before I realized what I was doing, I was running through the crowd, pushing people as I went. I ran straight to my car and slammed the door behind me, tears running down my face in torrents. Amber was running out the front door as I sped past her and out onto the main road.

CHAPTER TWENTY-ONE

SECOND CHANCES

I drove for miles and miles as I pictured the look on Drake's face when he sang to me. I had destroyed him without even realizing what I was doing. He had finally opened up to me, and I had pushed him away. I knew enough about Drake to know that he didn't do that often, and I had shut him down cold, ruining him for anyone else out there. I was a horrible person and deserved to be alone for the rest of my life for everything I had put him through.

I drove for over an hour before I was forced to pull up at a gas station and fill up with gas. I had been running on empty as I pulled in, and I cringed as the machine continued to put dollar after dollar into my car. I needed to get my head together before I made myself go broke with this nighttime driving. A thought hit me as I replaced the nozzle and pulled away from the station. I could go back to the spot Drake had shown me. I needed the peace that place brought me right now, and surely he wouldn't be out there this late at night, especially after everything that had happened.

I pulled my car back onto the interstate and made my way

slowly back toward West Virginia. I hadn't realized just how far into Maryland my travels had taken me. Finally, after what felt like hours, I crossed the state line and started watching for my exit. I was upon it quickly, and I breathed a sigh of relief as I gave my blinker. I was almost there. I pulled off the main road and onto the hidden path, driving slowly since there was so much fog.

I finally pulled into the clearing and shut my car off, enjoying the total silence that came with it. I sat there for a moment before getting out and making my way down the path to the edge of the water. I sat on the same rotten tree as before, but decided against sticking my toes in the frigid water. I'd leave dying of hypothermia for another night.

I let myself drift away with the water, leaving my worries behind me. If I could stay here forever I would, there was nowhere else on earth as special as this place. I leaned back against the trunk of the tree as I began to feel sleepy.

Sometime later, I woke with a start as I heard footsteps approaching. I attempted to make myself as small as possible, trying to hide, as the footsteps grew louder. A figure stepped in front of me, and I nearly shrieked.

"Chloe?"

I peered into the darkness, trying to make sure I had heard who I thought I had. The moon was hidden behind the clouds and made the feat nearly impossible.

"Drake?"

A flashlight clicked on, and I shielded my eyes at the brightness as he pointed it in my face. "Yeah, it's me. I've been looking everywhere for you."

I held my hand in front of my face, trying to block out the light. "Do you mind? I'm going blind here."

The flashlight clicked off instantly, and we were plunged back into darkness. "Sorry, wasn't thinking. I'm relieved I found you. I came by here earlier, but you weren't here."

I nodded into the blackness even though he couldn't see me. "Yeah, I went for a drive. Had to clear my thoughts. I didn't realize until just a little bit ago that this was the perfect spot for it."

I felt him sit down on the log next to me. "I know what you mean. This place seems to have some kind of magic, doesn't it?"

"Yeah, I guess it does."

We sat in silence as I wondered why he had been searching for me. After the performance tonight, I had assumed he was done with me.

"Why are you here, Drake?"

He let out a long sigh. "I talked to Amber, she told me everything you guys talked about the other day. I wish you would have come to me, Chloe, instead of me having to search for you. You could have saved us both a lot of time."

I groaned as I let my head fall into my hands. "Amber has a big mouth." I pulled my hands away from my face as the moon moved out from behind a cloud and cast a beautiful soft light on the water and Drake. It almost looked like he was glowing.

"I'm glad she told me. I've been trying to stay away from you all this time. I thought you'd moved on."

"Drake, I'm never going to move on from you. Never."

I could see his lips turn up in a smile as the moonlight reflected off his lip ring. "I'm glad to hear that because I don't think I can move on from you either. I've missed you so much, you're all I think about."

My heart leaped at his words, but I forced my face to remain neutral. "We're not good for each other, Drake. You said it all tonight, we're a whirlwind and we destroy everything in our path when we're together."

He shook his head as he wrapped his hand around mine. "You're wrong. Everything that happened wasn't just us. Logan was in the picture and it just screwed everything up. We both made mistakes. But I think if you gave us a chance, I think we could really make something beautiful instead of so much destruction."

I watched as he ran his hand across my palm and up my wrist. I shivered at the sensation as I pulled away. "How can you think that? All we've ever caused is destruction. I can't think of two people who could possibly be worse than us together. We bring out the worst in each other."

He shook his head as he reached out and pulled my hand back into his. "That's where you're wrong again. You bring out the best in me. I've changed since I met you, all for the better. I don't know what it is about you, but you make me want to be a better person. I haven't felt that way since my parents died. I spent my teenage years making my uncle's life hell when all he did was try to raise me. I didn't care though, I refused to let him or anyone else in."

I squeezed his hand. "Will you tell me about them? Your parents, I mean."

He sighed and ran his free hand through his hair. "What do you want to know?"

I shrugged. "I don't know, just tell me what they were like, what they did, their favorite colors. I don't care, just something."

He was silent for a moment, and I thought for sure he was going to tell me no. Instead, when he spoke his voice was filled with emotion. "Their names were Diane and Landon."

My eyes went to his covered tattoo. "The initials in your tattoo, those are for them, aren't they?"

He gave me a small nod before continuing. "Yeah, they are. I needed something to remind me of them. But anyways, you wanted to know about them. My dad was an accountant for a local law firm, my mother worked as a nurse at University Hospital. They were great, the best parents anyone could ask for. I can remember my dad coming home every evening after work and throwing a football around with me. My mom would always sit down with me after dinner and help me with my homework. I never wanted for anything." He stopped and cleared his throat, trying to control his emotions. "They left me with a babysitter one night, something that was rare for them, to go out on a date together. I remember when Sheila, my babysitter, got the call about the accident. She just stared at me, unsure how to tell me. I instantly knew something was wrong and begged her to tell me. She whispered that some jackass who was drunk turned onto the exit ramp instead of the entrance and hit them head-on. They were dead before the paramedics even arrived on scene. I screamed at her, called her a liar, and destroyed everything I could get my hands on. Child Protective Services came and took me away a couple hours later. I was with them for a few hours until my uncle showed up to take me in. He's the only family I had left, both sets of my grandparents had died before I was even born."

I felt a tear slide down my cheek and hit our joined hands as he spoke. "Oh, God. Drake, I can't even imagine. You were only ten, weren't you?"

He nodded. "Yeah, I was ten when my entire world was ripped apart. My uncle took me in, but he was gone a lot with his job so I pretty much raised myself. He did his best to take care of me though, but I threw everything back in his face. I started doing drugs when I was thirteen, I was pretty messed up for a while. There were days, sometimes weeks at a time, that I can't remember. My uncle finally had enough when I had been arrested yet again on my sixteenth birthday, for possession this time. He put me in rehab and told me to clean up and get myself together or he'd put me in foster care. It took me a long time to get my shit together, but finally I did. I was released and found the band shortly after. I've never looked back since, never cared about anyone except them. I used the women to fill the void the drugs left and I gave no apologies, never questioned what I was doing."

He was silent for a moment. "Until you came along, that is. Everything changed the minute I laid eyes on you. I thought I was going crazy at first. How could one girl come into my life and make me question every single one of my beliefs?"

Tears continued to slide down my cheeks as I leaned forward and kissed him gently. "You've been through so much and then when you started to open up, I just tossed you aside. I'm so sorry, Drake. I never meant to hurt you."

My lips brushed his as I spoke. I felt him smile as he pulled away. "I think we both hurt each other. But I want a chance with you, Chloe. I want to put everything behind us and start over. Do you think we can do that?"

I smiled as I wrapped my arms around him. "I'd like that. I'm just afraid we'll hurt each other again."

"We will, I have no doubt. We'll fight and slam doors and then we'll make up. Every couple in the world does it, Chloe. I'm willing to take all that hurt to be with you if you are too."

"I am," I whispered as he pulled me close and kissed me gently.

"Glad to hear it. Now let's get out of here, I'm freezing. We can talk more in my car."

He stood and held his hand out to help me up. The moon was shining brightly as I made my way slowly up the trail with him following close behind me. I slid and nearly fell several times on the way up, but Drake was always there to catch me. We were giggling and covered in mud by the time we reached the top of the hill.

"I don't think I've ever met someone as clumsy as you. Although, seeing as how I got an awesome view that first night, I guess I should be thankful."

I lifted my hand to slap his chest, but he caught it and used it as leverage to push me onto the hood of his car. The engine was still warm, and it helped to thaw out my legs and ass as he pushed me further up onto the hood.

Before I could ask what he was doing, he was on top of me, kissing me roughly. I let myself melt into the hood as he continued to kiss me. He finally pulled back slightly and we were both gasping.

"Wha— What was that for?"

He gave me that devilish smile of his as he leaned down to attack my mouth again. "I've waited long enough to do this guilt-free and I'm not waiting another minute."

I pushed him back as his words sunk in. "Wait! Wait a minute! You aren't serious, are you? We can't do *that* on the hood of your car!" I felt myself blushing at the thought alone.

"Of course we can, no one is around us for miles. The hood of my car is a perfect spot."

I started to argue, but stopped when he cupped my sex through my jeans. I let my head fall back against the glass as he slid my work pants off and threw them to the ground. Next went my underwear, then my shirt and bra. I propped myself up on my elbows and grinned at him. "How is this fair? I'm completely naked, on top of your car just so we're clear on that little fact, and you're still completely dressed."

He grinned wickedly as he pulled his jeans and boxers off, but seemed to hesitate at his T-shirt.

"What is it? You're not shy all of the sudden, are you?"

He smirked at me. "No, definitely not shy. I'm just not sure how you're going to take this once you see it."

I gave him a confused look. "What are you talking about? And hurry up already, I'm freezing here!"

He hesitated a second longer before pulling his shirt off and tossing it with the rest of our clothes. My breath caught as I saw what he was talking about. Directly over his heart was the exact same tattoo that adorned my wrist.

I sat up and pulled him closer. "Drake, this is beautiful."

He gave a weak smile as I traced the outline of the tattoo. "I wanted something to remind me of you, of us, and I figured there wasn't anything better than this. So I went back to Katelynn and she hooked me up."

I pulled back so that I could look him in the eye. "I guess these tattoos are wrong now."

He trailed his fingers down the side of my arm, and I shivered. "Why do you say that?"

"Because they mean *Never Loved*. I think we took care of that problem for each other." I leaned forward and wrapped my arms around his middle, pulling him down on top of me. "I love you, Drake Allen, and I always will."

No words were spoken after that. His lips were on mine as the world around us faded away. Every touch, every brush of his lips sent me into an oblivion of passion and love. My head fell back against the glass with a dull thud as his lips tasted every inch of me. His tongue snaked out and rolled over my nipples, wetting them before blowing his breath over them.

He trailed kisses down my stomach, my hips, until he finally stopped at my thighs. He kissed the inside of each one before moving to the spot I most desired. I cried out as he kissed me there before probing with his tongue ring. My hands flew to his hair as he moved up to my clit and started sucking. I made sounds I didn't know were possible as he worked me into my perfect oblivion.

I opened my legs wider to allow him better access as I came around his fingers, his tongue never stopping its attack. My body finally came down from heaven as he kissed his way back up my body until he was on top of me, positioned at my entrance.

"I love you, Chloe, so much it hurts."

I moaned as he thrust inside me. He grabbed both my wrists and held them above my head to hold me in place as he thrust deeper than I had ever felt before. Without me asking, he felt my need growing and drove deeper, harder. I shattered underneath him as he continued to pound into me to the point where pleasure was mixed with pain. It was the most amazing pain I had ever felt.

I felt him shudder, and he yelled my name as he released his seed into me. We lay there, still connected, as we tried to figure out how to breathe again. He slowly pulled out, and I groaned. I felt empty without him inside me. He chuckled as he bent down to kiss me. "That was the best car sex of my life."

I smacked his bare chest as I sat up. "Gee, thanks. You're going to have to take your car to the car wash tomorrow. Pretty sure my butt print is permanently dented into it."

He laughed as he helped me off the car. "Not a chance. I

plan to drive around with your ass on the front of my car as long as I can."

We dressed quickly, the cold night air stinging our dampened skin. I gave him one last kiss as I turned to walk to my car.

"Where do you think you're going?"

I looked at him, confused. "Um, to my car. I can't just leave it out here all night."

He raised an eyebrow. "And why not? You can ride back to my house with me tonight and we can come back out here tomorrow to pick it up. Maybe if you're lucky, we can break in your car the same way we just did mine."

I laughed. "Not a chance on your life, buddy. That was a once-in-a-lifetime event, but since it's so late I guess I can ride with you."

I smiled to myself as I grabbed my things from my car and locked it up. Drake held the door open as I slid into his before walking around and getting in himself. He took my hand as he turned the car around and made his way back down the road and onto the interstate. He held it until we reached his house, and I smiled to myself at the feel of it. We were together now, and yes, we still had several issues to work through, but nothing could tear us apart.

DRAKE

Three months later

I smiled to myself as I watched Chloe making dinner in my kitchen. Well, our kitchen now that she had finally agreed to move in with me. It had taken me almost three months to talk her into it, but she finally gave in. I glanced around the kitchen and the entrance to see several of her possessions already littering my house: her shoes and purse by the door, her books on my table, her jacket thrown over the back of the couch. The sight of her so engrained into my life made me smile. Since she would be leaving with me in a couple weeks to go on tour, we had left most of her things boxed up in the basement.

It had taken us so long to get to this point, almost a year, and I counted my lucky stars every day to be with this gorgeous woman. She was everything that I needed, that I wanted out of life, even if I hadn't realized it before. She had her back to me as she bent down to take our dinner out of the oven, and I took advantage of the chance just to stare at her ass in those tiny shorts of hers.

She glanced back and noticed me staring. "And just what are you looking at, Mr. Allen?"

I rose from the table and walked over to her. I waited until she closed the oven and set the food on top of the stove before pulling her into my arms. "Just the sexiest, most amazing ass I have ever seen. *Woman,* I mean *woman* I have ever seen."

She smacked me with her oven mitt and laughed. "Nice

save, buddy. Now go sit down so I can bring our food over to the table and we can eat."

I happily obliged. Her cooking was amazing, far better than anything I had ever attempted to make. She sat the plate in front of me and turned back to the cabinets to grab glasses just as the doorbell rang.

"Can you see who that is, babe?" she asked as she rummaged through the cabinets to find a clean glass.

I was on dishwasher duty, and as usual, I was slacking. I made a mental note to do it after dinner as I rose from the table and walked to the door. I opened it to find a vaguely familiar woman standing there. She was in her late thirties or early forties, but years of self-neglect had made her look years older.

"Can I help you?"

She gave me a smile that made my blood run cold. "Yeah, I'm looking for Chloe. I was told I could find her here."

As soon as the words left her mouth, I realized who was standing in front of me. Before I could reply or slam the door in her face, Chloe came around the corner.

"Babe, who's at the do—"

Her face instantly drained of color as she took in the woman standing in front of us.

"Hello, Chloe."

She was still holding one of the glasses from the kitchen, and I watched in slow motion as it slipped from her hand and fell to the floor, shattering into a million pieces. She just stood there and stared as blood started dripping from the cuts covering her bare legs.

"Mom."

Follow Drake and Chloe as their story continues. . . .

Twisted

SHOUT-OUT!

I really don't think I could name everyone that I want to send my thanks to at this point—there are enough of you to put in a book!

First—to all of the bloggers whom I've met and who've welcomed me into this crazy author/blogger world with open arms: I'm proud to call several of you my friends.

Second—to my fans. I have received SO MANY comments and emails, and I want you to know just how important those are to me. I always have a silly grin on my face when I read them, so thank you for that. You've pulled me out of some really bad moods more than once.

Third—to my book club for making me laugh until I cried. No words can express how much I love you all.

Fourth—in a category all her own, Dirty Molly. You have sent me some of the most AMAZING fan art a girl could ever ask for. And yes, I know you're blushing right now.

Fifth—to my parents. I couldn't have done any of this without either of you. And the fact that you've dealt with me on a daily basis for the past twenty-two years without murdering me, well, that deserves a medal. I love you both.

Thank you to every single one of you reading this. You've touched my life so much. I love you all!

RESOURCES

For more information on some of the topics covered in this book, please check out the following links:

Childhelp National Child Abuse Hotline: http://www.childhelp .org/pages/hotline-home

Drug Abuse Hotline: http://drugabusehelpline.net/

National Suicide Prevention Lifeline: 1-800-273-TALK (8255)

No one should ever have to suffer alone.

ABOUT THE AUTHOR

K.A. Robinson was born and raised in West Virginia, where she still lives, next door to two of the most wonderful parents she could have ever asked for. When she's not writing, she continuously has her nose buried deep in a good book. Most of her favorites are new adult, dystopian, or paranormal. She works full-time at a Kubota Tractor dealership. She is happily married to her high school sweetheart, together with whom she has a two-year-old son. She has major weaknesses for Starbucks and for Cocoa Pebbles.

For more information, please visit her Goodreads page at:
K.A. Robinson Goodreads Author Page

Or her Facebook page at:
http://www.facebook.com/KARobinson13

Or her Twitter:
https://twitter.com/KARobinsonAutho